What the critics are saying:

"…Lovers of the vampire genre will relish Michelle's sensual tale. A soulful romance, an intricate plot and an intense sexual dance make for an adventure readers will definitely enjoy sinking their teeth into!" – *Susan Mitchell, Romantic Times*

"…Ms. Michelle has written a masterpiece of love and revenge that is incomparable! It isn't often that the plot, characterization and sexuality of a book come together so completely they result in a truly fantastic work of art. A Taste For Revenge is one of those books…cover to cover…" – *Amber Taylor, Just Erotic Romance Reviews*

"…A Taste For Revenge is a terrific vampire story filled with action, suspense, heartwarming romance and sensual love scenes. The dynamic characters will captivate you…This is one of the best vampire romances I've read and well deserving of a 5-ribbon rating…" – *Brenda Lee, Romance Junkies*

D0400705

A TASTE FOR REVENGE
An Ellora's Cave Publication, March 2004

Ellora's Cave Publishing, Inc.
PO Box 787
Hudson, OH 44236-0787

ISBN#1-4199-5003-7

ISBN MS Reader (LIT) ISBN # 1-84360-783-2
Other available formats (no ISBNs are assigned):
Adobe (PDF), Rocketbook (RB), Mobipocket (PRC) & HTML

Edited by *Martha Punches*.
Cover art by *Darrell King*.

A TASTE FOR REVENGE

Patrice Michelle

Acknowledgements

I wanted to say thank you to my family for supporting me and the crazy writing hours I keep. I couldn't do it without you!

A special thank you goes out to the wonderful friends I made while researching the Irish language for my book. *Go raibh míle maith agaibh, a chairde* for your inputs while teaching me to love and appreciate the complexity and the beauty of the Irish language.

To the fans of *A Taste for Passion*...finally, Ian's story.

Chapter One

"Man, this hunter's good. Damn good." Ian Mordoor mumbled to himself as he squatted next to the body and touched the arrow imbedded in the center of the man's heart. The bolt was top of the line, meant to kill. He squinted against the setting autumn sun. If the man hadn't been a transer, his body would be scarred ash by now.

Transers. The fact they even existed made Ian's blood boil. Leave them human or make them vampri but don't leave them in that needy in-between state. Only a rogue vamp created transers because he knew a transer would follow his every command at the promise of being turned vampri.

Glancing up, Ian surveyed his surroundings and noted the deserted train station that stood thirty feet away. The yellow paint on the building peeled with age and neglect. He surmised the smaller building off to the right, with its windows and door boarded up, was probably the control station. His heightened senses on full alert, he sniffed the air around him. In the abandoned atmosphere, he detected no unusual scents stirring in the air other than the stench of the dead man at his feet.

Considering the body before him, the place was eerily quiet. Somewhere the vampire hunter lay in wait. He heard the faster-paced beat of a human heart, heard the blood coursing through the man's veins. Shifting his gaze back to the man on the ground, he noted the skin felt cold to the touch. Rigor mortis had already set in. He checked his watch. Based on the body's condition, he had to have been dead at least fourteen hours.

Ian couldn't help but smile. He gave the vampire hunter one thing—the man had tenacity and stamina by the cartloads. The hunter must have chased Drace here because Ian knew Drace. The vamp was used to life's luxuries. Drace never would've come to an abandoned train station of his own free will. His gaze settled on Drace's BMW. All four tires had been slashed. The hunter must have chased Drace here on the brink of dawn. Like a rabbit into a snare.

His smile turned to a grin as his admiration for the hunter grew. No wonder Drace remained here. The abandoned train station held no food source for the rogue vamp and the longer he went without a food source, his vampire powers diminished to a glimmer of his full power. He couldn't shape shift into a raven or turn into mist to get away. For now, he was bound to earth, just like his human hunter, and forced to remain hidden until the sun disappeared from the sky. Right now the hunter had the advantage.

Ian had been on Drace's trail for a month now. From Chicago to Florida he'd chased the ousted vamp. Before he officially took over his newly appointed position as leader of the Ruean clan, Ian vowed to eliminate Drace for his role in the brutal killing of a vampire hunter named John Markson. It shouldn't have taken him this long to track the bastard down, but several Rueans had helped Drace escape him on more than one occasion.

Many of the Rueans weren't happy Ian had been appointed their new leader once their original leader, Kraid, had been killed—Drace, most of all, since Kraid was his brother. Never had a hunt for a rogue vampire been more important to him, especially now that eliminating Drace would go a long way in establishing his leadership over the Ruean clan.

Between Drace and the vampire hunter, all Ian had to do was follow their trail. They each left a path of bodies behind—humans Drace killed after gorging himself on their blood, and transers, killed by the vampire hunter. Ian considered himself one of the best trackers, but for some reason this vampire hunter always seemed to have the jump on him when it came to Drace.

Standing up, he fisted his hand. He respected the vampire hunter for his tireless efforts, but Drace was *his* to hunt down. The thought spurred him into action. Ian might have the advantage of being able to walk in the sunlight, but he fully recognized the limitations of his hybrid—half human-half vampire— powers compared to a pureblood vamp. Instead, he depended more on his hunting skills to catch his vamp prey. The signs were always there, if one knew where to look.

As he inspected the soft dirt around the body beside him, the booted footprints told the tale. Whoever killed the vamp had checked to make sure he was dead. Ian followed the footprints. The prints were smaller than he expected, but then, size wasn't a requirement to be a good hunter.

Peering around the corner of the building, he caught sight of a woman crouched near the abandoned train cars ten feet away. Two chopsticks speared through the mass of jet black hair on her head, keeping it out of her face while giving him a nice view of her slender neck. She wore a man's white tank top that clung to her generous breasts, her chambray over-shirt tossed to the ground. As she raised her arm, his gaze locked on the gun in her hand.

God, a *woman* caused all this? He chuckled inwardly. Drace must be chomping at the bit that he let himself be trapped by a mere woman. Ian crossed his arms and, in a casual stance, leaned against the wall to admire the rest of her shapely form.

While she checked her weapon, he appreciated her toned arms. His gaze dropped to her lower body, past her khaki cargo shorts where the muscles in her thighs and calves, clearly cut and defined, caused him to harden instantly. As much as he wanted to take inventory of the rest of her assets, it was her choice of weapons that drew his attention and ultimate respect.

She checked and reloaded her crossbow pistol with practiced ease, almost as if she could do so in her sleep. A weapon known for its deadly accuracy, the crossbow pistol was slow to load compared to a semiautomatic with a clip. And with her enemy's known speed, the fact she chose such a weapon spoke of her confidence in her abilities as well as her courage.

Nor was she stupid. He grinned as he surveyed the arsenal of other weapons on her person. She had a throwing knife clipped to her belt and a thicker, longer Bowie knife strapped to her thigh. When she turned and rolled her shoulders, as if to ease the fatigue from a long night of lying in wait, he caught a glimpse of the semiautomatic handgun tucked against her spine in the waist of her pants. *Good girl*, he thought.

As if she sensed his presence, the woman looked up and turned her head until she spotted him. He stared at her, meeting her steady gaze. She narrowed her eyes and slowly turned her body to face him. Ian checked his watch with unhurried movements. He looked up at the setting sun, then met her gaze as he mouthed "show time".

* * * * *

Jax Markson stared at the man leaning against the train station. A warning vibrated through her body the way it always did when a vamp was near. But this time the sensation seemed fainter and accompanied a tremor that skidded down her spine, causing her to jerk herself upright and face him head-on.

She pegged him at around thirty-one, only a couple years older than her. Jax took in the tall, physically fit physique, the close-cropped, light brown hair, and serious eyes. His thick brows, a shade darker than his hair, gave him a rugged, rough-around-the- edges look. Of course, that look might have to do with the five o'clock shadow he sported or the black t-shirt he wore tucked into his well-worn faded jeans.

Her pulse raced when he pushed off the wall and started toward her. She knew he wasn't a vamp, but she hadn't survived this long on her hunting skills alone. Being prepared was half the battle. She raised her weapon. Just then, a vamp leapt toward the stranger from the roof of an adjacent building. The stranger didn't take his eyes off her as he pulled a gun from the holster strapped to his shoulder and held it straight out to his side, pegging the oncoming vampri. His attacker crumpled to the ground, dead.

Damn, that was good, she thought as a small smile of appreciation played at her lips. The stranger must be a hunter, too. She'd chased Drace and two other vamps here. The other hunter had just taken care of the second bloodsucker. Now there was just Drace left. Adrenaline pumped through her veins. Her stomach tensed as he continued his slow, measured pace toward her.

A grating sound off to her left, drew her attention as one of the train car doors opened. Drace jumped down to the ground, spotted the hunter coming toward her, and immediately vaulted to the roof of the car. *Damn vamp powers!* she thought as Drace drew his gun and fired. The stranger dove the remaining distance and landed next to her against the locomotive.

Well, shit. The idiot just gave away her one advantage. In his weakened condition, she doubted Drace knew she was so close. He hadn't even looked her way. If she hadn't been so distracted by the other vampire hunter, she would've had the vamp by now.

Jax wasn't taking any chances. Drace was hers! The murdering fiend had to pay and she'd earned this kill. She started to climb the ladder leading to the top of the train when a strong hand clamped around her ankle, yanking her back down.

"What'er you? Nuts? He has a gun and he'll be waiting for you," he hissed quietly in her ear from behind her. The deep timbre of his voice combined with the faint accent tracing his words rolled across her nerves like warm honey. The sound made her want to hear him speak again to see if she'd imagined the slight inflection in his tone. She shook off the curious sensation and instead landed a well-placed elbow in his solar plexus. His muffled grunt surprised her. Jax expected a whoosh of lost breath for her efforts. Apparently, the man was made of steel. Long fingers clasped her upper arm in a firm grip.

With deft speed, she turned to him, placing her crossbow pistol over his heart, finger braced on the trigger. "Unless you want to become a statistic, I suggest you let go of my arm."

The man stood a good seven inches taller then her five-eight frame. Jax had to look up just to meet his gaze. At first his golden eyes narrowed as if he planned to refuse her, then his gaze darkened as he openly assessed her. He pressed his lips together, giving evidence to a mouth that could be both hard or sensual, depending on the mood of the man. And from his current, unyielding stance she had a feeling he *could* be both types of men if the situation warranted it.

"Fine. I was just trying to help you," he ground out and released her arm. Backing away, he raised his hands, his weapon dangling from his thumb.

She lifted her eyebrow as if to say, I don't need your help. "You're the one with the gun trained on you."

He flashed a smile. "Look again."

When Jax lowered her gaze, he had his gun pointed at her, laser light pegging her in between her breasts. Man, he was fast. She hadn't even seen him move!

The hunter drew a slow circle with the red light around her left breast before stopping right over her heart. Smartass show-off, she thought, gritting her teeth.

Somehow she knew the guy wouldn't actually shoot her. She decided to test the theory, but just in case, she kept her gun trained on him while she climbed the ladder. When she neared the top of the train, she slid her gun in the specially made holster on her shoulder and pulled her thick-bladed Bowie knife out of its sheath from her leg. Using the blade as a mirror, she raised it over her head to look around the top of the train car.

When the setting sunlight glinted on her blade, shots rang out as Drace fired off more bullets. Before she pulled her knife down, Jax saw Drace turn and vault over to the next train car in a full run. Slamming the knife into its sheath, she climbed to the top in time to see the other vampire hunter running down the train cars after Drace. How the hell did he get up here ahead of her?

No way was this guy getting the jump on her. Jax took off after the men while she pulled a three-stoned bola out of her fanny pack. Whirling the weapon in her hand, she let the strings and weight of the stones build in momentum, then flung the weapon toward the hunter's legs. He went down hard as the bola's strings ensnared his knees, wrapping tight.

Just to make sure he didn't grab her as she passed and also for some extra in-your-face, Jax jumped on his butt, bounding over the rest of his body like a graceful gazelle. "Better luck next time," she called over her shoulder as she kicked his dropped gun off the top of the train and continued after Drace.

* * * * *

Ian yanked at the offending leather strings entangled around his legs until they snapped, jumped to his feet, and took off after the female hunter. He clenched his jaw in anger that he'd been so thoroughly one-upped. But then, he'd never run into another hunter quite like this woman either. What was her name anyway? Lara Croft? If he could've put a face with that popular computer game heroine, it would have to be the fascinating beauty streaking across the train several car lengths ahead of him.

His boots made dull thumping sounds as he sped over the metal train cars. He held back his running speed, not wanting to give away his vampire status to the trigger-happy hunter. Who knew what the woman's motivations were. Maybe all it took was hearing the word "vampire" for her to turn on him. He could see it now. As he's lying in a pool of his own blood, she would say, "Oh, sorry I shot you. You're a good vamp? There's such a thing?"

He shook off the amusing, yet morbid thought as he finally caught up with her. She stood in a firing stance, crossbow pistol trained on Drace. Drace had reached the end of the train cars and held his pistol on her as well. They were fifteen feet away from one another and clearly at a standoff.

Drace gave an amused laugh when Ian stepped next to her. "I can't believe the 'great' Ian has let a woman catch up to me first."

She turned a surprised gaze his way, but then quickly masked her expression as she faced Drace once more, her eyes narrowed. "Quit talking to him, Drace. Face your death like a man. Or should I say, like a sorry excuse for a man, Vampire," she sneered.

Ian gave Drace humorless smile. "This *woman* has you earthbound and using a gun at the moment. I'd say she's a formidable foe." Ian glanced her way. "As good as you are, he's mine," he told her with a steely look.

For a brief second, Drace's cruel mouth thinned in response to his deliberate dig before his lips curved in amusement. This time he laughed harder, holding his belly in mirth, his black eyes full of delight. "It feels so good to be fought over." Once he spoke, he sobered quickly and focused his gaze on them, his dark brows slashing downward. "But it seems to me that I have the advantage here." As if to punctuate his words, he lifted his chin toward the woman's one-shot pistol and then jerked his semiautomatic weapon in a mocking fashion.

Ian couldn't help the tilt of his lips at Drace's assumption. While she stood there, crossbow trained on Drace, her other hand held the grip of the handgun tucked in her belt behind her back. No doubt about it, the woman was ready. To Drace, she appeared to be laying her hand on her spine to balance herself.

Drace noticed his grin and his bravado faded from his eyes. He looked directly at the woman and pulled the trigger. Anticipating his move, Ian dove toward her, knocking her out of the way and right over the edge of the train.

Chapter Two

"When you pull me up from here, I'm going to kick your ass," she railed once she regained her breath from being slammed into the side of the train.

As her body dangled toward the train tracks, Ian held her hand and thanked his lucky stars that Drace held up to his true coward status. As soon as he'd fired at the woman, Ian heard Drace's feet hit the ground and take off running. Otherwise, holding her over the side, Ian would've been a sitting duck for Drace's target practice.

He looked down at her, gun still in her hand, the muscles in her arm straining under the full impact of her weight. She could've dropped her weapon and grabbed onto him with two hands, but instead she chose to hurl death threats at him. What a woman!

He said in a calm voice, "Now is that any way to treat your rescuer?"

"If it weren't for you, I wouldn't even be in this position, you idiot."

Ian stiffened at her insult. If he had to guess, he'd say her gritted teeth were more from her anger then the pain in her arm. Respect. She needed to learn a little respect. All amusement fled his expression. "Your name."

"What?" she panted. She was finally wearing out.

"Your name," he repeated slowly. "I won't pull you up without a name." No better time than the present to find out the woman's identity.

"Jax!" she hissed out.

"Your whole name."

"Jax! Now pull me up from here and I won't kill you."

He couldn't help but chuckle at her moxie. "You don't seem to be in a position to negotiate, Jax, love. So how about showing a little gratitude, hmmm?"

And damn if, with her last ounce of energy, she didn't grunt, turn, and maneuver herself until she had her crossbow pistol pointed at him.

"I said pull me up. Now, damn you!"

The woman had a stubborn streak a mile long. Ian pulled her up. Not because he thought she'd shoot him, but because he wanted an excuse to touch her. As soon as her feet touched the top of the train car, he put his hands on her arms, noting the blood on the curve of her shoulder.

"You're hit," he commented while staring at her superficial wound. He couldn't tear his gaze away. The blood. He smelled its sweet, inviting scent. If lust wasn't already surging though his veins from the vision of those gorgeous breasts rising and falling with each breath she took, the sight of her blood just about undid him. He had to taste her. Ian met her startled green-eyed gaze, felt the tremor run through her body as he gripped her arms tighter, and pulled her closer.

Before his lips touched hers, she shoved away from him. Holding her crossbow gun between them, she said, "I'll live. Keep your hands to yourself, bud."

As she glared at him, he heard the unmistakable rev of a car engine. They both turned their heads toward the train station in time to see Drace taking off in a car, his car, while dirt stirred up behind the wheels. Fuckin' hell.

Jax focused her accusing gaze on him. "He was *my* kill. Not yours."

Ian indicated the gun with a tilt of his head. "What are you going to do?" He raised his empty hands from his sides. "Shoot an unarmed man?" He wanted Drace, but right now he wanted her more. Cocking his head to the side, he taunted her, hoping to goad a reaction, "You're pretty tough when you have all those weapons at your disposal."

"Oh, is that what you want? Man to man?"

The smirk she gave him only heightened her natural beauty, but he noticed the half-smile on her full lips didn't quite reach her striking emerald eyes. *Why?* he wondered.

"Then by all means..." she trailed off and walked away to set down her gun. The fanny pack came next, along with the gun from her back.

Ian's stomach tensed and his cock rose to throbbing attention in an instinctual, primal response to the sound of the Velcro strap being pulled open as she removed the Bowie knife from her thigh, then unsnapped the throwing knife from her waist. The idea of her stripping her weapons, her defenses, away ricocheted in the forefront of his mind while his body reacted in pulse-pounding awareness.

His gut clenched when she removed her belt, the act reminiscent of undressing in front of him. He noted the larger gold buckle had an unusual design, two snakes on a pole or something. Ian resisted the primal urge to pull her into his arms and challenge the false bravado she held so tight around her like an invisible cloak of armor. Did she realize how seductive her actions were?

Not if the determined look in her eyes was any indication. She met his gaze and positioned herself, feet apart, arms raised in a "ready" stance. One hand in a fist, she beckoned with her other hand. "Come on, let's go, Ian the Enforcer. The winner gets Drace."

Ian raised an eyebrow at her use of his nickname. How much did she know? Obviously, she didn't know he was a vampire or she'd have shot him already.

He swiftly knocked one of her hands down, moving so fast he knew she didn't see it coming. Ian held back the smug look that threatened to spread across his face. But he didn't have time to savor the small victory, for she whirled and slammed him in the lower chest with a powerful roundhouse kick, throwing him back a few feet, right to the edge of the train car.

As his feet teetered on the lip, he raised his arms to regain his balance. Yeah, vamp powers notwithstanding, he could've saved himself, but it was more fun to watch the expressions of shock, then guilt cross Jax's face before she reached over, grabbed the waistband on his pants, and yanked him back onto the train car.

Ian took advantage of her momentary lapse out of "battle mode" and grabbed her upper arms. But before he knew what hit him, he was laid out flat on his back, her foot on his chest, his arm twisted, and his hand bent backward.

"Say it. Drace is mine," she demanded.

He shook his head.

She twisted his hand back further. Man, that had started to hurt. Enough fucking around.

"Uncle," he said with a grin and twisted, kicking her legs out from underneath her. As soon as she landed, he pounced, covering her body with his while he pulled her wrists above her head. Never had he met a woman who fueled the fire in him as this one did.

"Give, Jax, love. You've been outmatched."

The pulse in her wrists quickened underneath his fingers, while the pupils in her eyes dilated. If it weren't for those almost imperceptible indicators, he wouldn't have known that Jax was just as turned on by the situation as he was. She kept her expression carefully guarded. But the vampire side of him was never out of tune with his immediate surroundings. He listened to her heartbeat change from quick thumps to staccato thuds. The sound fueled his desire, calling to his basest instincts.

* * * * *

Jax instinctively bucked to knock him off, but he just pressed his hips against hers, pinning her to the train car's metal surface. She was trapped. The man was an immoveable rock and so was the unmistakable rigid flesh pressing against her lower belly. Unable to stop her intake of breath at his obvious arousal as well as her own, Jax forced an unaffected expression.

"I'm not 'your love'," she bit out. Where'd this jackass get off calling her that? Just because he'd saved her and she'd saved him? They were even as far as she was concerned. Love had nothing to do with it.

Pinned underneath him, his body over hers, she couldn't help but study his angular face and the dark stubble gracing his strong jaw line. She wondered what it would feel like against her skin, the rough drag adding friction in just the right places. His woodsy scent reached out and fueled her libido further, making her throb with desire. God, it had been a while for her if she was fantasizing about a complete stranger.

But, damn, he had the most mesmerizing eyes. The golden color reminded her of a lion's, their intensity seemed to stare right into her very soul, to know her every thought and desire.

He didn't say a word. He just held her there, staring into her eyes. Her heart rate jumped tenfold when his intense gaze drifted to her lips and then her chest. Heat emanated off his body, but he wasn't breathing hard like she was. As a matter of fact, he was calm, very calm.

Her anger rose as the realization hit her. She'd exerted herself and he hadn't even broken a sweat. "You were playing with me, weren't you?"

"Not like I'd like to play with you." He smiled then as his gaze returned to her mouth. The sensual curving of his lips coupled with the deep timbre of his voice sent a jolt of awareness coursing through her. She let her anger temper her desire.

Spreading her legs wide, she quickly lifted her hips and wrapped her limbs around his neck. Locking her ankles underneath his chin, she pushed his neck back to the limit. Unless he released her arms, they were at an impasse.

"I don't play nice," she gritted out and twisted her hips to the side, slamming his head into metal roof of the train car.

While Ian rubbed his head, she scrambled to her feet and collected her gear. As she climbed down the ladder, she paused and met his disgruntled gaze, her voice steady and calm, "Drace is mine, Ian. Go find another vampire to hunt.

* * * * *

"Where the hell have you been?" Blake bellowed into the phone.

Jax shifted the cell phone between her shoulder and ear so she could sign the check-in form. Thanking the hotel attendant, she turned toward the elevators, duffle bag in hand.

"Blake," she sighed, "what are you doing at my uncle's house?"

"It's lucky I was here to answer the phone," he ground out, anger evident. "You were supposed to check in two days ago."

Jax stiffened as she punched the elevator button. "You're not my keeper, Blake."

"That was your choice," he countered, sounding frustrated.

Jax shook her head. Blake hadn't been thrilled when she'd broken things off with him a few months ago. But as angry as he'd been, they'd managed to remain friends.

"This is something I have to do on my own."

"Going after the vampire that killed your father makes you a sitting duck, Jax, a beautiful sitting duck." The protective tone in his voice made her smile. Blake would make some woman a fine husband one day. That woman just wasn't her even though that was one of the reasons her father recruited him into their vampire hunter group, the Trackers.

She chuckled as she slid her key card into the hotel room's door. "I can take care of myself. I always have."

"I know that too well," he grumbled. "But you'd better check in once a day, Jax, or I swear I'm coming after you."

She tossed her duffle bag on the bed and lay back on the mattress. "I'll be a good little soldier from now on, Herr Commandant."

"See that you are," he warned, ignoring her jibe.

She snapped the cell phone closed and dropped it onto the bed beside her, contemplating Blake Grayson. He was the perfect man to fill the leadership role her father vacated. As soon as she'd taken care of Drace, she'd set her uncle James straight. He'd expected her to take over as leader of the Trackers after her father was killed. Jax knew herself better than anyone. She wasn't a team player. She worked alone. She always had.

All her life her father had done the same—he'd worked alone. But when he grew older and his reflexes weren't what they once were, he decided to recruit others to his cause. That's when he found Blake.

She rubbed her hand over her aching temples, the pain of a killer headache threatened. Man, she was tired. She'd been awake for 26 hours straight. A couple hours of shuteye and she'd think about food. She sat up, unlaced her boots, and toed them off. Climbing to the top of the bed, she laid her head down on the pillow, her head throbbing.

If I'm not going to join Blake, what am I going to do once I get Drace? she wondered. Her heart ached at the reason for this quest. She missed her father. If he were here, he'd remind her of "the quest for revenge"—that all vampires were evil. *Weren't they?*

Ah shit! She lifted her head and punched her pillow before laying back down. She only got all sappy and weak like this when she was really tired and down. A few hours of shuteye and she'd have her verve back, full force. With that last thought, Jax succumbed to exhaustion.

* * * * *

Like clockwork Jax surfaced from a deep sleep two hours after closing her eyes. She dragged her tired butt out of bed and sought a much-needed shower. Refreshed and feeling cleaner than she had in weeks, she dried her hair and pulled the red silk dress over her shoulders, enjoying the feel of the soft material as it whispered down her curves to settle against her waist and swirl around her thighs.

She looked in the mirror and smiled. The one and only time she allowed herself this type of indulgence—to be a woman—was when she was among strangers. In this upscale hotel, no one knew she was raised without feminine influence, in a life where a dagger in her hand felt more familiar than a tube of lipstick.

She ran her hands over the expensive silk against her body, appreciating the gliding rub of material against her skin. Sometimes being an heiress had its good points. Her mother may not have been there to raise her, but the one thing her mother did leave behind was the considerable Wellington legacy.

Tonight she left her hair down and applied a little mascara and lip gloss. No need to overdo it, she thought. Plus, she wouldn't know how to apply blusher if her life depended on it; good thing it didn't. She stuck her tongue out and winked at herself in the mirror before heading out for dinner.

* * * * *

"Thank you," Jax murmured to the waiter as he handed her the menu and walked away. She could've eaten in her room instead of the hotel restaurant, but having dinner downstairs was part of the "indulgence" fantasy for her, even if she ate alone.

As she browsed the meal selections all her senses suddenly kicked into high alert and a zinging sensation rippled down her spine. She lowered her menu to see Ian standing in front of her table. Unexpected intense awareness slammed through her at the sight of the fine gauge forest green sweater that stretched taut against his bulging biceps and the black dress pants that clung to his trim hips. He'd shaven and the faint aroma of masculine soap clung to him, making her want to move closer so she could inhale deeply.

His gaze met hers as he laid her bola—or rather the remnants of her bola—on the table in front of her. He didn't say a word, but let his gaze skim over the spaghetti straps of her dress, lingering on the curve of her shoulder, the swell of her breasts, before boldly returning to her eyes.

His golden eyes, hot, hungry, and intensely predatory, locked with hers. Without words, the man told her exactly what he wanted and damn if her body didn't react in kind. Her heart rate sped up, her stomach clenched, her nipples tightened, hard pebbles against the silk material. Hot moisture dampened her panties. She had to fight the urge to squirm under his close scrutiny. He dropped his gaze to her breasts once more and the corners of his lips quirked upward.

Ian turned and walked back to the bar across the room, settled on a stool, and picked up his drink. As his eyes met hers over the rim on his glass, his bold act with the bola told her in a very blatant way...

He was the hunter.

He'd found her.

And now…he wanted her.

Jax looked down at the bola on the table, a reminder that she'd been so distracted from the hunt, she'd left a weapon behind. Damaged, yes, but fixable. She gritted her teeth and clenched the bola's strings in her hand, angry with herself for being so close only to let Drace get away. Her anger simmered, dampening her spirits, until she realized Ian the Enforcer, the vampire hunter who "always got his man", had failed, too. The thought brought a small smile of satisfaction to her lips.

As soon as Drace called him Ian, she knew. The hunter that stood beside her on the train was Ian the Enforcer; the man she'd overheard a couple of vamps talking about in a bar she'd scoped out as a well-known vamp hangout a couple weeks ago. Many vamps feared Ian and with good reason, apparently. She'd heard he never lost a prey. Ever. But if he was so good, why had her dad never mentioned him?

Jax ignored Ian as she ate her meal, refusing to acknowledge his presence. But she felt his heavy gaze on her, watching her every movement, every bit of food she ate, every sip of drink she took. Any other woman might have frozen at being the object of his forceful inspection, but Jax, well…she was Jax. She never cowed and she *always* met a challenge head-on. Her meal finished, she ordered a fruity drink with a smile on her lips. Delay tactics were her specialty.

The waiter brought her drink and lingered at her table. "Is there anything else I can get for you?" he asked, his dark eyebrows elevated.

She shook her head. "No, thanks. The bill will do."

He smiled and his handsome face brightened. "Wanna grab some coffee? I get off in a half an hour."

You and me both, bud, if Ian gets his way, she thought with an inward chuckle, even as she realized how much the waiter's invitation surprised her. She was so used to men seeing her as one of the guys. But then, she remembered her outfit and fantasy. He'd seen her as a woman, nothing more, nothing less. Tucking her hair behind her ear, she met his questioning blue gaze with a smile on her lips. He had to be at least seven years younger than her. "Thanks for the invitation, but…"

He stiffened and immediately cut her off, looking at his watch and then back at her with an apologetic smile. "Oh, sorry, I just remembered I have plans."

Talk about a one-eighty. Indian giver. This time Jax chuckled out loud as he scurried away. Her chuckle died on her lips, however when her gaze locked with Ian's. His jaw clenched, he looked downright pissed. What the hell was his problem?

She finished off her drink and picked up the cherry sitting on top of the ice in her glass. Holding the stem, she used her tongue to suck the plump bulb between her lips. She met his unwavering gaze with a bold one of her own as she chewed the delectable fruit, shot full of alcohol.

Why not indulge in some anonymous, guilt-free sex? Her entire body felt tense, perched on the edge of...what? She didn't know. Maybe it was the weeks chasing Drace. She needed a physical release and Ian...well, the man certainly had a body she'd love to explore. His prowess as a hunter called to her most primal instincts. He met both her physical as well as professional requirements. No fuss, no muss. He wanted her. She wanted him. No strings attached.

She couldn't ask for a better circumstance to assuage her sexual needs. She smirked. At least she didn't have to worry about her own protection. Thanks to bitchin' cramps since she was thirteen, the pill became her very best friend. Ian better damn well have some condoms.

The waiter seemed to have all but disappeared, so Jax left cash on the table and stood up, collecting the bola in her hand. As she passed the bar on her way out of the room, she called over her shoulder, "Night, Ian."

At the narrowing of his eyes, she both hoped and feared he would follow her. She held her breath as she stepped on the elevator, her heart thudding in her chest. Would he follow?

Just then Ian stepped into the elevator, moving directly behind her. As she reached toward the panel of elevator buttons, he leaned over her and punched the button to her floor. He didn't bother to ask, but once again he showed her in his own deliberate way — he'd found out which floor she was on and he intended to follow her there.

The brief brush of his shoulder against the bare skin on her back, the heat that emanated from him, made her shudder. He didn't touch her again, nor did he move away. Instead, he stayed in her personal space, almost touching but not quite. She never knew how much of a turn-on "almost" could be.

As the elevator zipped upward, Ian bent his head and inhaled close to her neck. Desire swirled in her stomach, clawing its way down to her sex. She bit back a moan of anticipation. When his large hand settled on her lower belly, she resisted the urge to jump at the contact. Splaying his fingers, he drew her back against the hard planes of his chest just as the elevator doors slid open.

Chapter Three

Yikes! Too much, too much. The man made her feel way too much and he hadn't even kissed her yet. Jax pulled out of his grasp and headed for her room. *Bad idea, Jax. Bad idea.* The words chanted in her head as she lifted the key card and tried to insert it in the lock, her hand trembling and clumsy. *Maybe I can get in my room before...*

Ian pressed his entire torso against her back. His hand landed over hers to steady the key card and insert it in the lock as he whispered in her ear, "You know what I want. I smell your desire, Jax. You want this, too." He planted a tender kiss on her neck and finished, "Don't second guess yourself."

Jax closed her eyes. God, did she want him. He was right. She should enjoy the here and now while she could. She might not survive her self-imposed assignment of tracking down Drace. She could hear herself bitching as she lay there dying from a mortal wound, *I should kick my own ass for not taking a romp with that sexy Ian guy while I had a chance.*

Ian opened the door and put his hand against the small of her back, leading her into her room. As he shut the door, he moved around Jax and set her against it. Laying a hand on the wood surface above her head, his expression turned intense and focused as he leaned over her. He didn't smile. He didn't flirt. But his smoldering eyes told her everything. He *wanted*, and God, so did she.

Ian lightly brushed a finger against the strap of her dress. "This dress becomes you, Jax. Why do I have the feeling it's a rare occasion to see you in one?"

She stiffened, ready to be offended by his remark when she saw his gaze had locked on her lips. He touched her bottom lip with his finger.

"Did you know that there is an erogenous zone from here," he drew a line straight down her chin to her neck, "to here," he said in a husky tone as he continued his seductive path between her breasts.

She whimpered that he'd bypassed her breasts until his finger moved lower down her stomach, stopping once he reached her sex.

"To here?" He pressed against her clitoris through the silk of her dress and Jax thought for sure she'd have an orgasm right then and there. She resisted the urge to buck against his hand. No way. He was going to have to work harder than that.

She met his gaze head on, her breathing turning shallow. Her eyebrow raised, she quipped, "Hadn't heard that one."

The corners of his lips canted upward in a pleased smile. "Good." He slid his hand around and cupped her backside, pulling her full against his erection. "I like the idea I'll be the one to show you."

Jax drew in her breath at his aggressive action while the thrill that zinged through her body caused moist heat to pool between her legs. He slid his hand down her buttocks to the back of her thigh, but stopped when his fingers brushed against the knife strapped to her leg.

Ian clenched his jaw and anger reflected in his gaze. "One more thing." He pulled the knife from the sheath and jammed it forcefully into the wood door a few inches from her head. "Drace stays out there. Got it?"

A jolt of awareness shot though her at his words. Jax reached over, grabbed his erection through his pants, and pulled him flush against her. "I couldn't agree mo—"

She didn't get a chance to finish her sentence. Ian's mouth came down on hers, hard and hungry, demanding and aggressive. The sensual slide of his tongue against hers turned that earlier jolt of awareness into bolts of electricity, shooting to all of her extremities. Where hot moisture gathered earlier, now a throbbing ache took over.

Ian's kiss slowed as he pulled her into his arms and cupped the back of her head for a deeper, more intimate kiss. His first kiss, she expected, but this thorough, measured mating with her mouth took her breath away. The masterful play of his mouth over hers told her this man didn't skimp in the oral category. He seemed to savor every touch of skin against skin, every brush of lips against lips, every glide of tongue against tongue as he explored her mouth, completely dominating her. And for once it felt good to be dominated.

Jax slid her hands under his shirt, up his sides, and around his back, savoring the feel of hot skin stretched taut over rippling muscles. She swiftly lifted his sweater over his head and tossed it on the floor. Meeting his hungry gaze, she traced a path across his powerfully built chest with her palms, skimming her hands around his six-pack abs and trim waist. Ian groaned his approval when she dropped her hands to his buttocks and pulled him closer to her, pressing her belly against his erection.

He stepped into her then, backing her up against the door once more, his hands moving to her shoulders and then her breasts. Jax arched into the large hands that palmed her soft breasts through the silk of her dress.

His lips soon followed a path down her neck, leaving a trail of hot fire behind them. Ian stopped kissing her and stared into her eyes as he eased the straps down her shoulders. Her stomach tensed and her breasts tingled as she waited for him to slip her dress down her body. When he slid the material down, she kicked her shoes off along with her dress and stood in front of him, clad only in her red silk underwear.

Ian's gaze skimmed over her body, stopping along the way to appreciate a curve here, a swell there. Everywhere he looked she tingled in response. "*Tá tú go h-áileann,*" he said, his tone rough and low.

Though she didn't know what he'd just said, the look in his eyes told her it was a compliment.

When his gaze dipped to her stomach and lower, his expression hardened. "Never with me," he ground out, his gaze intense as he ripped at the Velcro strap and pulled the knife's sheath from her leg.

She knew what he implied. Never with him would she feel the need to protect herself.

He was the hunter.

The alpha.

The protector.

He spoke as if they would have more than one night together. The fantasy made her shudder, her heart jerk, and thighs tremble in response. He was wrong, but she'd enjoy the fantasy for one night at least. When he stepped close to her once more, Jax put her hands on his shoulders.

His golden eyes blazed, focusing on her breasts. "Red cherries," he murmured. He licked his finger, then brushed a pebbled nipple with the wet, blunt tip.

She moaned at his brief touch, saw the desire flicker in his eyes as he traced his hand down her belly, touching each firm muscle in turn.

Ian slipped his finger inside her underwear and slid it against her clitoris. "And sweet cream," he finished as he dove his finger deep inside her channel, wrenching an unbidden pleasure-filled moan from her for his efforts. She dug her fingers into his shoulders and watched in fascination as he withdrew his finger and slid it in his mouth, sucking away her juices, while his gaze locked with hers.

It's just not right. Not right at all that one man could make her feel so much. But she'd be damned if she would pass this up out of fear over her own emotions. Ian was turning out to be every woman's wet dream and she soooo wanted to get thoroughly drenched.

Jax's heart skipped several beats as she unbuttoned Ian's pants. God, she had to see him, to know if he was as large as he felt. She kept her eyes focused on her hands. She didn't want Ian to see how much she wanted this—to see her need.

"I'm on the pill, but I don't take chances," she rambled to hide her own desire. "Please tell me you have a condom or three in your pants," she finished as she unzipped the zipper.

Ian clasped her wrists, stilling her movements.

Jax met his gaze with a questioning one.

"I want to feel your warm flesh around me Jax. I don't want anything between us."

As much as his sexy words excited her, Jax's heart plummeted, disappointment setting in. Well, damn.

Ian clasped her neck, rubbing his thumb along her jaw. His gaze searched hers. "I didn't save your life today just to throw it away. I carry no diseases, Jax."

"How do I know—?" she started to ask.

He leaned over and whispered in a husky voice next to her ear, "You'll just have to trust me as I do you."

Trust me. Trust me. His words echoed in her mind.

For some unfathomable reason, she did trust he would never hurt her.

Jax nodded and Ian backed away to step out of his underwear and pants.

She couldn't stop the gasp that escaped her lips. Good Lord. Not only was his erection long and thick, but it curved slightly toward his hard stomach. *Nonononono*, there's no way they would fit together. When she shook her head and said, "I'm thinkin', no," Ian chuckled.

"I'm thinkin', hell yes," he replied, his tone adamant.

The deep timbre of his voice vibrated up her spine when she met his gaze.

"Remember, I've seen just how limber are." He grasped her hand and placed it over his hard erection. Wrapping her fingers around him, he guided her hand from the plump tip to the base, groaning as she reflexively squeezed.

When Jax slid her grip back up and down, he grabbed her wrist and gritted out, "You'll be asking for all of me before it's over."

Jax raised her eyebrow at his arrogance. "Oh, you're so sure, are you?"

He gave her a sexy grin. "I'm sure of these." He twirled her nipples between his fingers, applying just the right amount of pressure. When the pain came, her breath hitched as lust surged through her. He released her breasts and moved his hand to her underwear, sliding his hand inside once more. Finding her moist entrance, he dipped his finger inside her hot center. "And I'm very sure of this."

Desire shot through her body as he pressed as deep as his finger could go, touching her cervix. When he drew a lazy circle around the sensitive tip, she felt her own warm juices rush to coat his finger, aiding his titillation. His eyes flamed at the added lubrication and a pleased smile tilted his lips.

When he started to walk backward toward the bed, Jax grasped his shoulders, trying to lift herself off of him. "No," he demanded, clamping his palm around her mound to keep his hand inside her.

Jax met his challenging gaze with one of her own until he touched that sensitive spot deep within and tapped on it, pulling her along. Of its own accord, her body jerked forward at his expert manipulation. Talk about being led around by the balls...well, in her case that saying would be entirely different, but at least now she truly understood the meaning behind it. He had her so wound up right now if he asked her to jump, she'd say, "Honey, from whatever bridge you ask, I'm there."

When they reached the bed, he pressed the back of her legs against the mattress and, *Holy Toledo!* The man lifted her up on the raised bed with just his finger and hand against her. She grasped his shoulders and bit back the moan from the friction and subsequent pleasure his action elicited. God, he was strong. What a turn-on!

Ian slid her underwear off as she crawled backwards on her elbows. Then he followed her onto the bed, towering over her, every bit the hunter, every bit the predator. She tried to slow her breathing, to hide the excitement that coursed through her body—excitement that had her heart pounding a zillion beats a minute. But when Ian kissed her thigh and inhaled deeply near her sex, growling his appreciation, she lost her hold on her composure.

Her breathing turned choppy, her chest rose and fell with her rampant breaths at the thought of what he made her feel—wound up, horny, insatiable. And the man hadn't touched her. He'd just sniffed her for crying out loud. *Get a grip, Jax!*

But she couldn't. Her body wanted, no, needed *his* touch, *his* dominance, *his* primal mating. She'd never felt anything pull at her quite as much as this man's potent magnetism. The thought scared her back to that protected place she kept around herself.

She put her hands on his chest, ready to push him away, when his hand swiped across her slit and gathered her warm juices. His action shocked her into stunned immobility. With measured and precise movements, he rubbed her essence along the insides of both thighs.

She looked up and Ian's seductive golden gaze held hers, causing her heart to ram against her chest when she realized his intent. Never had a man turned her on like this one did, nor made her feel so completely rapacious in her need for him to taste her. Her stomach clenched in fierce, spiraling desire when Ian lowered his head and licked a path along the soft skin he'd just coated, tasting her, savoring her.

Jax moaned at the combination of hot moisture with the rasp of his tongue. His groan against her thigh sent tiny shivers shooting through her body. She'd never survive this, she thought as she tossed her head back and forth at the sexual tension building inside her.

When he'd thoroughly cleansed one thigh and moved to the other, her legs began to tremble. She grabbed his hair, forcing him to look at her. "Taste me, Ian, I can't stand the suspense."

He gave her a roguish grin. "Not yet, *a chroí.*"

Arrgh! In anger and frustration, she clamped her thighs together, locking his head between them.

Ian grabbed her knees, forcing her thighs apart and against the bed. His intense gaze met hers. "Keep them there or you won't get what you want."

Jax clenched her teeth and grasped the covers underneath her as he continued his sweet torment. This time as he neared her moist entrance, he slid his tongue across the folds ever so slowly before he plunged inside her. She almost jumped off the bed at the contact, but he held her hips firmly against the mattress as he resumed his slow torture once more.

Jax balled her hands into tight fists. She wanted to tell him where to go, but at the same time she'd beg him to stay if he decided to leave.

The last few strokes of his tongue brought his mouth closer and closer to her throbbing heat. When he finally lifted her hips and devoured her sex, Jax let the moan of pleasure she'd been holding back escape her lips. God, he knew just how to take her to the edge of orgasm, keeping her in humming, gut-wrenching anticipation.

Ian murmured against her as he licked a path to her clit, "You taste so good, Jax. Your cream is rich, the sweet flavor such a turn-on. You make me want more."

His sensual words made her juices gather again and Ian groaned, saying as he laved and sucked, "That's it. I want all you can give, *a ghrá.*" He continued speaking to her, encouraging her in his lilting language. She'd heard Blake say similar sounding words before. Irish, yes, he was speaking Irish as if it were a second language to him.

Ian slid two fingers into her slit, stroking her in a slow, tantalizing rhythm as he sucked her clitoris with his tongue and lips, teasing and pulling.

"Oh, God." Jax shut her eyes as her body began to shake with her impending climax.

"Look at me, Jax," Ian demanded.

Jax opened her eyes as Ian let go of her hips and hovered over her, his erection pressed against her moist heat. She grasped his shoulders and spread her legs, lifting her hips as she accepted his hard shaft.

Ian thrust inside her slightly, pulled out, and shafted her again. Jax keened in pleasure, but before she could move against him, he withdrew.

"Ian," she warned, her insides clenching and knotting at her delayed orgasm.

His golden gaze met her frustrated one. "You have to be ready, Jax."

She clutched his shoulders, digging her fingers deep. Through gritted teeth she said, "I'm ready."

He pushed inside her once more, slow and steady, the look on his face serious and focused.

Jax clenched her muscles around him and smiled in satisfaction when her efforts elicited a low growl from him. This time, when Ian tried to withdraw, she was prepared. Jax quickly put her hands on his buttocks and held him inside her. Canting her hips against him, she moaned her gratification at the tight feel of his hard flesh—a perfect pressure against her warm walls.

Ian moved so quickly she didn't have time to react. He grasped her hands and held them beside her head. Lacing his fingers with hers, he pinned her still as he withdrew once more. "Not yet. I want you delirious with need."

"Screw you," she hissed out as anger grappled for dominance over her highly charged desire. She was taut with unfulfilled need and the man wanted to string her along. No way in hell would she beg. She tried to shift his weight off of her.

A smirk crossed his face. "I think you're ready now." He thrust inside, filling her completely, rending a scream of pleasure-pain from her as the full length of him stretched her taut, touching her cervix. Ian pulled out and slid back inside, pressing his hips against hers. "Come, *a ghrá*. I want to hear you scream."

Jax closed her eyes and bit her lip. She didn't want to give him the satisfaction even as she felt the first tremors of her orgasm begin.

"I feel you tightening around me, Jax," he ground out as he withdrew and thrust back in, his own breathing turning ragged.

She shook her head, not willing to let him know just how good it felt.

"Liar," he rasped, thrusting forcefully against her.

"Oh, God," she whispered before she could check her words. He felt so damn good, the sensations both thrilled and scared her. She wanted to scream her pleasure. She'd never screamed during sex.

"Come for me," Ian said, his tone hoarse as he pistoned into her. He kissed her throat, then clamped his teeth on the sensitive curve of flesh between her neck and shoulder. His primal branding, coupled with the sensation of his hot semen coating her insides, sent Jax over the edge, causing her to scream his name as pure ecstasy rolled though her body in erotic, climatic waves.

When their breathing slowed, Jax kept her eyes shut as Ian planted tender kisses on her neck, skimmed his lips to her jaw and then kissed her mouth while he murmured Irish words. Words she didn't want to know the meaning of. She didn't want him to make this personal or talk to her like they were lovers. She couldn't allow herself to feel anything for him.

They were adversaries.

When the blush of needy arousal waned, she realized how much she needed space. Ian's presence unnerved her more than she cared to admit. Mumbling her desire to use the bathroom, she slid out from underneath him and started toward the bathroom.

He grasped her wrist before she could move away from the bed. "Jax?"

Jax refused to look at him. When he released his hold, she walked into the bathroom and closed the door behind her. Leaning against the door, she slid to the floor and wrapped her arms around her bent knees. Why did he have to be so attentive, so tender, so damned irresistible afterward?

Chapter Four

Ian lay back on the bed and contemplated Jax. The whole experience with her shocked the hell out of him. He'd enjoyed many women but never like this. Stubborn, brave, naturally passionate yet purposefully distant. She was a complicated woman, his mate. His mate. Fuckin' hell that sounded weird. He never thought in a million years he'd settle on one woman. And such a resistant one, too. He sighed when he realized the uphill battle he'd have to face with her. It bothered him to see her withdraw so quickly from him after their lovemaking as if she were ashamed to have let her feelings be known.

He chuckled to himself when he realized the irony of the fact that Ian the Enforcer, the blunt speaking, rough-around-the-edges Ruean leader, would be the one to teach his *Sonuachar* how to love and be loved. And he would. He might not know what happened in Jax's past to make her so afraid to share her feelings, to be touched and loved, but one thing he knew for certain, she was his vampire mate and he couldn't do any less for her—for them.

Never had he wanted to bring a lover to pleasure more than with Jax. He'd had to fight the urge to take her blood. At one heightened point during their intense lovemaking, his incisors had unsheathed on their own. That had never happened to him before. Ever. He'd always been in control. It was as if his body craved her, knowing her blood would taste spicy and sweet, yet he knew identifying her exact flavor would be as elusive and hard to describe as Jax.

Having made love to his mate, his protective nature kicked into high gear. Never had he felt more defensive over another. She'd laugh if she knew his thoughts, tough as she thought she was. But facts were facts. He was a better hunter, if for no other reason, because he was a vampire.

And therein lay the crux of the problem. Somehow he didn't think revealing his vampire status would benefit either one of them at the moment. He wanted Jax to learn to trust him before he sprung that little surprise on her. *Guess what?* The guy you share mind-blowing sex with? He's a vampire. Ian shut his eyes and his entire body tensed at the thought of her reaction. No. Not yet.

Jax opened the door and walked out. Her hair now hung in one long thick braid over her shoulder. She'd washed her face and brushed her teeth. Ian's keen senses kicked in. He could hear her beating heart, smell her arousal. She smelled delicious.

"You're still here?" She stood beside the bed with her arms crossed over her naked breasts, a scowl on her face.

Ian folded his arms behind his head in a casual pose. "Where else would I be?" He knew she really wanted to be rid of him.

"I assumed you'd left already."

Ian chuckled. "What? Wham, bam, thank you, mister?"

"Well put." Jax smirked.

When Ian sighed in resignation, he noted the breath of relief she let out. He held out his hand and said, "Help me up, will you?"

Anything. Anything to hurry him the hell out of my bed, Jax thought as she offered her hand to help him. Instead of taking her hand, he grabbed her wrist and grinned before yanking her down onto the bed. Man, he had fast reflexes. Jax's heart pounded in her chest at the abrupt change in her locale now that her body was ensconced against Ian's broad chest, spoon style.

When she started to struggle, he threw a muscular leg over hers. "Guess what?" he whispered in her ear and kissed her neck. "That's not how I operate."

"Let me up, Ian. You got what you wanted," she bit out, anger bubbling to the surface at his presumption.

Ian clamped a large hand over her breast, pulling her closer to his body, his hard erection pressing against her backside. "And so did you," he chuckled.

"Cease your struggles, Jax." His tone sobered. "You're exhausted. You've tracked Drace for two days straight now with little if any sleep. You couldn't have rested very long before you went to dinner tonight. I want you to sleep without worrying about protecting yourself."

Jax strained against his hold. "I can protect myself just fine, Ian. I've been doing it all my life."

"Why would you need to do that *all* your life?" he asked. "Tell me about yourself."

The softening of his tone, the concern it held, jerked at her heart. The foreign feeling set off another bout of struggles to be free of his hold.

He sighed, but tightened his arm around her. "Okay, just rest, *a chroí.*"

Jax pulled at the hand on her chest, but Ian spoke against her hair, kissing her neck and that sensitive spot behind her ear, lulling her with his beautiful Irish words. Before she knew it, her eyelids started to droop and her body relaxed against his much larger one. She didn't even have the energy to move when he slid his hand down her stomach and rested his palm possessively on her thigh. The last thing she heard before falling asleep was Ian saying, "*Oíche mhaith.*"

Ian compelled Jax to sleep. She needed her rest. He needed to know she was safe. As he slid the band out of her hair and ran his fingers through the black silk, unbinding her braid, he couldn't believe he had found his *Sonuachar*, his soul mate. He never really expected to find a woman who pulled at him both mentally and physically. There was just something about Jax, something elusive, and it wasn't because she held her emotions at bay. No, he'd get to the bottom of it.

First thing tomorrow, he'd have Mark Devlin check out her background. Well, after he found out her full name. He chuckled to himself. Damn, she'd managed to never tell him that part. He had to compel the bellhop to find out what floor she was on since Jax had made her hotel reservation under a fake name.

He yawned. In the morning, while she showered, he'd search through her things and find out her identity. He wanted answers. He wanted to know why she became a vampire hunter and why she'd set her sights on Drace to the point of losing sleep over the hunt. Tomorrow they'd talk. But tonight...tonight he wanted to enjoy the peace he felt while holding her close.

Ian awoke the next morning feeling rested and content. He reached for Jax and opened his eyes when he found the bed empty. He scanned the room, his heart skipping beats as he noted all her clothes were missing.

Jumping from the bed, he darted into the bathroom. Empty. Damn it. How had she given him the slip? Twice he'd had to compel her back to sleep last night. Somehow she'd managed to come awake on her own as if out of habit, even breaking through his mental stronghold over her sleep. The woman had a will made of steel. He knew she would test every bit of patience he thought he never had.

Ian rubbed his chin and considered where she might go next, thanking his lucky stars for the homing device he'd attached under her car fender at the train site.

* * * * *

Jax smiled as she sheathed her Bowie knife and hopped into her car. She surveyed the flat tires on Ian's rental car in her rearview mirror as she drove away. Served him right for presuming to stay in her room all night long. Plus, she needed a little head start on the man.

When she awoke and realized she'd slept practically the whole night without waking, she freaked out. She'd always woken several times a night.

Jax picked up her cell phone and dialed her voicemail. A cultured, male voice came across the line. "Miss Markson, I see you've let our friend Drace slip through your fingers once again." He gave a bored sigh that made Jax grit her teeth in frustration. "I've just heard he's made plans to be at the Red Satin club tonight. Looks like our rogue vampire is turning bolder. He's heading home."

"Shit." Jax threw the cell phone into the passenger seat and jerked the wheel, turning the car around. Now she needed to book a flight back to Chicago. Damn vamp. Trying to eliminate his ass had cost her way too much of her own personal time and money. When she caught up with him, she'd roast him good just on principle.

Jax still hadn't figured out the identity of the man who'd been leaving her anonymous messages for a month now. The first phone call came a week after her father's death. The man on the phone claimed to know how to find the vamp who'd killed her father. She was leery of trusting him, but his information on where to find Drace had always been accurate. If only she knew what his motives in helping her were. But she'd never been given a chance to ask. After that first phone conversation, he'd only left her voicemails.

* * * * *

Ian followed the homing device's signal straight to the airport rental car parking lot. "Shit," he hissed as he kicked her rental car's tires. After discovering his slashed tires, he'd *borrowed* a car from the parking lot to track her down. This was the last thing he needed.

"Uh, can I help you, sir?" A tall, thin blond-haired man stood in the doorway of the rental car booth.

Ian turned to the man. "Yes, can you tell me where the lady went who dropped off this car?"

"She was in an awful hurry. Said something about catching a plane."

"Did she say where she was going?"

"Nope."

Ian walked closer and met the man's gaze, compelling him. "Can you tell me her name?"

The man looked down at the register and then flipped through the paperwork. "Hmmm, that's weird. She only signed it Jax."

"What about the credit card receipt?"

The guy shook his head. "She paid in cash."

Ian ran his hand through his hair, frustration mounting. "What form of ID did you require for the rental?"

"Driver's license. "

"You didn't require a credit card?" he asked, incredulous.

He got a blank stare in response. Ian set his teeth, his patience growing thin. He compelled the rest of the answer from the man.

With a sheepish look, the attendant replied, "She slipped me a hundred."

Ian took a deep, irritated breath. "Write down her license number for me."

After the attendant handed him the driver's license number, Ian stopped off at a payphone to call his friend Mark Devlin. Frustration mounted when he got Mark's voicemail.

"Mark, Ian here. Listen buddy. Need a favor. Check out this Illinois driver's license number L4568JD, City: Chicago. Name: unknown. Nickname: Jax. Female, white, around twenty-eight years old. Let me know what you can dig up on her present as well as her past. And I need the information as soon as possible. Leave a message at my home phone with the info. Thanks Mark. I owe you one."

Ian hung up the phone and headed inside. The lines to the ticket counter were excruciatingly long. He shifted his feet, waiting for the line to move up. After fifteen minutes of waiting and the line had only moved inches, Ian leaned over and met the ticket person's gaze across the room.

"You sir," she called out.

Ian looked around, an innocent expression on his face, and pointed to his chest. "Me?"

"Yes, sir. Could you please come forward?"

Ian picked up his overnight bag and walked to the front. When he got to the counter he asked, "I need to know what flight out Drace Kovac took yesterday." If he couldn't find Jax, all he had to do was look for Drace, then he'd be sure to find her.

The woman checked the system. "I'm sorry, sir but no Drace Kovac flew out of here yesterday."

Ian almost turned away in frustration when a thought struck him and he turned back. "What about Kraid Kovac?"

The woman checked the flights again. "Ah, yes. He took the 9:00pm flight to Chicago yesterday." She looked expectantly at him. "Would you like to book a flight to Chicago as well?"

Ian smiled and pulled out his credit card. "Yes, I would."

* * * * *

"Hey ya, Unc." Jax leaned over and kissed her uncle's balding head as she threw her duffle bag in the burgundy wingback chair in his office.

"Well, well, my prodigal niece returns." His blue eyes twinkled as he looked up from the paperwork on his walnut desk.

"She does indeed," Blake announced from the doorway.

"Do you live here now?" Jax's gaze skimmed across the deep plum carpet, past the walnut bookshelves to land on Blake's tall frame blocking the doorway. Not an ounce of fat graced his lean, muscular body. With thick black hair, leaf green eyes, and sculpted features, she'd never seen a more handsome man. So why did Ian's rugged good looks draw her in so much?

Blake walked in and handed her uncle a glass of water. Jax noted James' hand shook as he put the glass to his mouth and swallowed the water along with his heart medicine. The sight pulled at her heart. When had he aged on her so quickly? She squatted down beside his chair. "Hey, I just came by to get some fresh clothes. But if you need me to take some time off, I will."

"No!" her uncle said, his tone vehement. "I'm fine." He cut his gaze over to Blake. "Though I'd prefer you to take Blake with you. He's hovering over me like a worried mother."

"I am not." Blake looked highly offended to be compared to a woman. "I'm here to go over my latest plans to expand the network with you." He let his gaze roam over Jax's form, pausing at her curved backside before returning to her face. "Though, I wouldn't mind being Jax's backup on this case."

Jax straightened and smoothed the wrinkles out of her cargo pants. "No thanks, Blake, I've got it covered. I'm going to get a shower before I head out again." Jax left the room before her uncle could insist on Blake accompanying her. Not that it would do any good, but she just didn't want to upset her uncle any more than necessary.

As she crossed the foyer and took the curved staircase that led to the east wing of the house, she considered moving into the guesthouse at the edge of the Wellington estate. That way, she'd have her privacy but still be close enough to watch over her uncle. Thank goodness for Blake. Otherwise she'd feel guilty leaving her uncle, even though he was the one who insisted she had the right to avenge her father's murder.

Once in her room, she quickly undressed and stepped under the shower, letting the hot water soak through her skin. Sighing her contentment, she realized she felt truly rested. Something she hadn't been in a very long time. Ian did that for her.

Thoughts of Ian brought back memories from their night together. The warm water beating on her back, sloshing between her legs made her sex begin to throb in renewed interest as her body reminded her just how much she had enjoyed his touch, his tongue, his mouth. What would it feel like to have sex with Ian in a shower? Jax moaned as her mind wandered down that sensual path—Ian laving at her sex, Ian pressing her against the shower wall while driving his hard shaft into her. Frustrated at her traitorous thoughts, she turned the water to cold before shutting off the faucet.

Stepping out of the shower, she inhaled sharply at the sight of Blake leaning against the doorframe, his arms crossed over his chest.

"Blake!" Jax pulled the towel down off the shower rod and wrapped it around herself, tucking it between her breasts in quick, jerky motions. "How long have you been standing there?" She narrowed her eyes on his grinning face.

He raised his dark eyebrows. "Long enough to wish I had been in the shower with you. The noises I heard made me think you might want company."

Jax felt her cheeks grow hot at his close scrutiny. Ignoring his comment, she picked up her hairbrush and began pulling the bristles through her wet hair. "You have no right to be in here. What do you want?"

"I want to help you with Drace. I don't like you doing this alone."

"We've been though this before, Blake. I work alone. Period."

Blake's concerned expression turned hard, angry. He reached over and swiped his hand across the mirror, wiping away the fog. Turning her shoulders until she faced the mirror, he touched the space between her neck and shoulder. "I don't think you did this alone, Jax." Turning on his heel, he walked out of the room.

Jax leaned over and looked at the place he touched. A perfect bite-mark bruise showed through her skin. God, Ian truly had branded her. Why did that knowledge both thrill and disturb her?

Chapter Five

Jax entered The Red Satin nightclub among a group of college-age students. She'd even had her ass grabbed as she squeezed through the crowd. She chuckled at the look on the young guy's face when she grabbed his hand before he could whip it away.

"I'm a bit old for that."

"But you're dressed just right for it." He had the nerve to reply.

Jax couldn't help it. She laughed at his ballsy statement and let him go. He was right. She had dressed in the best damn "fuck me" outfit she could find. Well, when one goes looking for trouble, one needs to fit the part.

She walked over to the bar and smoothed her hand down her outfit's short skirt. The red, long-sleeved, fitted dress clung to her curves all the way to her hips where a skirt floated around the tops of her thighs. A keyhole cutout over her breasts allowed for a good view of her cleavage. Dangle diamonds in her earlobes, her requisite chopsticks in her hair, and red, three-inch spike heels completed the outfit.

She even attempted the impossible, putting on lipstick. Blood red at that. As she surveyed the decadent red furnishings of the nightclub, the three-tiered dance floor, and the crowd of people dancing to the latest rap song, Jax had to smirk at the fact she got dressed in a hotel room. Wouldn't Blake have a cow if he saw her dressed like this? Good thing he wouldn't be seeing her.

Her body's internal warning system hummed with the vibrations of vampires all around her—the bartender who handed her a drink, the guy sitting at the bar, about to grab her ass. Jax sighed and deftly moved away. As she put the drink to her lips, her eyes met Drace's across the crowded dance floor.

He sat in a circular booth right off the dance floor, flanked on either side by women. A redhead kissed his neck while a blonde dipped her head under the table. Jax had no trouble discerning her intent.

As she watched them, the rap song *In Da Club* by 50 Cent started up, the gangsta beat thumping through her body. Jax couldn't help but tap her foot to the body-rockin' rhythm. When she met Drace's gaze once more, he raised his glass in mock salute to her.

Care to join us? Drace spoke in her mind while the loud bass in the music made her heart jerk in time to the song's steady thump.

As a hunter, Jax was familiar with many of the vampires' vast powers, from compelling humans and animals to their ability to speak in one's mind. Still, the sensation of his voice in her head surprised her, since this was the first time Drace had deemed to use his powers to communicate with her.

Jax gave him a seductive smile then mouthed very slowly so he couldn't possibly misunderstand, "Kiss...my...ass."

And it's such a lovely one, too. Drace's cruel lips twisted into a smile.

If you want it, come and get it, Jax thought. She smirked at her thoughts, knowing he couldn't read them, and set down her glass. Turning away, she walked through the crowd surrounding the dance floor and headed toward the bathroom. Squeezing through the crush of people outside the bathroom, she finally made it inside.

Once she finished up in the bathroom, Jax checked her makeup in the mirror and straightened her skirt before opening the bathroom door.

Before she made it more than two steps her throat was grabbed in a vise-like grip and Drace slammed her against the wall outside the bathroom.

"You've hounded me long enough," he hissed, displaying his fangs as he leaned closer. His gaze dropped to her neck. "I've wanted to taste you for quite a while now."

How convenient that the long hall to the bathrooms she'd had to claw her way through were now empty and dark, Jax thought. Drace must've compelled everyone to leave. Great, where's an annoying crowd when you need one?

"Don't you know you're supposed to savor your food? You know, take your time, maybe toy with it a bit before you devour it?" she quipped.

Drace leaned back and contemplated her. "Why are you so fixated on me?"

Jax glared at him and he tightened his hold on her neck for a brief second.

"Answer me."

She knew he could compel her but instead he chose pain. Just like he did with her father. The bastard. "You killed my father."

Drace threw his head back and laughed. "You'll have to be more specific than that. I've killed many humans."

He tightened his hold further, making her reach up and grasp his fingers around her throat in an effort to pry them away.

"Who are you?" he demanded.

"Need some help?" Ian asked as he casually crossed his arms and leaned against the wall a few feet away. Dressed in gray slacks and a black shirt, he looked just like any other partygoer.

"No, thanks. I got it covered," Jax rasped out as she managed to get some reprieve from Drace's tight hold around her throat when he looked up at Ian.

Both men laughed at her bold statement. Drace turned to Ian. "You have to admit, the woman has balls."

"Oh, I've got balls all right," Jax said, "Yours, right where I want them."

* * * * *

While she pulled at Drace's grip around her neck with one hand, Ian noted the laser light from Jax's gun made a brilliant glow against Drace's crotch. Ian chuckled at her brash move as Drace hissed at her in anger.

"Release me or I'll pull the trigger," she managed to choke out.

Just then, Ian heard a sound a few feet behind him.

"Have her release Drace, Ian, or I'll blow your head off," a vamp said from behind him.

Jax narrowed her eyes on Drace. "Looks like we're at a standoff. Have your vamp release Ian, then I'll let you go."

Ian noted the anger and frustration reflected in Drace's expression before he turned to her. "Why are you protecting him?" Then he paused as if realization dawned. He looked from Jax to Ian. "Ah, two adversaries after a common foe...is that it?"

Ian would've ignored him, but Jax chimed in, drawing Drace's attention back to her. "Something like that."

Drace let go of her throat only to draw a finger down the smooth column. "I think I like the idea of being the hunter instead of the prey. I'm a *much* better predator. And you're a human worthy of a good fuck. What did you say your name was?"

Ian's stomach clenched at the idea that Drace now saw Jax as prime meat and not just a hunter to be avoided.

"Jax Markson, you murdering bastard. You killed my father, John. Remember my name because you're already fucked as far as I'm concerned."

Jax's true identity was the last thing Ian expected. He still hadn't heard back from Mark. To discover Jax was John Markson's daughter blew him away. But the information did explain her driving need to eliminate Drace.

Drace's laugh was rich and unconcerned as he turned to Ian. "So, you two really *are* going to have to fight over me, aren't you, Ian?"

"We're—" Ian started to speak, to show a united front, when Jax interrupted him.

"You're mine, Drace."

Drace turned back to her and extended his fingernail at the tip of his finger. Pressing it into her neck, he drew forth several drops of blood. "And you," he tasted the red liquid on his finger, "Mmmm, you taste good. You are mine, Jax Markson."

"No," Ian bellowed as bloodlust coursed through his veins. No one touched Jax or tasted her blood but him. Ian didn't think, but moved purely on instinct. Without turning, he shot the vamp behind him with the gun he had tucked under his arm, then aimed at Drace, but it was too late, the vamp had shifted into mist.

Sensing more vamps would be on them in seconds, Ian took two long strides, grabbed Jax by the wrist, and broke into a run down the hall, saying as he pulled her behind him, "Come on. We've got company coming,"

Jax made him stop long enough for her to kick off her heels. Once she'd tossed her shoes, Ian pushed her in front of him when they heard the vamps enter the hall and Drace ordering them to hunt them down.

Jax's heart raced as she darted down the long hall. Oriental rugs, oil paintings on the walls, and sconces that gave off a low yellow glow were the only markers she had to go by. The hall ended with a dark cherry console table against the far wall. Now she had to make a decision to turn left or right. Right. Listening as gunshots reverberated down the hall, she waited until Ian saw which path she took and then took off ahead of him.

She'd passed several opportunities to turn left or right and had looked back over her shoulder to make sure Ian followed when she ran right into a wall—a tall, vampire wall of muscle. The impact knocked her back, sending the gun flying out of her hand. Fear for survival made Jax attempt to retrieve her gun, but the dark-headed vampire grabbed her arm before she could react, ripping her dress as he jerked her against him. While she struggled, he quickly lifted her and wrapped his arms around her waist, squeezing until she was almost out of air. "I think Drace wants to talk with you."

Gasping for breath, knowing she was on the verge of losing consciousness, Jax reached up, pulled a chopstick out of her hair, and jammed it into the vampire's jugular. Blood spewed as he howled and dropped her to grab his neck.

She dove for her gun, sliding across the floor. Turning over, she aimed for the vamp's chest as he pulled the chopstick out of his neck and staggered toward her, his face contorted in pain and rage. She had to fire three times before the man went down.

Once the vamp fell and stayed down, Jax leapt up and realized she was once again at a crossroads. Man, she'd studied the maps of The Red Satin, but this was all new. It was like being in a rat's maze. She looked back down the hall and didn't see Ian, but she did see several vamps making their way toward her at lightning speed. Where the hell did Ian go? She ducked as a bullet whizzed past her head.

Served her right to depend on anyone but herself. Trusting her instincts, Jax took the right turn and ran as fast as her legs would take her.

She'd almost made it to the end of the hall when she was suddenly jerked to a halt and pulled behind a wall. The wall quickly closed, suffusing the small room in total darkness. Jax lashed out with her foot, connecting with something hard.

She heard a grunt and then a voice hissed, "Stop it, Jax, it's me."

"Ian! Where the hell—?"

His hand covered her mouth and pulled her in front of him, further into the cramped space and away from the entrance.

She couldn't see him, but she felt his rock-hard chest pressed against hers as the space was barely big enough for the two of them. Jax started to shrug his hand away, but Ian cupped his hand behind her neck and put his lips near her ear. "Hush for a sec."

Ian's watch let off a high-pitched sound and the glass face glowed indigo blue. He twisted the dial and the light disappeared and the sound made a higher and higher pitch until it faded away as well. He leaned close to her ear once more. "The high- pitched sound my watch emits will confuse the vampires. They won't be able to hear our hearts beating." He put his arm around her and pulled her close, laying his wrist against her back. "But it only works as long as there's direct contact."

Jax had put a hand on Ian's chest when he pulled her to him. She whispered in his ear. "I want to fight."

"Know when and where to pick your battles, Jax. This place is crawling with vamps."

Jax sighed. She knew he was right. "I guess having vamp blood on my clothes is a good thing, too. The smell should cover our human scent."

"Good point," Ian said amusement in his voice.

Jax's body stiffened and her grip on her gun tightened when she heard vampires pause on the other side of the wall, talking, deciding where she and Ian might have gone. Adrenaline surged through her at the danger that lurked just outside. Her heart thudded, making her very aware of Ian's hard body pressed against hers. In the pitch dark, she felt the warm stirring of his breath, the steady beating of his heart against her chest. Her breasts tightened and her nipples pebbled in response to his heat.

When Ian's lips brushed against her jaw, she held back a gasp. *Surely that was an accident? He wouldn't be so careless as to —*

Ian pressed his lips more firmly against her throat, right over the vein that pulsed to the rapid beat of her heart. With the counter pressure of his lips against her pulse, she could feel her own heartbeat's rapid rhythm. Her lower belly clenched in response when he pressed his hips to hers, pinning her against the wall. His erection, hot and hard between them, caused moisture to gather between her legs.

The vampires moved off and Ian took her gun and laid it on a metal-sounding shelf to her left. Jax held her breath when he pulled the lone chopstick out of her hair and set it on the shelf as well. The rest of her hair tumbled around her and Ian brushed it over her shoulder. His fingers lingered on her skin and he whispered, his voice hoarse and raspy, "I'm sorry, Jax," right before he pulled the torn fabric away from her collarbone and planted a kiss on the curve of flesh between her shoulder and neck.

He kissed her right on the bite-mark bruise, but there's no way he could see it. Jax sighed at the intimate gesture, regardless. Shivers shot through her when Ian slid his hand up her neck and threaded his fingers through her hair, grabbing hold as he trailed his tongue from the base of her throat upward. His hips rocked against hers as he slowly made his way to the gash that Drace had inflicted. With tender swipes, he laved his tongue over her wound.

The primal gesture, as if he were the male lion, lapping the wound of his female mate, was a heady turn-on. Jax clutched his thick shoulders and let him pull her head further back, exposing her throat to his attentive ministrations.

Ian made a low growling sound and laved at her injury once more before he kissed her lips, slanting his mouth over hers. He slid his tongue into her mouth as he stepped into her body, seeking the most intimate connection.

When Ian's tongue touched hers, the steady, unhurried pace of his tongue tracing inside her mouth, gliding against and tangling with hers, surprised Jax. She expected him to kiss her with savage intensity, not this almost reverent exploration of her mouth.

Jax threaded her fingers in Ian's thick, silky hair, pulling him closer, changing the rhythm of their kiss to a more urgent, I've-gotta-have-it-now kiss. Ian groaned quietly against her mouth and lifted her thighs around him as he thrust his cock against her damp panties. Jax bit her lip, wanting to moan at the exquisite feeling of his hard shaft rubbing against her aching clitoris. The fact that she had to keep quiet only made her want to scream at the top of her lungs.

She felt Ian's knuckles brush against her mons as he moved to unbutton his pants and her heart rate soared knowing he had to have her right then, that she'd put him that out of control. The anticipation of waiting for his thick, long cock to slide inside her, to fill her fully, made her breath catch in her throat.

The sound of her underwear ripping as Ian grabbed and twisted the thin strap at one hip and then the other made her sex ache in response to his savage need. Jax wrapped her arms around his neck and waited in tense agony. Her heart pounded as he clasped her bare buttocks and effortlessly lifted her, lowering her over his cock.

Inch by delicious inch he filled her body, stretching her sensitive outer skin while he filled her walls completely until the tip of his cock hit the tip of her womb. Ian held himself perfectly still, his breathing ragged, his shoulders and body tense.

"You feel so good, *a chroí*. So damn right," he whispered, his voice so low she almost didn't hear it.

Jax clenched her muscles around him and smiled at his swift intake of breath. But her smile faded, replaced by an involuntary gasp when Ian withdrew and thrust back in so hard and so fast her body started quaking before she even realized her orgasm was upon her. The force of their passion, the intensity, shocked her, making her orgasm that much more pleasurable.

Ian covered her mouth with his, muffling her cries of ecstasy as he continued to pump in and out of her body, taking her from one orgasm to another and another until she pulled her mouth from his and begged, "Let go, Ian."

Ian groaned and pressed her harder against the wall as he ground his hips against hers. Jax clenched her sheath muscles tight around him, wanting to hold him inside her as long as possible, never wanting the mind-blowing sensations to end.

"Jax," Ian whispered her name forcefully as his entire body tensed and then shuddered. Jax clutched him tighter, riding him until he came.

A low, primal sound escaped her throat when she felt the warmth of his cum coating her walls. Her body trembled with her final orgasm, shaking her senseless. Never had another person made her lose such control, made her reveal so much raw emotion.

When they were both spent, Ian lifted his head from hers as if he were staring at her face. Jax was so thankful he couldn't see the rapid expressions of confusion, shock and amazement she knew had to be flitting across her face.

He leaned close and rubbed his cheek against hers, whispering in her ear, "Are you okay?"

She swallowed and nodded, her arms trembling. She flexed her fingers tighter on his shoulders to release some of the tension. *Man, had he rocked her world or what?*

Ian lowered her legs to the floor and then she felt his hand, rubbing something across her labia. *What was that?* Oh, God. He was cleaning his semen away. He was being so attentive. The intimate gesture frightened her. Self-preservation kicked in.

"Uh, was that my underwear you just used?" she snapped.

His body tensed underneath her fingers and then relaxed. "Yes." He chuckled. "I don't think it was good for much else at this point."

"No thanks to you," she grumbled.

"If you insist on another method..." he began as he started to slide down her body.

When Jax realized his intent, she amended her tone, saying quickly, "Um, no, the underwear will do just fine."

Ian stood back up and finished his task. When he was done, he leaned close to her ear and said, "Now apologize."

Jax stiffened. "For what?"

His hands closed over her shoulders and his thumbs rubbed her collarbone in a gentle massage. *Hey, why wasn't his wrist touching her body?*

"For trying to make what just happened between us less than what it was."

No way would she admit it meant more. That would give Ian too much power over her. She reached up and moved his arm until his watch touched her skin before she answered him. "It was just sex, Ian, hot I-almost-died-and-I-want-to-celebrate-life sex."

Ian stopped rubbing her shoulders and his fingers clutched her tighter, his voice on edge, "What do you mean you almost died?"

Whew! I'm pretty good at getting out of these hot spots. "Where'd you think the vamp blood on me came from?"

"I just assumed it was from a gunshot."

"No, a vamp tried to break my spine by giving me a great big bear hug. So, I had to show him that I'm not into vamp lovin'."

There was a pause and then Ian asked, "If you didn't use your gun, how did you get free?"

"I used one of my chopsticks, of course," she said in a matter of fact tone.

"Of course," he repeated, his chest rumbling with low laughter. She could tell he was shaking his head at her, but he still moved his hands over each of her shoulders and then up and down her arms as if assuring himself she was okay.

* * * * *

Ian started to remind Jax she still hadn't apologized when he heard vamps coming back their way. He pulled her close and whispered, "Not a word, *a chroí.*"

He expected Jax to balk, but instead she stood perfectly still, holding on to his waist. Ian wrapped his arms around her and leaned back against the wall, pulling her with him. When the vamps walked away, he kissed her temple and said in a hushed voice, "They'll be back. We're going to be here for a while, probably until sunrise. Why don't you rest?"

Jax lifted her head and started to pull away, but Ian held firm. "No, Jax. You have to stay close." He knew she intended to withdraw from him. No way. He needed to keep her close, touching him. If nothing else, the contact would work on her physical response to him. He knew it did for him. Her lush body had him hard as a rock again, wanting more.

When he'd cleansed her blood from her neck, the honeyed, erotic taste thrummed through his body, making his fangs unsheathe of their own free will. He had no control when it came to Jax. God, he'd wanted to sink his teeth into her sweet flesh, to take what was his! He'd never felt so physically connected to another before, and the out-of- control emotions he experienced with this woman only solidified his belief that Jax was his *Sonuachar.*

He felt no guilt about making up that bullshit about his watch. Whatever excuse he could use to hold her close, he'd employ to his full advantage. The physical pull between them was a start, but he had to find out why she resisted giving anything of herself. He needed a glimpse into her mind, to find out about her past, find out what made Jax who she was today.

Vamps continued to run up and down the hall reminding him there would be no more talking for the evening. He sighed and cupped the back of her head, pulling it down to rest on his chest. Jax resisted. She was such a stubborn woman! Ian compelled her to relax. When her head finally rested against his chest and her body snuggled into his, a sense of rightness washed over him, yet at the same time fierce protectiveness roared through his mind, tensing his body.

His adrenaline pumped all over again at the thought she'd been in such a precarious position with a vamp, that she could've died while he tried to find a safe place for them to hide. Ian liked a good battle as well as the next vamp, and he would have stuck this one out if he'd been alone. But he had Jax to consider and they were outnumbered at least five to one. Getting Drace came second in his mind. Jax was his number one priority. When dawn came and they were free to walk out of The Red Satin club, he'd take her somewhere safe so they could talk.

Chapter Six

"Wake up, Jax," Ian whispered in her ear. "It's dawn."

Jax came awake quickly, surprised she'd been able to sleep at all, especially standing up. Man, she really needed a vacation when all this was over with Drace. She was slipping. She pushed away from Ian so fast, he fell back against the wall behind him. She heard him grunt and then sigh heavily. "Um, sorry about that. I'm just jittery," she explained in an attempt at an apology.

Ian grabbed her hand and she started to jerk it away, when she felt the cold metal of her gun thrust against her palm. "Here, take your gun. It's time to go." She heard a click and a whooshing sound as Ian shifted her out of the way so he could open a panel on a wall beside them.

Cool air rushed in, refreshing the still, warm air in the room. Ian turned his watch's dial and the indigo glowing light brightened, lighting the stairway deep into the dark passage.

"Come on." He walked ahead of her down the steep steps.

"Hold a sec," Jax called out as she felt around on the wall for the shelf and her lone chopstick. Setting her gun down on the shelf, she hurriedly wrapped her hair up and jammed the chopstick through the fast French twist. Her hair secure once more, she grabbed her gun and exited the room.

Jax skipped down the steps behind Ian, trying to catch up. "Hey," she called out in a whisper, "If you knew about this exit, why didn't we leave by this way earlier?"

"Because I had no guarantees Drace wouldn't have vamps waiting to ambush us," he replied without turning.

Eventually the steps stopped and they took a long passageway that led to a dead end with a door. Bright sunlight peeked through the side seams of the door. Ian unlatched the lock and pulled open the heavy metal. The door made a loud creaking sound and Jax sensed the coiled tension in Ian at the noise.

He peeked his head outside and then pulled open the door. As they walked up the steep inclined driveway from the back of the nightclub Jax stopped, realizing she'd have a hard time getting a taxi this time of the day. Ian stopped and turned to look at her as she asked, "Can I hitch a ride?"

He gave her a quizzical look. "How'd you get here?"

Jax started walking again while she pulled the clip out of her gun and checked the number of rounds left. "I took a cab."

"How did you expect to make a fast getaway?" Ian jogged up beside her, his tone slightly admonishing.

Jax slipped the clip back into the chamber, double-checked the safety and answered, "I didn't expect there to be anyone left to chase me."

Ian grabbed her arm, stopping her in mid-stride. His intense golden eyes met hers. "You're playing with fire. You heard Drace. He has tired of being the prey and his first victim in his role as hunter will be you."

Jax pulled her arm free and walked away. Without looking back, she quipped, "Good. At least I don't have to find him anymore. Saves me time and effort. I'll just wait for him to come to me."

As the reached the top of the incline at the front of the nightclub, Ian said from directly behind her, his voice stern, "Jax, this isn't a game. Drace will kill you."

Jax rounded on Ian, anger rising. "Don't you think I know —?"

"Jax!" A man's voice calling her name interrupted her rant. Jax turned to see Blake approaching, the expression on his face not a happy one.

"What are you doing here, Blake?" She faced her comrade, her shoulders squared, spine ramrod straight. *Did she have a homing device on her or what? How the hell did these men keep finding her?*

Blake's gaze roamed her skimpy outfit, his overnight beard making his expression appear that much harder when his gaze shifted from her bare feet to her torn, bloody top. He grabbed her shoulders and ground out, "Are you all right?"

Conscious of Ian's probing gaze and stiff stance, Jax shrugged out of Blake's hold. "Yeah, this isn't my blood. Unfortunately it's not Drace's either." She met his green gaze with a narrowed one. "You didn't answer my question. Why are you here?"

He pulled a long, narrow jewelry box made of smooth black lacquered wood from his pocket and handed it to her. His eyes flicked to Ian briefly before he spoke. "You left the house before I could give you the gift I purchased while I was out of town."

"You followed me all the way here to give me a gift?" She stared at him incredulously then ground her teeth. "Blake, I don't appreciate being tailed."

Blake gave her an unrepentant, humorless smile. "Yes, I did. And I don't give a shit if you don't appreciate it, Jax. I don't like you risking your neck without backup. Needless to say, I got worried when you didn't leave before the club closed for the night. This place was crawling with vamps. I could smell them." He looked purposefully at Ian before he returned his gaze to her.

Jax turned to Ian to make quick introductions. "My colleague, Blake Grayson." She indicated Ian with her hand and introduced him to Blake, "Ian..." She stopped and frowned when she realized she didn't know the man's last name. *Holy shit! I've had sex with the man twice and I still don't know his last name?*

Ian gave Blake a curt nod. "Ian Mordoor."

"He's a hunter, too," she supplied in haste as she felt the mounting tension build between the two men.

Blake jerked his gaze back to her and stared at her with a penetrating gaze. "I thought you wanted to work alone on this case."

"Ian's just giving me a lift," Jax said.

"I can do that," Blake insisted.

Jax started to speak, but Ian placed a hand on her shoulder saying, "We have unfinished business to discuss."

Blake's fists clenched by his sides as his gaze strayed to Ian's hand on her shoulder. *Oh, boy, I can see a pissing contest about to commence. All I want to do is have a hot shower and take a nap. I don't have time for this crap.* Jax sought a distraction and piped up as she shoved her gun in Blake's hand and lifted the box lid, "What did you get me?"

Blake met her gaze once more and his softened as he chuckled and reached up to pull the lone chopstick out of her hair. "Looks like you'll be needing them."

Jax gasped at the beautiful set of chopsticks. She lifted one in her hand, inspecting the black onyx-like semi-flattened shaft with the pointed tip and said, "It's surprisingly heavy."

He touched the amber round ball at the top. "Yes, but perfectly balanced with this."

Jax laughed. "Ah, I see." Blake was always the hunter even with his gifts.

Ian hadn't removed his hand from her shoulder. He squeezed gently, but firmly. "We need to get out of here, Jax. The vamps may be sleeping but as you well know they can have transers act on their behalf."

Blake put a hand on her arm and pulled, saying, "Excuse us for a moment."

When they'd walked a few feet away, he whispered in her ear, "I don't trust him, Jax. Something about him just doesn't smell right."

Blake had always had a keen sense of smell. That heightened ability had saved his life on several occasions. Jax glanced at Ian and then faced Blake. "He's covered in vamp's blood as am I. Of course he smells funny."

"No, the scent runs deeper." He inhaled and stared directly at Ian. "He's more than an average human."

Jax laughed out loud. "The same could be said about you and your sense of smell, Blake. Now I think you're being paranoid. Maybe his unique 'whatever' is what makes him so good."

Blake narrowed his eyes on her. "If he's so good, why haven't I heard of him?"

"Jax," Ian called in a firm tone.

"Keep your shirt on," she shot back before she turned back to Blake. Ian was rushing her, but there was one thing she wanted to find out. "I remember hearing you speak Irish. What does, '*a chroí*' mean?"

"It means, 'my heart.' Why?" Blake answered with a curious expression.

"Oh, no reason." My heart? That sounded way too sweet, a true endearment. Why couldn't it mean, babe or chick or even hotbox, just something guaranteed to get her feminist ire up? Jax thanked Blake for the gift, retrieved her weapon and walked away wishing she'd never asked.

Ian walked ahead of her with swift, purposeful strides. Jax had to run just to keep up. "Who lit a fire under your pants?" she called out right before she slammed into his back when he stopped abruptly in front of a black Hummer.

Ian turned around, his face set in hard lines, his shoulders tense. Before she could think to move away he cupped the back of her neck and yanked her against his chest, kissing her, plunging his tongue deep in her mouth in a blatant show of male machismo.

Jax stomped on his foot, angered when he leisurely pulled away and flicked his gaze in Blake's direction. She turned her head and sure enough Blake saw what Ian intended for him to see. She noted Blake's narrowed eyes before he climbed in his vehicle and slammed the door shut. Damnit.

Jax shoved him away. "Try that again and I'll shoot you where you stand. Got it?"

Ian set his jaw and opened her door before he turned on his heel and walked around to his side of the car. She climbed in the tall vehicle and Ian did the same.

Jax gave him her hotel location and after a long silence Ian spoke, his voice low, controlled, "Who is Blake to you?"

"Blake? He's as I introduced him," she answered being deliberately vague.

Ian cut his eyes over, his own golden gaze glittering at her. "He spoke as if he lived with you, Jax. Who!" he demanded.

His forceful words made her insides jump, but there was no way she'd let him know he'd gotten to her. "There's nothing to tell. I don't want to talk about Blake, Ian."

Ian turned back to the road, his lips set in a firm line. After a few minutes he said, "Fine. Let's talk about our partnership."

Jax's jaw literally dropped. "Partnership?" She gritted her teeth. "Nothing has changed. Drace is mine."

"Everything has changed," Ian said, his expression fierce. "Drace is gunning for you now. We need to work together to defeat him. Two heads are better than one."

After her initial gut reaction, which was to open the door and jump out of the moving vehicle, Jax had to admit Ian had a point. If it hadn't been for him yanking her in that hidden space, she would probably be dead right now. "I'll think about it," she grumbled.

As Ian pulled into the hotel parking lot and cut the engine, Jax rubbed her hand over the supple charcoal gray leather seat. Hummers weren't cheap vehicles. "Man, vampire hunting must be paying a lot more these days," she quipped.

Ian let his gaze follow her hand before he tucked his gun under his seat and climbed out of the car, saying, "Let's just say I've made some good investments over the years."

She strapped her gun back to her leg and climbed out of the car before Ian could come around to assist her. When he came into view, the sight of dried blood on his shirt reminded her of her own appearance. How in the world were they going to stroll into the hotel unnoticed in their condition? Granted it was around six in the morning. Most people would be asleep.

Ian must've surmised her thoughts from her expression. He clasped her elbow and turned her toward the entrance saying, "Come on. I've got a plan to get you upstairs."

When they walked into the hotel, the concierge looked shocked at their appearance. Ian wrapped his arm around her neck and pulled her close, kissing her temple. "Man, being an actor sure is fun, huh, hon?"

Jax caught on and wrapped her arm around his waist laughing. "Yeah, and no human was hurt during the making of this film either."

Realization dawned on the hotel clerk's face but then based on the changes in his expressions she could literally see his mind working, trying to place them. What movies had they been in? She chuckled as Ian led her to the elevators.

Ian punched the Up button and turned to her. "Grab a shower and I'll meet you down here in an hour and we can discuss our strategy."

"I didn't agree to become your partner, Ian."

The elevator doors slid open and he pushed her inside, completely ignoring her comment. "Go, get cleaned up. We'll talk over breakfast."

Before she could utter a word he walked off. As the shiny metal doors closed and the elevator rose Jax considered the ramifications of accepting Ian's offer. Offer? She snorted. The man didn't know the meaning of the word "ask". Would she be able to handle collaborating with another? She'd been used to working alone for so long, she wondered if she knew how.

When she entered her room, she felt too keyed up to immediately jump into the shower. Jax unstrapped her gun, laid it on the table, and opened her duffel bag. Pulling out her Bowie knife, she sliced through the ruined thin leather straps of her bola weapon and set about attaching new lengths to the stones.

Maybe she should go home tonight instead of staying in the hotel. Blake had already seen her a-la-slutty look. There was no reason to stay. Except the fact she'd already paid for the room. Plus, she may as well enjoy that hot shower and soft bed before heading home. She didn't relish her uncle's reaction when she told him she planned to move to the guesthouse. Sighing, Jax finished the bola and headed for the bathroom.

* * * * *

Ian used the payphone in the lobby to check his messages. He let out a deep breath as he heard Mark's voice over the line.

"Heya, Ian. It's been a while bud. We need to get together over a beer sometime. As for your lady friend, here's what I have on her. Lives at 1424 Oak Lawn Drive with her maternal uncle on a twenty-acre estate. An only child, her father raised her after her mother died during childbirth. While her father became obsessed with hunting vampires— Ha! Got a live one there, don't ya bud?...um...anyway, she grew up, graduated high school with top honors, and attended a military academy.

From there she served four years for her country and has worked for her father ever since, learning to be one of the best vampire hunters around. Her real name is Jacqueline Markson and she has just taken over her father's role fulltime since he was found brutally murdered a little over a month ago. Hmmm, wonder who might have killed John Markson?" His friend gave a humorless laugh. "Get the vamp who did this, Ian, all right?"

Ian replaced the receiver and contemplated Jax. What kind of life had she led growing up without a mother or siblings and a father who hunted vampires half the night?

His thoughts strayed to Blake and his blood boiled at the idea the man and Jax had been more than colleagues. Blake's familiarity with her spoke volumes. Ian had willed himself to remain calm while the man touched Jax when all he wanted to do was strike him down where he stood. Had Jax shown Blake any affection? Had she shared her secrets with him? Jealousy shot through him, digging into his gut. He wanted Jax to open up to him, give something of herself, trust him enough to let down her barriers.

Shrugging off his raging emotions, Ian needed to feed and get a shower before he met Jax for breakfast. He booked a room and returned to his car for his duffel bag.

* * * * *

"Tell me about your father." Ian looked across the table at Jax as she handed the waiter the menu. He'd noted everything about her when she'd met him in the lobby. From her fitted, long-sleeve white cotton shirt to the casual khaki pants she wore, held up with that unusual gold-buckle belt, the woman attracted him like no other. As she turned her head to watch the waiter walk away, he ground his teeth when his gaze landed on the two new chopsticks holding up her hair.

"Aren't you going to eat?" she asked, turning back to him.

"No, I grabbed something earlier."

Looking away, she picked up the linen napkin and spread it in her lap, saying with a catch in her voice, "Now you know why I want Drace so bad. He murdered my father."

Ian lifted his glass of water, took a sip and put it back on the table. "I'm sorry for your loss, Jax, but that isn't what I meant. I want to know what it was like being the daughter of a father with such an unconventional obsession."

Jax met his gaze with angry eyes. "My father wasn't obsessed. He was on a mission."

Did he say obsession? Shit! He'd meant to say profession. "What mission was that?"

She gave him an are-you-stupid look. "To rid the world of vampires, of course."

"Why?"

"What?" She let out an exasperated breath. "Because they are murdering, blood- sucking creatures, Ian." Jax sat back in her chair and put her hands on her hips. "That reminds me. Drace said, 'now we would really have to fight over him'. What did he mean by that?"

"I'm also after Drace for murdering your father."

"You are?" She looked surprised and then a smile crossed her face as she relaxed in her chair. "Good, then you can understand my need for revenge."

Ian shook his head. "No, Jax. My seeking Drace is about justice not revenge."

Jax flipped her hand in a nonchalant manner. "Revenge, justice, they're one in the same."

"No, they're not. Don't get me wrong. I understand your need to avenge your father's death, but for that very reason, you need a partner."

"No, I don't."

Ian gripped his glass tighter. He knew she was going to be stubborn about this. "Yes, you do. You're too close to this hunt, too emotionally involved. Emotions in the equation only lead to mistakes, often deadly ones."

Jax twirled her fork in a circle on the table. He could tell she was mulling over what he'd said. He decided to tilt the scales even more in his direction. "The two of us can divide and conquer, which will become even more important with Drace back on his home turf. You can bet he'll be soliciting more vamp help." He paused and fixed her with a penetrating stare. "For the last month, you seemed to have this uncanny ability to be right on Drace's trail, literally kicking him in the back of the heels to his next location." Ian raised his eyebrow. "How is that possible?"

Jax shifted in her seat. She considered partnering with Ian, but she wasn't about to give up her source. Not yet anyway. She gave him a winning smile. "'Cause I'm that good."

As the waiter set her plate in front of her, Jax laughed outright at Ian's doubtful expression. While she ate her omelet, he remained silent. Once again the man had the amazing ability to make her aware of his presence, even though no words passed between them. Goosebumps formed on her arms and her breasts tingled as his heated gaze seeped right into her pores. Jax refused to look at him while she ate, but when she finished and raised her glass to her lips her eyes invariably met his.

Partner with me. His gaze demanded and oddly enough she heard the words in her head, too. She resisted the shiver that threatened at the dual meaning. The man was one potent, "grade A", never-get-enough-of-him sex magnet.

Jax set her glass down. "Okay, we'll be partners." When he grinned and started to speak, she interrupted, "But for now," she pulled money from her pocket and threw the bills down on the table to cover her meal, "I've got to catch up on some much needed ZZZZs."

When Ian followed her out of the restaurant and over to the elevator doors, Jax punched the Up button and looked at him. "Where do you think you're going?"

He regarded her with serious eyes and replied, "Upstairs with you."

The elevator doors slid open and Jax walked inside. She turned and put her hand on Ian's chest, preventing his entrance. "I said we could be partners in crime, not in bump-and-grind, Ian."

He stiffened at her words, his jaw tightening.

The doors started to shut and Jax pulled her hand inside. Ian didn't try to stop the doors from shutting, but the look of sheer determination on his face before the doors closed caused a shudder to pass through her.

Chapter Seven

Jax's eyes came open at the sound. What was it? She gripped the knife she always kept tucked under her pillow. Earlier she'd closed the drapes in the room so she could sleep, but now the late afternoon sun behind the curtain cast the room in long, dark shadows.

She sucked in her breath when Ian leaned over her and kissed her neck. Pushing him back, she laid her Bowie knife against his neck, noting his bare chest. With an inward smirk she surmised that the rest of him was just as naked.

"I know you want me," he said in a self-assured tone.

Jax pushed the sharp edge of the knife further against his skin. If he moved at all, he'd have a nice slice across his neck. "Just because I'm tough doesn't mean I'm not a woman. You still need to ask."

She could see the anger in his eyes before he spoke as he curled his fingers around her wrist. "Then I'm asking, Jax. I want you."

When he finished speaking he slid his hand over hers and pulled the knife from her hand. He put the knife on the nightstand and before she could react, he'd turned and captured her wrists in his hand. Drawing them over her head, he wrapped the leather bola string around one wrist.

No way would she let him tie her up. She'd be too vulnerable. "I won't be tied," she gritted out as she started to twist away, but Ian quickly straddled her hips. When he let go of one of her hands in order to secure her wrist to the spindle on the headboard behind her, Jax took full advantage. She punched him in the arm and then went straight for his jaw, but Ian just dodged her blow and chuckled as he grabbed flailing arm and secured that hand to the bed as well.

Once he'd secured her arms, he put his hands on either side of her and leaned close. "I am your partner in *every* way. I want more from you than you're giving me, Jax. I want to make love to you and tying you is the only way I can guarantee you'll let me." He stroked his fingers over her breasts, a gentle caress, pausing to brush her nipples with his thumbs. Jax closed her eyes, shook her head, and willed herself not to respond. But her nipples tingled and tightened anyway.

"Who is Blake to you?" Ian leaned over and flicked her nipple with his tongue.

She let out a huff of exasperation. "I told you already. He's a comrade."

Ian's penetrating gaze met hers. "He's too familiar with you, Jax. *He* thinks there's something there." He pinched her nipples between his fingers, twisting them until she moaned and arched closer to his hands. Ian slid off of her hips and let his warm mouth hover over her nipple while he traced his hand down her abdomen to cup her swollen, moist folds. "Did you open up to him, share your deepest secrets?" His tone held a steel edge as if he were angry.

Jax bucked against his hand and pressed her breast closer to his mouth. Ian chuckled and captured the taut tip, sucking, then nipping the pink nub as he slid a finger over her clitoris. Spreading her lower lips with his fingers, he pushed a finger deep inside her. Jax panted, inching closer to his warm body, wanting more. Ian traced his tongue along the plump underside of her breast while he slid a finger inside her and rubbed his palm against her aching nub. When he slowly stroked his finger in and out of her body, her stomach clenched tighter and tighter as her climax drew near.

Ian lifted his head, withdrew his finger and laid his hand, warm from her moisture against her thigh, clasping the muscle firmly. His intemperate gaze locked with hers. "Tell me," he demanded.

"He didn't torture me the way you seem to enjoy doing," she spat out, angry with herself for letting him get to her.

Ian stared at her for a long moment and she saw anger flicker through his eyes. He put his hands on either side of her once more, drawing close. "I'm not trying to torture you, Jax, but I want more than you're giving me. I won't let you hide yourself from me. I want everything."

Jax shook her head at him. He scared her more than anything else she'd faced in her life. "I don't have any more to give you."

He kissed her, his tongue taking long, thorough strokes against hers. When Jax began to return his kiss, he pulled back, leaving her angry and breathless.

"Yes, you can give more of yourself, *a chroí,* and I won't settle for anything less."

Ian moved down her body and settled between her legs. Bending her knees, he pushed them outward as he slid his thumbs over her sex. Jax closed her eyes and clenched her fists, pulling on the ties around her wrists, trying to inch closer to him.

"Is this all you want from me, Jax?"

The surprising slide of his cock inside her made Jax arch her back and keen in pleasure.

"Yes!" she hissed out.

Ian withdrew from her and her eyes flew open in frustration until she saw his head descend between her legs. The rough rasp of his tongue against her clitoris and the fullness of his fingers sliding inside her brought her so close. She canted her hips toward his masterful mouth and tongue, but Ian shoved her back down on the bed, pinning her to still her movements.

"I want *more*, Jax."

Her sex throbbed, her nipples tingled, her entire body bowed in its need for fulfillment. Tears formed in her eyes, her chest burned. She couldn't give in to him. Never before had she depended on anyone for happiness, only herself and she never would.

"I can't, Ian."

He held his cock against her entrance, pushing in slightly. Jax's lower muscles contracted in response.

"Damn you, Jax. I want all of you, not just your body."

He slid inside her once more. "I want you to trust me." He pulled out and sank home again, this time staying buried deep inside her. "I want you to let me help you, to depend on me, to give something of yourself…" He paused and rocked his hips against her, pressing deeper. "I want you to open up your heart to me."

Her emotions raged within her: fear, desire, raging need, fierce, intense craving, surprising joy at his words. *I can't let someone else be responsible for my happiness.*

Ian stopped his movements and looked at Jax. He'd heard her words as if she'd spoken them out loud. She was projecting and she didn't even realize it. Joy filled his heart. The connection between them had already started and he had yet to take her blood. His heart rate elevated at the realization.

When a tear trickled down her check, Ian swore, grabbed the knife, and cut her free. Jax pulled him close and planted a kiss on his neck, whispering, "I'll try, Ian. That's all I can promise." She wrapped her arms tighter around his neck while she lifted her legs and locked her ankles around his hips.

Ian ground his hips against hers and groaned against her shoulder, murmuring in Irish, "*Go raibh maith agat.*"

"What does that mean?"

Ian lifted his head and ran a finger across her lower lip, then trailed his thumb along her jaw line. "It means 'Thank you'."

Jax smiled, then sucked in her breath when he swiftly rolled over onto his back, taking her with him.

Ian pushed her shoulders until she sat upright on his hips, his cock still buried deep inside her. Jax smiled, arched her back, and rocked against him. He skimmed his hands up her waist, touching each rib until his hands reached her breasts. Testing their weight and fullness, he rubbed his thumbs across the pink buds.

Jax leaned over and kissed him, tracing her tongue along the edge of his bottom lip. Ian reveled in Jax's acceptance of their lovemaking, the wanton nature she displayed without even realizing it. He slid his hands up her back and pulled her against him while he thrust inside. Sexual need coiled within him as she rocked against him, her pelvic bone applying pressure. Her soft body rubbed against his as her inner muscles clamped around his cock. He ground his teeth at the erotic feeling and concentrated on forcing his incisors back to their normal length. Soon he'd take her blood. It was only a matter of time.

Jax grasped the sheet underneath him and cried out, "Yes."

He skimmed his hands back down her spine and grabbed her ass. Cupping the firm cheeks, his fingers drew closer and closer until he pressed his fingers against their joined bodies.

Jax screamed as her orgasm rolled through her. As her sheath contracted around his cock, Ian kept up the pressure with his hands while driving into her until her tremors started all over again. God, the feel of her walls milking him as she came…her body felt so right, warm and wet, soft and tight, and ah, damn…

He groaned as his own orgasm hit him, causing him to thrust deeper, his movements intentional, dominat, possessive. In his mind, with each thrust, he claimed her as his. And this time, Jax didn't fight the emotions. She welcomed him, sighing in delight when her body spasmed around him once more.

Jax laid her head down on Ian's chest, the slick heat of their bodies from such passionate lovemaking felt so good. He ran his hands up and down her back, speaking to her in Irish. She'd never tire of hearing his voice. The low register seeped all the way to her bones, making her feel safe, protected, and happy.

Happy?

At the surprising thought, she rolled over and moved to get up. Ian's hand encircled her wrist and pulled her back onto bed. "No you don't. You promised, Jax," he reminded her as he snuggled her back against his chest.

With his chest to her back, he literally draped her in the warm cocoon of his body, making sure every part of his body touched hers. The warmth felt like heaven. She wanted to melt into him. Maybe just for a little while, she thought as she allowed her body to relax and accepted his gentle caresses down her arm and waist.

When he kissed her neck, then rubbed his nose into her hair and inhaled, her heart softened even more.

"Tell me about your childhood," he whispered in her ear.

She let out a deep breath, then answered, "My life started before I was even born."

Ian's heart contracted at the sadness in her words. He ran his fingers through her hair all the way to the ends. When she sighed he started the same process all over again.

"That feels good," she admitted.

Ian smiled and urged her on. "Go on."

"When my mother was nine months pregnant with me she was bitten by a vampire. Not long after that my mother went into labor. It was a difficult delivery. There were problems."

Her body tensed in his arms and Ian said in reassuring voice, "It's okay, Jax, I'm here."

She took a steadying breath and continued, "My mother died the day she delivered me. My father blamed the vampire for her death. No," she corrected. "He blamed all vampires. As do I, for I'll never know my mother. Or my father," she whispered the last.

If Ian hadn't had such keen hearing, he would have missed her last comment. His chest tightened at Jax's lot in life. God, her mother? Bitten by a vampire. Obviously rogue. No honorable vampire would take the much-needed blood of a pregnant woman. No wonder her father had hated vampires.

"Who took care of you?"

Jax stiffened in his arms. "My dad did, of course."

"How could he have always been there for you if he was out hunting vampires half the night?"

Jax closed her eyes at his caring question. Tears threatened. But she refused to let them fall. So what if during her early teenage years on more nights than she could count she went to bed to an empty house, hence her fitful sleeping patterns. Her father loved her, in his own way. "My uncle was there for me," she said, her tone defensive. *Well, only until I was fourteen. Guess they figured I was old enough to leave alone overnight by then.* "Sometimes," she whispered to herself.

Ian rolled her over and kissed her temple, then her cheek and her jaw. "I'm sorry, Jax."

He kissed a tender path down her chest, her stomach, her inner thigh. When he kissed his way back up, Jax opened her legs as he braced himself over her. Ever so slowly he eased inside her moist channel while he continued kissing her shoulder, her chest, her neck, her jaw—every part of her body he could reach as if by kissing her he could erase her lonely past.

Jax slid her hands over his sculpted chest, loving the feel of his warm skin covering the muscles bunching and moving underneath her fingers. When his mouth covered hers and his tongue gently enticed and seduced hers, his erection seated fully in her body, making Jax sigh against his mouth. Ian pulled out and slid back inside. He set a slow, poignant pace, one that brought her to the edge only to start back over again.

The feeling of his hips pressing hers to the bed, his hard body over hers, dominant, but gentle made her want to weep that such a strong, powerful man cared enough about her to make love gently, reverently, passionately. In his own way, Ian showed her that he cared about her feelings.

"I care for you very much," he whispered in her ear as if he'd heard her thoughts. Laying his chest on hers, he thrust deep and stayed buried, pressing into her. "No matter what, Jax, know I speak the truth."

Jax didn't know how to respond, but her body answered for her as his intense act and sincere words set off a series of tremors within her, causing her moist walls to contract around his shaft. "Ian…"

"I feel you, *a ghrá*," he said in a husky voice near her ear.

He jammed deeper, causing her breath to hitch and her orgasm's pleasure to peak.

"You are no longer alone. I will always be here for you."

Jax sobbed and clung to him, wrapping her legs around his hips. He made her feel so safe and loved.

"Always," he repeated as he withdrew and thrust back in once more until he shuddered and groaned as he succumbed to his own climax.

* * * * *

Ian opened his eyes as soon as Jax closed the bathroom door behind her and turned on the shower. Early morning sunlight slipped through the crack in the drawn curtain, slicing a line of warmth down the covers on his waist. He yawned and stretched as he considered the merits of joining Jax in the shower. Better not push her too soon too fast or he'd lose all the ground he'd gained last night.

He'd lost count of the number of times they'd made love. Until the wee hours, until they both passed out in sheer exhaustion. All he knew was he'd never get enough of her. And this was without tasting her blood! His cock hardened instantly when he imagined the heightened intensity of their lovemaking once they mated in the vampire way. After last night he knew she'd come to care for him even if she wouldn't admit it right now. Soon he'd tell her about his vampire status.

When the shower turned off and he heard her moving around in the bathroom, Ian rubbed his jaw, ready for a shower himself. The rough sandpaper sound rasping against his hand reminded him he'd left his bag of toiletries in his room. He hoped Jax didn't mind sharing her razor. Then he smiled at the idea of sharing such simple things with her.

He got up and walked over to the bathroom to ask if he could borrow her razor when he heard the sound of a dial tone coming from within the bathroom. Why would Jax use her cell phone in the bathroom?

He didn't give a damn about ethics as he concentrated so he could hear who she called. The hair on the back of his neck stood up when he clearly heard Sebastian Gauthier's calm, cultured voice come across the line.

"Good evening, Jax, my dear. I heard things didn't go so well at The Red Satin club…"

The Norriden leader had been Jax's source? Disloyalty and dissention among the leaders was hard enough to discover, but to learn Jax had held back from telling him the truth…blind rage suffused him as he slammed open the bathroom door.

Jax looked up at the crash of the door against the wall. A surprised expression crossed her face when Ian grabbed the phone from her hand and curled his fingers around it.

His shoulders tense, his face set in hard lines he said, "Is this how you've been one step ahead of me when it came to Drace?" He snapped the phone closed. "Cheating," he finished as he raised his voice in anger.

Jax met his gaze head on, an angry look on her face. She pushed off the counter she'd been leaning against and made a grab for the phone.

"Give me my phone back, Ian," she bit out.

"No," he thundered and threw it against the wall, splintering the cell phone into hundreds of little pieces. As he turned back to her, he finished, "You will learn to track vamps the old-fashioned way, by using your head and your hunting skills."

Before he could anticipate her next move, Jax grabbed the counter top behind her, lifted her body, and shoved both of her feet into his solar plexus, hard. Ian slammed back against the wall, hitting his head against the tile with such momentum, he actually saw stars.

"I do things *my* way," Jax said before she bolted out the door.

Ian lay there for a good five minutes before he could see straight again. Once he no longer saw two of everything, he quickly got to his feet, pulled on his clothes and took off after Jax. He knew that his anger must have seemed unwarranted to Jax, but the idea that the Norriden leader had chosen to provide Jax with information on Drace sent him off the deep end. Why had Sebastian gotten involved?

Ian took the steps leading to the lobby, knowing with his vamp speed he'd be faster then the elevator. When he reached the parking lot, he breathed a sigh of relief that his Hummer's tires were all still intact. As he opened the door, he noted two things sitting on his car seat along with a note.

He picked up the homing device he'd planted on her car fender while she showered yesterday. Then he picked up his watch or pieces of his watch rather. It appeared as if she'd run her car over the platinum piece of jewelry as it was now suspiciously flat.

No gadgets. Find me the old-fashioned way. Her note taunted him.

Ian crumpled the note in his hand. The woman would be the death of him.

Where would Jax run? His gaze narrowed as he climbed in his car and turned the key in the ignition. Home and straight to Blake. Intense jealousy sliced through him. Tamping down the urge to drive straight to the Wellington estate, Ian decided to pay Sebastian a visit first.

Chapter Eight

The distinct clicking sound of a bullet being loaded into its chamber brought Sebastian quickly awake. He stared at the semiautomatic weapon no less than an inch from his nose and then met Ian's furious gaze.

Ignoring the gun stuck in his face, Sebastian touched Yvonne's lush rear, wanting to know she was safe. She woke, groggy and sexy, throwing her long blonde hair over her shoulder.

"What?" she said in a sleepy voice.

"It's time for you to go home," Ian said to her in a matter of fact tone.

Yvonne clutched the covers to her naked breasts as she eyed the gun in Ian's hand.

"Go. Now," Ian said once more and that's all it took. She bolted from the bed, grabbed her clothes, and left before he could even say goodbye.

Sebastian narrowed his gaze on Ian once Yvonne had left the room. "Not only do you break into my home, you disturb my sleep, and send away my bedmate?"

Ian put his booted foot up on the hunter green Egyptian cotton sheets. "You don't seem to have a problem interfering in my life. Why shouldn't I return the favor?"

Ian's humorless smile told Sebastian that the hybrid knew exactly what he'd been up to.

Sebastian let his gaze slide from the mud Ian's shoe left on his sheets, up Ian's khaki pants and black turtleneck, to his face in a slow, purposeful manner. When his gaze met Ian's once more, he put an invisible hand around the vamp's neck and squeezed. A smile of satisfaction curved his lips when he noted Ian's body tensing. Sebastian used his powers to reach inside of the vamp's body and grab hold of his heart.

Don't think I won't get off a point-blank shot before you stop my heart, Ian said in an imperturbable tone that impressed the hell out of Sebastian considering the vamp had to be in considerable pain.

He released his hold and gave Ian a disinterested look. Shrugging, he said, "Miss Markson deserves to avenge her father's death."

Ian snorted. "Let me translate that for you. You want Jax to beat me in getting Drace so I fall flat on my face as the new Ruean leader."

Sebastian couldn't help the smile that played on his lips. "Astute for a mongrel."

Ian narrowed his eyes. "And that's what this is really all about isn't it? My hybrid status."

Sebastian curled his lip in disdain. "Only a pureblood should lead a clan."

"Pure doesn't automatically mean worthy," Ian shot back.

They stared each other down, each measuring the other's worth. The man *had* managed to get past his security and his wolves. Plus, the hybrid could have killed him at any point during their conversation. Sebastian's respect for Mordoor grew.

"I concede your point. Kraid obviously came from bad blood and Drace as well."

Ian laughed, arching his eyebrow. "And pureblooded the both of them, imagine that."

Sebastian met Ian's steady golden gaze. "All right. I won't provide Miss Markson any more clues." When Ian gave him a curt nod and turned to leave, Sebastian couldn't help one last dig, "And may the best man or *woman* win."

* * * * *

Jax pulled her Land Rover to a halt in front of the Wellington gates and pushed the remote button on her sun visor. The gates didn't budge and soured her mood further. What the hell was up with Ian? Why had he been so angry at her? She climbed out of her car and punched in the security code on the gates. Once they opened she climbed back in her car and drove through.

As she drove up the long driveway, she noted the gates didn't close behind her and sighed. Damn gates. They were temperamental when opened with the security code. She'd have to close them using the code once she got to the house.

Walking inside she punched in the code on the security panel and called out for her uncle. When she received no reply, she checked his office, the kitchen, the study, his bedroom. Where could he be? Jax walked back into his office and noticed a piece of paper on his desk.

Jax,

Don't know if you'll be home today or not, but just in case I thought I'd leave you a note. Blake and I are off to pick up some new weapons he scouted out on his last trip. Be back around dinnertime.

Uncle James.

Speaking of weapons. Jax realized she'd left her bag out in her car in the driveway. As she walked toward the front door, she noted the red light blinking on the security panel. Odd, it should be green now that the gates were closed.

Jax's senses kicked into high gear as she lifted a picture frame on a wall in the entryway and pushed a panel behind it. When the panel slid out of the way, she grabbed the gun she knew her uncle kept stashed in a hiding place. Holding the gun behind her back, she opened the door a crack, her body tense, ready for attack.

"Good morning, miss," a man called to her from the driveway.

Jax tucked the gun between her spine and the waistband of her jeans, pulled the door open, and stepped onto the porch. "Can I help you?"

A young man with a friendly smile shut the door of his florist van. He touched his baseball cap as he walked toward her with a bouquet of blood red roses in his hand.

"Hope you don't mind, but the gate was open."

"I believe you have the wrong house," she said in a clipped tone.

He frowned and checked the clipboard attached to his waist. "It says here to deliver to Miss Jax Markson at 1424 Oak Lawn Drive. Are you Miss Markson?"

She nodded and stepped down the steps.

He handed her the flowers. "These are for you. There's a card inside."

As Jax pulled the card from the holder, she noted that the man squinted against the sun. The hairs on her arms stood up and her body started to tingle.

She reacted on reflex, throwing the glass vase, flowers and all, at him as she reached to pull her gun. She'd just retrieved her weapon when a sudden pain slammed into her neck, followed by a searing sting.

"Son of a bitch," she hissed out. Grabbing at the source of pain, her hand encountered a small tranquilizer dart imbedded in her neck. Pulling it out, she turned her furious gaze toward another man standing off to her right, training his tranq gun on her. As her vision began to blur, Jax lifted her arm, gun aimed at the offender, and crumpled to the ground.

* * * * *

When Jax came fully awake she realized two things: her mouth felt like the Sahara and she was tied up in an uncomfortable position. She shook her groggy head and blinked to clear her vision as she surveyed her surroundings. A dresser, a nightstand and a wooden chair were the only pieces of furniture in the room other than the double bed underneath her. She cast a glance toward the window. Rain pelted the glass pane, casting a dim light into the room. *What time was it?* she wondered. How long had she been out? She craned her neck to see the clock on the dresser against the wall. Four? She'd been out for hours and no one would know where she was.

She lay there on her side, her mouth gagged, her hands bound behind her back and her ankles tied as well. The doorknob rattled as if someone were unlocking it and then the door opened. Jax shut her eyes, pretending to be unconscious.

Heavy footfalls approached the bed. A man. He stopped in front of her and her entire body vibrated at his presence. A vampire. Drace. She didn't have to see the bastard to know he stood before her.

"Open your eyes, Jax. I know you're awake."

Jax refused to give him the satisfaction. She kept her lids closed and her body perfectly relaxed as if in sleep.

When his large hand clamped on her breast through her button-down shirt, her eyes flew open and she tried to squirm backward while her gaze shot daggers at the vamp. His laugher, sinister and wholly evil made a sliver of fear skim down her spine.

He clasped her buttock to keep her from moving away as his other hand slid over her breasts and her waist until he reached her belt buckle.

"I hope you like pain, Jax." His dark eyes skimmed her body, lust evident in his gaze. "I like inflicting pain when I fuck a weak human."

To prove his point he pinched her nipple hard, causing tears to form in her eyes. But she refused to let him know how much he'd hurt her. Instead she railed out at him through the cloth gagging her.

"What was that?" A malevolent smile spread across his face as he pulled her gag away.

"You son of a bitch. When I'm done with you, you'll be begging me to end your miserable excuse for a life."

Drace laughed at her threats. Amusement showed when his gaze met hers again. "Your complete audacity actually attracts me, Jax." He leaned over until his mouth touched her ear. "And I'm going to enjoy every last lesson of taming you, my little unworthy human."

"You won't lay a hand on me, Drace. I'll guarantee you that," she said as anger simmered to the surface at her predicament.

Before she could pull away, he clamped his teeth on her neck. Holding her still, the threat of his incisors sliding into her skin, he spoke in her mind, *Oh, but I already have and will any time I please. Make no mistake, you're mine to toy with, Jax Markson.*

Drace kept his mouth on her neck as he slid his hand up her thigh.

No! her mind screamed.

A loud knocking on the door followed by a man's concerned voice interrupted his hand's assent. "Drace, the wolves are howling. Another vampire is about."

"Fuck!" Drace said after he released her neck. Straightening, he pulled the gag back over her mouth. "Not a peep from you or I'll have to punish you later, got it?"

Jax just glared at him. Drace grabbed her hair, chopsticks and all, and yanked her head back. "Am I clear?" he demanded.

Pain seared through her skull as he pulled her neck until she felt it might snap. Finally she blinked and tried to nod.

A pleased smile touched his lips. "See, you're learning already."

Drace let go of her hair and walked toward the door. Jerking it open, he said to someone on the other side, "Go inside and keep a watch on her. I'll take a couple of men and check it out."

Before the guard came into the room Jax arched her back and pulled her feet through her tied arms. It hurt like hell to contort her body at such a fast pace, but she needed to be ready before the guy saw what she'd done.

When the man entered, his machine gun in hand, Jax rolled over, facing away from him, hoping the guard thought she turned away in an effort to snub her captors. She heard him grunt and settle into the chair. With slow movements, she lifted her hands to her mouth, pulled away the gag and started to bite at the knots tying her hands together.

When a hand landed on her shoulder, Jax rolled over prepared. Her wrists completely free, she swung hard only to have her fists caught in a much larger hand. Jax stared in shock at Ian standing over the bed. He immediately clamped a hand over her mouth and shook his head, telling her not to speak.

She nodded her understanding and Ian withdrew his hand to work on the ropes at her ankles. When Jax sat up, she looked at the man who'd been her guard. He slumped over in his chair as if in sleep, but she knew better. His head hung at an odd angle. She noted the open window and the rain pouring in. Is that how Ian got in? Had to be. His hair looked damp.

Ian pulled the pistol out of the holster strapped to the dead guard's body and handed it to her. Then he picked up the man's Uzi from the floor and signaled her to follow him. Peeking out the door, he slowly opened it the rest of the way and stepped into the hall. Jax followed close behind.

They crept down the hall, heading toward the back of the house. A door slammed off in the distance near the front of the house and she heard Drace bellow, "Find the son of a bitch, Mordoor's here somewhere. I smell him."

Ian put his arm back behind him, pushing her against the wall. Even wet, the warmth of his skin comforted her. When he pulled his arm away, Jax frowned. His skin? But he wore a thick, black cable sweater. How'd she feel his skin?

His entire body tensed as he poised, waiting. He swept his gaze back down the hall behind her and then returned his line of vision toward the front of the house.

When voices came from a direction behind them, her heart rate picked up. In front and behind, either way they'd face vamps. Jax straightened her spine, raised her gun, and turned her back to Ian's to face their enemies behind them. Ian grabbed her arm and said, "No, Jax."

Right when he said her name, Ian jerked her to the side as a knife embedded in the wall near her head. Jax's heart rate quadrupled as adrenaline pumped through her veins at the close call.

Then the yelling commenced. "Drace, they're in the hall!"

Ian yanked the knife from the wall and with swift, precise movements, flung the knife toward their pursuers. As soon as the knife left his hand, he flowed into battle mode as he pivoted and turned his Uzi toward the front of the hall. Pulling Jax behind him, he headed straight toward the front of the house as he held down the trigger, the machine gun peppering their path as they exited the hall and entered the main foyer.

Trying to avoid the shots, transers and vamps alike dove left and right behind couches and dining room furniture. Only Drace remained standing. And he stood right in the middle of the foyer between them and the front door, blocking their exit.

"Going somewhere?" he asked, machine gun trained on Ian.

Ian pulled Jax behind him, saying in a calm, even voice, "Yes, thanks for the brief visit, but we're all bushed out and ready to head home." Jax made a huffing sound and tried to move beside him, but Ian grated out, *Stay put, Jax.* The fact he'd just spoken those words in her mind stunned Jax into immobility.

She didn't like the fact she couldn't see Drace, but the tone of Ian's words told her it wasn't a request.

"Surely you don't think I'll let you leave here with my human do you?" Drace drawled.

Come to me, my pet, Drace whispered in her mind, compelling her. Of their own accord, Jax's feet started to move.

She noted the look of surprise on Ian's face as she moved out from behind him. *No, Jax. You've got it in you to fight him. Do it!* Ian insisted in her mind.

Jax locked her jaw, closed her eyes and leaned her head back, fighting the strong will that called her to Drace's side while her mind screamed at the realization Ian wasn't who she thought he was. No, he couldn't be a vampire! But then she felt another presence keeping her feet grounded. The extra help was all she needed.

When she regained a level of control she opened her eyes and her gaze focused on the huge crystal chandelier hanging from the ceiling. Jax smiled as she lowered her gaze and met Drace's livid one.

"See, I can fight—" Cutting her own words off to glare at the vamps in the room surrounding them, Jax said as her hand holding the gun began to rise, "Okay, which of you bloodsuckers is playing puppet with my body," she continued in an indignant tone as her gun rose higher in the air. "You know," she went on, pretending to become more livid by the second, "I really don't appreciate being treated like a voodoo doll."

I've only got one chance, Ian, she whispered in her mind and hoped somehow Ian figured out her ploy.

"Enough," Drace scowled at the vamps and transers who had started to rise around them, apparently believing her.

Then you'd better make it count, a chroí, Ian whispered into her mind.

Jax pulled the trigger and hit the chain holding the chandelier directly over Drace. Everything happened so fast she couldn't believe her eyes. Ian turned and nailed the vamps standing in the hall, mowing them down with his machine gun.

She turned just in time to see a vamp dive toward her. Jax pegged him, getting a shot off, point blank to his heart while he flew through the air. She stepped out of the way and let him fall hard on the mosaic tile floor.

Drace let out a horrific roar, threw the chandelier off of him, and dove for his dropped gun.

"Time to go," Ian said in a cheerful tone as he grabbed her around the waist and literally jumped them fifteen feet over Drace, landing near the front door.

Once they landed and she got her bearings from being catapulted through the air, Jax turned and trained her gun on Drace. "Ah, ah, ah," she mocked pointing her gun at Drace's head while Ian opened the door.

Noting the vamps who stood around the room, their guns now trained on her, she ground her teeth that she couldn't take Drace out without becoming Swiss cheese herself. "I think we'll be leaving now." She narrowed her gaze on her captor who'd frozen in the process of retrieving his weapon. "The next time we meet, Drace, I'll be the one inflicting pain."

Come on, Jax. Let's get out of here. We need to move.

Once she followed him outside, Ian pulled the door closed behind him and wedged the machine gun between the curved handle and the door jamb, buying them scant seconds of time. Jax didn't need any urging. It was late afternoon and heavily overcast with the rain. The vamps could follow them outside at this point without fear of bursting into flames. As soon as Ian indicated where they should go, she dashed through the rain, across the yard, past the white floral delivery van to a black truck parked beside it.

Shots rang out around them as she scrambled in the passenger side while Ian climbed in the other. Jax looked on in amazement when Ian ran his hand over the ignition. No key. No nothing and the engine rumbled to life. Ian gunned the truck and they lurched forward down the driveway.

Driving rain blurred the windshield and Jax reached over to flip on the wipers.

"Put your seatbelt on," Ian barked out as he gripped the wheel and headed straight for the iron fence now only fifteen feet in front of them. Leaning over, she tried to put his seatbelt on first. "Do it, Jax. Now!" he ordered. Jax swiftly sat back and buckled her seatbelt. As they careened toward the fence, she closed her eyes and said a small prayer.

The impact jarred the vehicle but by sheer size and velocity, the truck won out and the gates swung open. Her eyes flew open at the impact, but as they sped off down the road, Jax closed her eyes once more, this time in shock.

In rapid succession, all the little things about Ian, things she chose to ignore: the insistent humming of her body while he was around, his strength, his sense of timing, his speed, the fact she'd never seen him eat and the mysterious aura about him... Now it all made sense. He was a vampire, yet different in that he could abide full sunlight.

How could she have been such an idiot? Blake saw it. Why didn't she? *Because you didn't want to, you fool,* she berated herself.

When they'd driven a few miles down the road, smoke started billowing out of the radiator. Ian pulled the truck up behind his Hummer saying, "At least it got us here."

Jax didn't say a word as they climbed out of the truck. She passed him as he came around the front of the truck and then turned back to him saying, "Where are the keys?"

Cold rain pelted down on them as Ian gave her a wary look. He said with a nod, "They're in the Hummer."

Jax turned toward his vehicle and heard Ian start to follow her. She faced him once more and lifted her gun toward him. "Keep your distance, vamp."

Rain poured over his face as Ian stopped walking and narrowed his gaze. She tilted her chin a notch. "Follow your instincts, don't use gadgets," she mocked. "You're a vampire. *You used your powers.*"

Ian clenched his fists by his sides. "I'm half vampire, known as a hybrid. My mother was human at the beginning of her pregnancy. My powers aren't near that of a pure blooded vampire. I have to depend on my human skills as well."

"Oh, yeah," she said in a sarcastic tone. "That walking in daylight thing. Kind of comes in handy. You must have all the other vamps shaking in their boots."

Ian took a step toward her and she tightened her hold on the gun. "Stay back." Emotions ran high. She'd had mind-blowing sex with a vampire. She knew her face reflected some of her conflicting emotions. Her lips trembled as she said, "I can't believe I—"

"What? Fucked a vampire?" Ian's anger emanated from him in powerful, unrelenting currents. His expression hard as granite, he continued, "And it was the best damn fucking you ever had. You said so yourself."

"I did not!" she said her voice rising in indignation.

Ian glared at her, his golden eyes glittering even in the dim light. "Your body told me, Jax, even if you won't admit it yourself." He took two more steps toward her, his expression thunderous.

Jax lowered the gun and pulled the trigger.

Chapter Nine

"Sonofabitch," Ian hissed out and grabbed his thigh. For a second, his jeans disappeared and she saw his bare leg, blood seeping out of his wound and then his jeans reappeared. Jax blinked. Were his clothes an illusion?

His gaze, the color of shards of amber, jerked to hers as he roared, "You shot me."

"It's just a flesh wound. You'll heal." She gave a hollow laugh. "Faster than most, but that ought to slow you down some," she finished with a smirk and turned toward his Hummer.

"Fuck it!" Ian bellowed and before she could react, he'd grabbed her arm and wrenched the gun from her hand. "You're coming with me."

When she landed a blow to his solar plexus, Ian took a deep breath, then curled his fist around her wet shirt and jerked her close, and lifted her off the ground until her face was level with his.

"One more physical assault on me and I'll return the favor, Jax. I swear it," he said through gritted teeth.

He yanked her around to the passenger side of his car, opened the door and then the glove compartment, pulling out a pair of handcuffs. Slapping one side on her left wrist, he attached the other side to his right wrist and slammed the passenger side door.

Jax stumbled behind him as he limped to his side of the car. Opening the door, he shoved the gun under his seat and bit out, "Get in and I don't want to hear one word out of you or I won't be responsible for my actions."

With Ian's stiff stance and clenched jaw, the man positively radiated fury. The atmosphere between them became so charged with high emotions she could almost reach out and feel the friction in the air. Jax climbed into the car and slid across the seat as best she could while she waited for Ian to enter the vehicle.

As Ian climbed in, he ground out, *"Damnú air!"* followed by a few other angry words in Irish while he pulled his hurt leg inside and slammed the door.

She knew his leg had to be killing him. Guilt shot through her at her impulsive act brought on by her own anger. The man *had* just saved her life. She turned her head and bit her lip while she looked out the window. He had also lied to her, made her feel wrong for using help to hunt Drace, and worst of all, he'd made her care for him, this man she could never be with—a vampire. Jax straightened her shoulders now that her mental pep talk had absolved her of her crime. Ian deserved to be shot. Better yet, he deserved to be tarred and feathered.

Jax concentrated on her anger as Ian drove for what seemed like hours. Once her anger simmered to a low boil and the adrenaline pumping through her body leveled off, she shivered at the cold, wet clothes clinging to her body.

Ian glanced over at her and turned on the heat, the only indication he was aware of her presence. He didn't look at her again as he kept his gaze on the road, his jaw set, and a tight grip on the steering wheel.

When Ian turned off the main road onto a dirt driveway surrounded by trees, Jax asked, "Where are we going?"

Ian didn't even glance her way as he spoke in her mind, his voice a steel edge, *I said not a word, Jax.*

Ian parked the car in the back of the two-story house set deep in the woods and cut the engine. Jax's nerves jangled on high alert. What did he plan to do with her? Once Ian shut off the car lights, complete darkness engulfed them, and only the sounds of crickets and frogs and other night animals permeated the air. The house was just as still and dark, which meant she'd be alone with Ian. A sliver of fear skimmed down her spine. She had no doubt she'd somehow have to pay for shooting him.

"My uncle's going to be out of his mind when he sees the broken vase and flowers and my car in the driveway. He needs to know I'm okay," she rambled, nervous to know what Ian planned to do with her.

"I'll call him later," Ian said in a detached tone as he grabbed the gun, shoved the weapon into his duffle bag, and pulled the bag's strap over his left shoulder. Opening the door, he stepped down and yanked her none-to-gently after him. He might be favoring his hurt leg but that didn't make his steps any less purposeful. Jax trudged along behind him, tripping up the couple of steps that led to the front door.

Her knuckles dragged against the wood door as Ian used his right hand to unlock the deadbolt. Once inside he shut the door and locked it. Without turning on the lights he started walking, pulling her along.

"Ow," Jax called out when her knee slammed into a low table.

"Sorry," Ian grunted and flipped his hand. Lights came on in the room, causing her to wince at the stark change. Ian didn't give her a chance to look around. He immediately started up the stairs. She either had to follow him or be dragged up the carpeted stairs like a rag doll.

When they topped the stairs they stepped into what had to be the master bedroom. Loft-like in design, the bedroom took up half the upstairs. A wooden banister along the outer edge of the master bedroom allowed for a view of the living room below.

Ian walked further into the room and pulled her around to face him. "Strip," he ordered.

"I will not," she shot back, her anger overcoming her anxiety over what he planned.

Before she could move away, Ian's hand shot out and captured the collar of her shirt. His gaze focused on her face, he said in a low tone as if it took supreme effort not to explode, "Either you do it, or I'll rip them off of you. Considering they are your only clothes at the moment, I suggest you do as I ask."

Jax lifted their joined arms and said with sarcasm, "I think I'll have difficulty with these on."

Ian set his bag on the floor, pulled out his keys, and unlocked the handcuffs. When Jax just stood there, he said in a flat tone, "I know I didn't stutter a minute ago. I want you out of those wet clothes, Jax. Now!"

Jax's fingers trembled as she unbuckled her belt and slid the leather strap out of the loops on her jeans. She unbuttoned her pants, wiggling and tugging until she could pull the wet cloth off of her. Ian's gaze traveled every inch of flesh she revealed as she undressed. He didn't bother to hide his appreciation of her form. Though her breathing had turned shallow, Jax tried to ignore him as she unbuttoned her shirt.

Once she'd removed her shirt, he held out his hand for her clothes. Jax handed them to him and widened her eyes in surprise when Ian tossed them over the rail to the living room below.

"You're not done, Jacqueline." His use of her real name made Jax snap her gaze back to his.

"Yes, I am," she said, defiant.

"All of them."

When she didn't move, Ian scowled and took a step toward her.

"Okay, fine." She had to force herself to keep from jumping at his menacing look. Jax unsnapped her bra and slithered out of her underwear, tossing them to him as well.

She stood before him in nothing but the clothes God gave her and had never felt so exposed in her life. Ian knew her background. She told him about her mother, her past, her vampire-hunting father, and now he knew her quest. He'd taken her to heights of passion and made her want him in return. Jax clenched her fists by her side, digging her short nails into her palms. Never would she let him see how vulnerable she felt. She met his gaze with a bold, self-assured one.

Her underwear met the same fate as her other clothes while she stared in shock to see Ian's clothes shimmer and then disappear altogether. So his clothes had been an illusion. Jax gasped at his long, thick erection. He wanted her, even now. Her gaze dropped to his leg and the wound she'd inflicted. Dried blood made a bold red line down his muscular thigh all the way to his foot. Guilt washed over her until she noted that his wound had closed and had already started to heal. *Damn vamps!*

She braced herself as Ian stepped close to her, invading her personal space. When he lifted his hand, she reflexively jumped back.

She thought she saw deep hurt in his gaze before he let impassiveness fill his expression. Ian set his jaw while he pulled the chopsticks out of her wet hair. The damp curtain of hair hit her back, setting off a series of uncontrollable shivers.

"If I touch you now, I won't stop, Jax. I'll be rough and unforgiving."

Jax met his gaze with an angry one. "There will be no other times between us."

Tossing the chopsticks to the floor, Ian gripped her arms and pulled her to his hard chest, pressing his erection against her lower belly. "Yes, there will be many more times. You are my *Sonuachar*, Jax, my soul mate."

Jax pushed against his chest, shocked by his admission to the depth of his feelings for her. "No, I'm not."

Ian set his jaw and pulled her over to the bed. Grabbing the handcuffs he'd laid on the dresser, he shackled her left wrist once more and hooked the other cuff to a spindle on the wrought iron bed.

"Let me go," she railed at him.

"You're safe here. Drace doesn't know about this place." Ian walked over to the dresser and pulled out a pair of khaki pants and a hunter green sweater. Dressing quickly he said, "I'll be back in an hour."

Jax jerked at the cuff around her wrist. "You can't just leave me here. Defenseless."

Ian's expression reflected deep respect. "Jax, you're *never* defenseless. You're the most resourceful woman I've ever met."

Jerking at her restraint, she shook the bed in her anger. "Let me go, Ian. I'm going to kill you."

"I have to get you some food. Plus, I need to feed." He took a step closer as his predatory gaze locked on her neck. "That is unless you'd like to volunteer." He grinned, revealing his fangs with the full curve of his lips.

"Come near me with those fangs, Ian Mordoor, and you'll walk away with a few less teeth in your head," she threatened.

Ian threw back his head and laughed, a deep, full-bellied laugh—an infectious kind of laugh—but Jax was anything but amused at the moment.

He turned and walked down the stairs, calling over his shoulder, "Be back in an hour."

Right when she heard him open the front door, he said, "I think you should rest while I'm gone."

And that was it. Jax suddenly felt so tired she pulled the hunter green comforter back with hurried movements and flopped down on her belly before she fell over on the floor in sheer exhaustion. *I'm going to kill him for compelling me to sleep*, she thought to herself before her heavy eyelids closed.

* * * * *

Ian entered through the French doors behind a man sitting at his desk chair. The older man had his back to him. The phone rested between his ear and his shoulder while he jotted down some notes, his movements brisk, annoyed.

"I don't give a flying fuck what the hell you're doing tonight, Dawson! My niece is missing and you're going to get your sorry ass here on the double," the old man yelled into the phone.

83

"That won't be necessary," Ian said in a calm voice.

James Markson turned surprised eyes his way before he narrowed his gaze. "Let me call you back, Dawson." He slammed down the phone and turned in his chair to face him. His cheeks ruddy and blowing in and out, he said, "Who are you and how the hell did you get on my property?"

Ian started to speak when Blake walked into the room, his gun trained on him.

"What have you done with Jax?"

Even though his fingers itched to pull the gun tucked into his belt at his spine, Ian willed himself to remain calm.

Keeping on eye on Blake's gun and stiff stance, Ian addressed her uncle. "Jax is fine. A vampire named Drace Kovac kidnapped her, but I rescued her and now she's somewhere safe."

Her uncle released a deep breath of relief, but his eyes narrowed and he repeated his first question, "Who the hell are you?"

"I'm a vampire hunter. My name is Ian Mordoor."

Ian heard Blake's heart rate kick up, a clear indication the hunter planned to pull the trigger. Before either man could blink, Ian had pulled his gun and trained it on Blake saying in a low voice, "I wouldn't advise shooting me."

Ian met the man's hardened gaze. "I'm the only one who knows where Jax is right now."

Jax's uncle held up his hand and addressed Blake, "Put your weapon down."

Instead, Blake pulled another gun from his back and sneered, "James, this man isn't human. He's a vampire, one that can walk in daylight."

"Took you long enough to figure it out." Ian gave him a taunting smile.

"How is it possible for you to be out during the day?" James demanded, his expression fierce, angry.

When Ian looked at him, the old man had his own pistol trained on him. He addressed James in a calm voice. "I'm half human, half vampire, known as a hybrid."

"Jax would kill you if she knew," Blake hissed out.

Ian grinned. "But she does know, and it hasn't changed a thing." He stared the other hunter down and knew the man understood his meaning. Jax was his.

Ian rolled his shoulders, ready to be the hell out of there and back with Jax. "I'm here at Jax's request. She wanted you to know she was all right."

"If Drace kidnapped Jax, then I'd say a very deadly vampire is gunning for your niece, James," Blake addressed her uncle. "We know what he did to John. We need to step in. Jax is in over her head."

"I agree—" James started to say.

"No," Ian interrupted, his tone brusque.

"You don't have a choice in the matter." Blake gave him a satisfied smile.

Ian narrowed his gaze on the man. "Yes, I do. I know where Jax is and you don't. I'll take care of Drace."

"You were with Jax the other night and you obviously haven't been able to take Drace out before now," Blake shot back.

The man's barb, meant as a slap in the face, hit him in the gut. The truth was, he *had* let Drace get away too many times to count and now, when it counted the most, he needed to take this rogue vampire out as soon as possible. The trick was to do so without putting Jax in harm's way.

"Let him go," James spoke up, interrupting their standoff as he met Ian's gaze.

Blake looked shocked. "You're joking, right?"

The old man shook his head. "No. Let the vamp go. I believe he speaks the truth about Jax." His gaze left Ian's and met Blake's. "You can have your go at him another time when my niece's life isn't hanging in the balance."

Gee, thanks for the vote of confidence, James. Ian faced Blake and smiled, letting his fangs show just for spite. To his credit, Blake didn't bat an eye. His stance never wavered, but remained on the ready as Ian walked toward the French doors to leave the way he came.

Ian turned before he left and said to them, "Maybe one day I'll tell you how I succeeded in getting past all your top-of-the-line security."

"The next time we meet will be in battle, Mordoor," Blake threatened, his entire body poised, ready to attack.

Ian remained calm, not about to be drawn in by Blake's taunts. He met the man's challenging gaze. "I look forward to it, Grayson."

* * * * *

Jax awoke with a start and looked around the room. *Where am I and why am I sleeping on my stomach*? When her gaze landed on Ian sleeping on top of the comforter next to her, her groggy thoughts meshed reminding her of her current circumstances. With her arm still handcuffed to the headboard, Jax rolled her shoulder to loosen the knots in her muscles from the prolonged position. How long had she been asleep?

Keeping an eye on Ian, she slowly tilted her arm and looked at her watch. Seven o'clock. She'd been out for an hour and a half. She lifted her head, thankful Ian had turned on the bedside lamp, and surveyed the room. A deep cherry colored computer desk in a sleek contemporary design stood off to the left of the bed. A matching chest of drawers with silver handles graced the wall across the room. Five feet above her head, the ceiling tilted inward to accommodate the steep pitch of the roof. She looked for anything, *a-n-y-t-h-i-n-g* that could unlock the cuffs and get her out of Ian's bed.

When Jax's gaze landed on the desk beside the bed once more, a smile formed on her lips at the paperclip clamped to the stack of papers. Could she unlock the cuffs with a paperclip? Her uncle claimed it could be done. The tricky part was getting to the desk with her left arm handcuffed to the bed. She carefully slid out of the bed and stretched as far as her bonds would let her. Even then her fingertips couldn't quite reach the desk. Damn it! But wait, her legs gave her a longer reach. Balancing on one foot, she lifted her leg in the air and managed to put her big toe on the paper.

As she pulled the papers off onto the floor, her other foot slipped out from underneath her, causing her to lose her balance and fall face forward onto the bed, right next to Ian. Holding her breath, hoping he'd slept through her graceful belly flop, she lifted herself on her hands and knees. Her gaze traveled the length of his khaki pants past the obvious bulge at his crotch, to his bare chest and then up to his face. Jax's heart jerked in her chest when her gaze locked with his narrowed golden one.

"Going somewhere?" he drawled.

Chapter Ten

"No, I—"

"Damn straight, you're not," he growled as he circled her right wrist with his hand and pulled, yanking her face down beside him.

Her breath came out in a whoosh at the abrupt change, but Jax recovered quickly and tried to slide off the bed once more. Ian's large hands landed on her hips and lifted her up on her knees, his intent clear.

"No!" she said, her heart hammering in her chest.

"Yes," he demanded as his hands slid up to the indention of her waist.

Adrenaline kicked in, quickly followed by searing arousal that curled in her lower stomach and slammed into her sex in an aching, throbbing I'm-gonna-die-if-he-doesn't-give-it-to-me kind of need. The depth of her physical response to Ian's primal demands caused her to panic at her own body's betrayal. She slid her knees out from underneath her, laying flat on her stomach once more and said in desperation, "It'll be forc…"

Ian swiftly moved over her, laying his chest on her back, completely covering her body with his and said angrily in her ear, "Don't you dare utter the word, Jax."

Ian pulled away and Jax tried to move again, but he lifted her hips once more as he slid a knee between hers and spread her legs. Jax yanked on the handcuff, gritting out, "Let me go, Ian."

Ian's hands slid down her buttocks until his thumbs reached her labia. Jax tried to jerk forward, away from his tantalizing touch, but Ian wrapped an arm around her waist and held her still. Try as she might, Jax couldn't move. God, he was so freakin' strong.

Rubbing the sensitive, swollen flesh with his fingers he said, his tone harsh and unyielding, "Not until you admit you want me, vampire and all."

"Go to hell," Jax snapped back, but immediately sucked in an involuntary breath when he slid a finger inside her. As he turned his finger around and pressed on her hot spot, Jax bit her lip to keep from moaning at the intense pleasure his touch wrought.

"No, I want to go to heaven, Jax, and only with you," he said in a husky voice as he pressed a tender kiss on her rear end.

Large hands slid up her waist to fan around her body until firm fingers grasped her nipples and twisted them. A whimper escaped Jax when his hands slid back down her body. With one hand on her hip, he splayed another hand on her thigh, while his tongue lapped against her clit, flicking the tightened nub right before his sensual lips sucked the sensitive skin into his heated, moist mouth.

When he slid two fingers inside her body, Jax arched only to moan as another warm hand grasped her breast, then rolled her nipple between his fingers. Reason returned to Jax's brain among the bombardment of physical pleasure she received. The sensations she currently experienced weren't physically possible. Three hands working at the same time?

She turned her head, flipping her curtain of black hair out of the way to look back at Ian as her hips rocked of their own accord to his masterful play over her body. When her gaze landed on Ian standing beside the bed, his burning gaze on her exposed body while he unzipped his pants, his movements slow, determined, a primitive instinct to mate and be mated slammed through her. The knowledge that he wielded the kind of power to seduce her without physically touching her caused a burning fire to start at her rigid nipples and draw a direct flaming path down to her crotch, a path of intense craving need raging out of control.

Muscles rippled in his chest and stomach as he slid his pants down his thick, well-defined thighs. Jax's gaze locked on his long, hard cock and her heart rate kicked up, then skipped a beat. When she met Ian's mesmerizing golden gaze, she closed her eyes and turned her face away. Just as quickly as they had started, suddenly all the tantalizing sensations stopped as the bed dipped with his weight.

Ian grasped her hips once more and before her lust-induced brain reminded her she'd missed her chance to move away he pressed his cock against her entrance, causing her entire body to tense in heart pounding suspense. "Tell me you want me, Jax. I want to hear the words."

She bit her lip once more to keep from uttering the words he requested, words that hovered so close to the surface. God, she wanted him very, very much. But her resistance stemmed from the fact he'd misled her. Deep-seated hurt and resentment, along with a myriad of other emotions her heart and her mind couldn't reconcile, let alone recognize, swirled within her.

When Ian slid the tip of his shaft inside her body, Jax tightened her muscles around him and pressed closer. He groaned, whispering, "Damn you, tell me," as he rammed into her in one swift plunge.

Jax let out a scream of pleasure at the erotic sensation as his body forced hers to immediately accept him.

He withdrew and slid back in, wrenching a raw moan from her as her core tightened around him, ready to climax. "Tell me, Jax," he demanded, pulling out of her body. Frustration and tension literally radiated off him. The aura permeated her skin, zinging deeper into her tissue and muscles, jangling her nerves to the very depth of her being. How could she *feel* his emotions?

"No," she sobbed at the loss of their connection, but Ian misunderstood her response.

A low growl came from him as he nudged her knees even farther apart until her body hovered just a few inches from the bed. He slid back inside her, burying deep. When he moved to pull away once more, Jax couldn't take the exquisite torture any longer. She reached back and grabbed his wrist whispering, "Don't leave me, Ian."

Another growl rumbled in his chest as Ian rammed his erection as far into her as he could while he reached over her body and grabbed the iron bar that held her handcuffs in place. With a guttural roar, he yanked on the bar and Jax's adrenaline skyrocketed to see him pull the bar completely away from the headboard, to experience his raw strength firsthand.

Sliding the handcuff off the bar, Ian withdrew from her and rolled her over to face him. His shoulders taut, his expression intense, he cupped her face in his hands and searched her gaze with his intense amber one. "I have to hear the words, Jax."

Jax put her hands on his broad shoulders, the dangling handcuff brushed against his flesh as she said, "I want you, Ian." She spread her legs in invitation and finished, "All of you..."

She arched her back and keened in pleasure when Ian entered her as the last word died on her lips. As he withdrew and drove back in, Ian nipped her shoulder, his tone gruff, "That's for shooting me."

His bite only heightened her arousal. Jax dug her nails into his back and lifted her hips to meet his powerful thrusts. "You deserved it for lying to me," she panted out.

He thrust in once more and stopped his movements as he kissed her jaw and then buried his face in her neck, inhaling her scent. "I didn't tell you because you would have shot me without a thought. You wouldn't have given us a chance, and I needed that chance."

When he finished speaking he kissed her shoulder where he'd bitten her, then laved his tongue over the same spot. Sliding his tongue across her collarbone, he traced a searing path up her neck and suddenly his entire body tensed. He lifted his head, his expression furious. "I taste another. Did Drace take you, Jax?"

Jax shook her head, "No, he didn't get a chance to, he—"

Ian pushed deeper into her, causing her breath to hitch. He clamped his teeth on her neck as he rocked his hips against hers and spoke in her mind, *No one takes your blood but me. You're mine, Jax. All mine.*

The possessive tone of his words only intensified the erotic sensation of his teeth piercing her skin, locking onto her. Jax cried out and jerked at the foreign experience. Her body turned slick with sweat, her heart thudded against her chest while her breath came in rampant pants, causing her head to swim. Her sex began to spasm in orgasmic waves as Ian took her blood, drinking deep and full as if he'd gone too long without tasting her.

Ian's cock grew harder, pressing against her walls as he slid his hand across her cheek and sweat-dampened hair. Spearing his fingers into the thick mass until he reached the back of her head, he pulled her head back further while he withdrew and thrust his cock in her moist sheath hard and deep, once, twice more.

Mine, he said with finality in her mind as he came long and hard, groaning his pleasure against her neck while Jax screamed through her second, all-consuming, body-wrenching orgasm.

Jax lay there, surprised and amazed at the intensity of their lovemaking. Ian withdrew his fangs and gently traced his tongue over the wounds. Cupping the back of her head, he turned her face to his and asked, his voice concerned, "Are you okay, *a chroí?*"

She really cared about him. The realization that she wasn't heartless, that she had the ability to care for another person, combined with the deep ingrained guilt that her lover was a vampire, overwhelmed her into stunned silence.

Ian sat up on his elbows and frowned. "Jax?"

She blinked and tears rolled down her temples into her hair. *Ohmigod, I'm crying big freakin' wimpy-ass tears.* Jax shut her eyes. She couldn't let Ian see the tumultuous emotions she knew had to be mirrored in her gaze.

Ian rolled over and pulled her into his arms, laying her head on his chest. "I'm here, Jax. You are my *Sonuachar.* I will always be here for you." He gently stroked her hair, twining his fingers through the strands as he spoke soothing words to her in Irish.

She'd never been held with such tenderness. Her father loved her, but he didn't know how to show his feelings. He hadn't been a touchy person. Wiping the tears away, she snuggled closer to Ian, rubbing her hand across his sweat-soaked chest while she basked in his warmth and all male smell. God, she couldn't get enough of him. She felt satiated and tired and euphoric all at once. The sensations made her smile. Wouldn't her uncle be surprised to see such a broad smile on her face? Her uncle!

She lifted her head and asked, "Did you get word to my uncle?"

Ian smiled and pushed her head back down on his chest. "Yes, your uncle knows you're safe."

She lifted her head once more, knowing her uncle would go ballistic if he knew Ian was a vampire.

"What'd you do, plant the knowledge in his head, leave him a note?"

Ian raised an eyebrow. "I just walked in and told him you were fine."

She looked at him in shock. "And he didn't question you?"

He chuckled. "Yes, imagine that. Even when he found out I was a vampire, he didn't shoot me."

Her stomach felt suddenly queasy and she knew her face turned pale as she swallowed hard and managed to squeak out, "My-my uncle knows you're a vampire?"

Ian picked up a tendril of her hair and wound it around his finger. "Yes, both he and Blake know."

"Blake, too!" She couldn't keep the panic from her voice.

Ian's expression hardened. "Yes, and Blake knows you accept me." He met her gaze with his intense one and finished, "That you accept me in all ways."

"What!" She tried to push off of him, but Ian speared his hand through her hair and cupped the back of her head, holding her still.

"Do you have a problem with that?" he growled.

If Blake knew Ian was a vampire, he'd kill him the first chance he got. Why didn't he? For that matter, why didn't her uncle shoot him?

"How did you convince them not to kill you?"

Ian gave a nonchalant shrug. "I told them I'm the only one who knew where you were and that I'm the best protection you've got against Drace."

"And they bought that bullshit?" she said, with an incredulous look on her face.

Ian chuckled. "Yeah, they bought it."

She shook her head. "Blake will be after you, Ian."

His hand fisted in her hair. "He can't have you, Jax. You're mine."

Jax reached up and smoothed her hand over his until he loosened his grip. "Not that I'm some bone you boys can fight over, but I was referring to the fact that Blake feels protective of me. That's all."

"You're not his responsibility any longer," Ian said in a disgruntled tone.

Jax laid her head back on his shoulder and smoothed her hand over his chest saying, "Whether I am or not, Blake won't rest until he finds me. Knowing him, he'll have to hear it from me before he'll relent."

"And what will you tell him, Jax?" She felt his body tense underneath her as he awaited her response.

She grinned against his chest. "Oh, I'll just tell him I'm not done with you yet, so he needs to keep his distance."

A resounding smack on her rear end caused Jax to jerk her head up with a frown.

"That's not what I wanted to hear, Jax."

"Well, that's the best you'll get," she shot back while she rubbed her buttock.

Ian scowled at her answer, then sighed. "Much as I'd love to lay here and debate with you, love, you need to eat." With that said, Ian stood up and pulled her out of the bed, throwing her body over his shoulder.

Jax smacked his bare buttock, railing, "Put me down, Ian."

"Watch it," he said with a chuckle and smacked her ass, hard.

"*Ye-ouch!* You don't know your own strength, you damn vamp." Jax struggled against him as he descended the stairs.

Ian rubbed the spot he'd just smacked then copped a feel.

"Ian!"

"Hey, when this sweet ass is bared and in-my-face, there's no way I'm not taking advantage," he said, his grin obvious in his words.

Turn around was fair play. Jax grabbed the firm muscle of one buttock then bit down.

"Ow!" he howled.

"That's for biting me," she shot back with a smug smile.

Ian had reached the kitchen area and swiftly set her down. Grasping her arms, his expression serious, he said, "Jax, the exchange of blood during lovemaking is a vampire tradition, highly satisfying and incredibly erotic, especially with your mate." His grip tightened. "Didn't it heighten your pleasure?"

Was he nuts? Of course, it felt good...it...oh, just tell him. "I was referring to the bite on my shoulder." She gave him a sexy grin. "In answer to your question, yes, I found the experience very sensual and exciting." At his smug smile, she held up her hand. "But I'm not your mate, nor can I ever be."

His smile disappeared to be replaced by a look of confusion. "Why can't you be?"

Jax tried to pull out of his grasp, but he held fast. "Because I'm a vampire hunter, Ian. It's what I do."

He shrugged. "So what? I'm a vampire hunter, too."

She shook her head, looking away. "No, it's more than that. Vampires are my sworn enemy." *And that sworn vengeance against all vampires is my only link to my father, even if that link grows weaker and weaker the more time I spend with you.*

Ian grasped her chin. "Am I your enemy, Jacqueline?" he asked softly.

She stared at his chin, unable to meet his penetrating gaze. "No," she whispered. Straightening her spine, she continued, "But this runs deeper than you and me, Ian."

He frowned. "Because of your dad and what you were raised to believe?"

He'd hit the nail on the head. Her loyalty to her dad and her mother's memory ran deep, so deep that guilt at her traitorous thoughts churned in her belly, making her feel sick to her stomach. Ian's grip had loosened and she shoved away from him, needing space.

When she tried to take a step, her legs gave out from under her. Ian caught her before she hit the floor. Lifting her in his arms, he set her down in a chair at the table, saying gruffly, "You need to eat, Jax. I've taken your blood and you need sustenance and sleep to recover."

Ian turned away and picked up a loaf of bread. Jax squirmed in her seat, feeling more than just a little underdressed while Ian walked around the kitchen as if he paraded in his birthday suit all the time. Then again, she thought with a wry smile, he'd done just that yesterday, while in battle mode no less.

"Why didn't you have any clothes on when you rescued me yesterday?"

"Because I'd shifted to a raven to sneak onto Drace's property undetected."

Jax's eyebrows drew together. "But by shifting you had to leave your weapons behind, right?" She shook her head in amazement. "I could never willingly leave my weapons."

Ian opened the fridge to pull out some meat and cheese. Facing her once more, he said, "Weapons are only tools, Jax. It's the hunter who does the stalking."

Jax admired Ian's self-confidence. Well, sometimes that part of his personality grated on her nerves, but other times his arrogance made him downright sexy.

As he pulled out slices of bread a thought occurred to her. "Why do you have a refrigerator if you don't eat food?"

He looked up from making the sandwich and laughed. "Vampires can eat food for purely social purposes. I do have human friends, Jax," he said, cutting the sandwich in half and setting it on a plate in front of her.

She lifted the sandwich to her mouth and even that small act seemed to take supreme effort. Man, why was she so damn exhausted? Jealousy sliced through her as she chewed, not really tasting the food. Friends? Ian didn't strike her as the kind of man who engaged in small talk. There was only one kind of friend he'd probably bring all the way out here in the middle of nowhere. The idea of Ian with another woman made her blood boil. But she had no right to say a word, not since she'd just told him she couldn't be his vampire mate.

Instead she looked away to calm her jealous thoughts. She took in the entire living room area with admiration. The furnishings looked like something out of Restoration Hardware magazine. Walnut finished wood furniture gleamed beside a U-shaped, textured chenille sofa ensemble in soft taupe. Throw pillows in deep hunter green graced the couch and the cream-colored side chair. An entertainment center took up the entire far wall, each section filled with the latest in high-tech contemporary audio and video equipment. Two fully packed bookcases covered both sidewalls and a baby grand piano stood off in the far corner of the room.

A baby grand piano? That was *not* Ian.

She turned around to see him staring at her. "Who plays?" she asked, nodding to the piano.

Ian laughed, looking insulted. "What? You don't I think play the piano?"

Jax smirked. "Hardly."

Brushing his hands together Ian walked over to the piano bench and made a show of pretending he had on a tux with tails that he had to flip out of the way before he sat down. The comical scenario with his bare-assed naked, yet sexy, body settling on the bench made her smile.

He laced his fingers together and stretched, cracking his knuckles.

Well, I'll be damned, she thought as he laid his fingers over the keys.

When he tapped out the song, *Twinkle, Twinkle Little Star*, followed by an upbeat rendition of *Mary Had a Little Lamb*, she couldn't hold back her laughter any longer. Ian grinned as he slipped into the theme song from Jaws. When he started into the next silly song Jax had tears streaming down her face.

"Stop, stop the torture please," she called out holding up her hand.

Ian stopped playing, slid off the bench and walked over to sit in a chair next to her at the table. Lacing his fingers in hers, he said, "The piano belongs to my brother." He looked around the room. "We bought this second house a few years ago as kind of a getaway place. He picked out most of the furniture." Ian's brows rose up and down in a suggestive manner as he finished, "But I chose the bedroom suit."

"Now why doesn't that make me feel any better?" she grumbled.

Ian pulled her onto his lap and nuzzled her neck. "Because you're tired and you need to sleep."

She noted his marble hard erection brushing against her thigh. Jax smiled and wound her arms around his neck, kissing his jaw, enjoying his rough evening beard against her skin. "Well, you're right about one thing. I do want to go back to bed."

Ian's hold on her tightened. "You have no idea how much I want to taste you again, Jax, how much I want to feel that warm, perfect pussy of yours contracting around my cock while I take your blood."

The effect of his explicit words shot straight to her sex. Hot moisture gathered, followed by swift, aching need. Jax shifted on his lap to straddle his thighs. Rubbing her damp entrance along his hard shaft she said, her voice seductive and husky, "I think I'm up for it." She made a growling sound in her throat and finished, "I *know* you are."

His broad hands slid to her buttocks and cupped the cheeks, pulling her tight as he rocked against her. She did feel tired, but Jax didn't care. Ian stirred her libido like no other. She let her head fall back and moaned at the delicious friction his movements created.

Ian wrapped his arms around her waist and stood up. Jax laughed and held on for dear life while he took the stairs two at a time.

When he laid her back on the bed and leaned over her, she sighed and let her hands roam over the firm hardness of his chest. Sliding her palms over his muscular biceps, she said, "I love everything about your body."

Ian smiled and kissed her, his tongue thrusting deep, tasting her mouth in thorough, hungry swipes. Pulling back he said, "I can't wait to explore your beautiful body from head to toe, *a chroí*. But first, you need your sleep."

What? She dug her fingers into his shoulders. "You're not planning on leaving me like this are you?"

Ian traced her jaw line with a finger, then kissed her neck, causing her to arch toward him. His passionate gaze locked with hers. "Now that I've tasted your blood, our bond is too strong. I won't be able to make love to you without following my primal instincts to mate in the vampire way. I *will* take your blood, Jax."

She sighed in relief. "Whew, is that all?" She arched toward him once more, rubbing her nipples against his chest. "I love how my body responds when you slide your fangs in me, Ian. Take away."

Ian grasped her wrists, his nostrils flaring as he stilled her roaming hands. "If I take your blood three times within as many days, you'll become a vampire. I would expect you to take my blood, Jax, to become my mate."

Jax's eyes widened. Though taboo, the idea of becoming his mate and being tied to Ian forever stirred something deep inside her. But the fact that she'd become the very enemy her father fought so hard to eliminate raced though her blood, chilling her to the bone.

"You did say three times, right?"

Ian nodded.

She pulled her hands free of his grasp and wrapped her arms around his neck. "Kiss me, Ian."

Ian could no more resist her request then stop breathing. He touched her soft lips with his, tenderly at first, then the need to taste her intensified. His tongue teased, then parted her lips, demanding a closer connection. He wanted to bury himself in her soft, giving body so deep he'd be locked to her for eternity. But he could tell Jax was truly exhausted. He wanted her body to recoup first. He felt responsible for her welfare now whether she realized or accepted the fact or not.

With his lips still on hers, he whispered in her mind, *Tá grá agam dhuit, Jacqueline,* as he compelled her to sleep.

Ian laid her down on the bed and pulled back, looking at Jax. What an exquisite beauty his *Sonuachar* turned out to be. He turned out the light and let his gaze feast on her luminescent skin. The moonlight streamed in the room through the angled windows, enhancing his night vision and making her body seem to literally glow. He reached out and stroked the soft skin above her breast and then trailed his hand down her firm stomach muscles. She must work out constantly to achieve such firmness.

He teased the dark curls between her thighs and Jax whimpered in her sleep. His smile faded as his entire body reacted on instinct. Unbidden, Ian's shaft turned even harder and his fangs unsheathed at the faint sound. Jax's naturally responsive nature—that same innate sensuality she'd tried so hard to deny them both—charmed and seduced him.

Curling his hand into a fist, Ian stood up, putting distance between them. His chest burned as he inhaled in long drawing breaths to calm his body that raged for another full vampire mating with Jax. His cock throbbed with his need to take her body and her blood again and again, to ensure the binding of their souls to one another for a lifetime.

"We will mate, Jax," he said aloud, his tone firm, full of resolution. Unable to bear being in the room with her without rousing her luscious body, he headed for the stairs. He needed to give Mark Devlin a call anyway. He smiled when he realized just how much Mark would like this particular request.

Chapter Eleven

Warmth and security. The feelings surrounded her in a blanket of heat, making her feel buoyant and protected all at once. Jax surfaced from her deep sleep, feeling so relaxed she snuggled closer to the source.

Ian's chuckle brought her fully awake and the sensation of waking in a warm bath, had her gripping the sides of the tub for a much needed grounding while she assessed of her surroundings. Water splashed over the sides of the claw-footed tub from her frantic actions, hitting the terra cotta colored tile floor with a loud *splat*. Daylight streamed through the frosty block glass windows, adding to the sunny warmth in the bathroom.

"Easy, *a chroí*." Ian's hands, full of scented soapsuds, came around her body and pulled her back against his chest. Jax gasped when Ian cupped her breasts. The soap in his hands only added to the sensual slide as he closed his fingers together to pluck at her nipples. The rough pads of his fingers caused her to moan and lay back against his him, closing her eyes.

"I should rip you a new one for compelling me to sleep last night," she said, unable to muster an ounce of anger behind her words.

"Open your eyes and see, Jax, really see how well we fit together."

Jax opened her eyes and looked beyond the tub. A floor-to-ceiling mirror graced the far wall opposite them. She saw Ian, his light brown hair, mussed and damp from the bath, his golden gaze intense and focused on hers in the mirror. Her long black hair fanned over his upper body and the rest dipped into the warm water.

Her skin looked so fair against his much darker coloring, her muscles slimmer and less defined than his bulging biceps and muscular shoulders that appeared even bulkier crammed into the narrow tub. Large hands with long fingers and wide palms cupped her breasts. Everywhere he came into contact with her, she burned.

Ian's hand slid between her legs until he reached her mound. Rubbing his finger along her sensitive nub, he said in a seductive voice while his palm applied just the right amount of pressure, "Can you forgive me since I have such a wonderful way of waking you up?"

She smiled at him in the mirror. Arching her back, she looped one arm around his neck and pulled him close. Ian nipped at her neck and slid his hand up the inside of her right thigh, where he lifted her leg from the water and hooked her lower calf over the edge of the tub. Skimming his fingers back down her thigh, he cupped the juncture where her leg met her body while his other hand lifted her left leg out of the tub in the same fashion.

She moaned as the water swirled around her, bathing her exposed labia and swollen clitoris in perfumed, decadent warmth. Steam rose up from the water and the smell of roses wafted through the air, further seducing her.

"You are so beautiful, Jax. Embrace your sensuality. Feel the warm water lapping at you, bathing you, preparing your gorgeous body for my entry," Ian whispered in her ear as he rubbed his thumbs back and forth along her labia, opening her body further. Jax nudged closer to his exploring fingers, but Ian splayed a hand over her lower belly, pushing her back against him. The contact, along with his hard shaft burning against her lower back, caused her breath to escape in short, choppy pants as her body tightened in anticipation each time his fingers neared her clitoris.

Jax's skin tingled with each brush of flesh against flesh. Her breathing turned more erratic and she noted every single sound around them, echoing to the beat of Ian's movements coming closer and closer to touching her—the gentle swoosh of the water as he moved his hands in a rhythmic motion against her, the *plunk* of the water dripping off her feet onto the floor. Her stomach knotted and her clitoris throbbed almost painfully. All the sensations worked in tandem to drive her body to a heightened frenzy of coiled, heart-pounding desire.

"Ian," she barely managed to get out his name, she'd become so incoherent in her need to have him touch her.

Ian plunged two fingers deep inside her channel and Jax screamed with the pleasure his penetration brought. Her nipples tightened and her inner muscles clenched around his fingers, desperate to keep them inside as long as possible. Ian groaned as he slid his fingers in and out of her body, saying, "You feel so tight, so ready for me."

Searing lust clenched her stomach, causing her skin to prickle, then flush as her climax neared. When Ian withdrew his hand, she sobbed, "Touch me, Ian."

In response, he slid his hands under her buttocks and lifted her body, rasping out, "I want to be inside you, *a ghrá*."

Jax sucked in her breath when he pressed his erection against her entrance. She started to move to lower her legs and Ian ground out, as the head of his cock slid inside her, "No. Keep your legs where they are."

She stiffened at his autocratic tone, but her body couldn't help its reaction to the sensation of his marble hard shaft gliding inside her, filling her...taking her. She clenched her inner walls against him and moaned at the sensation.

Ian kissed her neck, his lips tender, his words, a velvet brush against her skin, "The position will heighten your pleasure, Jax. Lean closer to me."

Jax used her arm wrapped around his neck to pull him as close to her as she could. As her body adjusted to his thick cock, allowing him full, deep entry, she moaned in ecstasy, rocking against him.

Sliding his hands back around the front of her body, Ian clasped a nipple, twirling, then pinching the tight bud while his other hand traced down her stomach and found her clit, rubbing the tiny rigid flesh between his fingers as he pumped into her.

With each upward thrust, Ian sank deeper into her body. Mindless bliss, she thought, the only description to express her current state of being.

That's it, Jax, take all of me, he whispered in her mind. *I've waited a long time for you. Only with my true mate have I found the lovemaking be this untamed, this raw, and explosive,* he continued as his hot tongue laved at her neck right before he plunged his teeth into her skin. Jax keened her pleasure, then gasped in delight when he used his arm to jerk her closer so he could clamp down more forcefully on her neck. With each dragging pull he took on her throat, her body tightened around his cock.

Ian shuddered at the taste of Jax's blood sliding down his throat. The second taking even more potent than the first, he knew he'd never get enough of her sweet wine. The flavor held pure temptation in the form of an erotic aphrodisiac. He wanted to drown in all that was Jax.

When she laid her head heavily on his shoulder, sighing in pleasure as she succumbed to him, Ian felt like roaring in satisfaction at her acceptance of his need to taste and savor her. No, he wanted to devour her, she tasted so good. Never had a thirst gripped him like it did with Jax and not for sustenance, but for deep sexual and personal satiation.

His grip on her tightened further, his thrusts became more powerful as he spoke in her mind, *I want to feel you accepting our destiny. Come,* a ghrá mo chroí.

Her breath hitched and she whispered his name. Threading her fingers through his hair and fisting her hand in the short strands, she pulled his head closer. The slight pain from her tight grip caused lust and possessive need to rage through him. He tightened his bite on her neck until he felt her muscles began to contract around his cock as her orgasm spiraled through her. Ian shut his eyes and reveled in their union, the mutual, sensual sharing of their bodies.

As explosive as their coupling felt, the act only primed him for a full vampire mating. He couldn't wait for her to sink her vampire teeth into his neck and take his blood while he came inside her soft, warm, inviting body. Groaning at the thought, he cupped his hand possessively over her mound and increased his pace, thrusting deep and hard until she screamed in ecstasy once again. Only then did he give in to his own long, drawn-out release.

When the bath water turned cold, Ian lifted Jax out of the tub, laying her on the towel he'd spread out over the large rug near the cabinets. Jax smiled at the pampering and attention he'd lavished on her while in the bath. He'd bathed her entire body, even her hair. But the one intimate act he did that melted her heart was to shave her legs, underarms, and even her bikini line before he shaved his own overnight beard away.

Butterflies scattered in her stomach as he used a fluffy cream-colored towel to dry off her body. Kneeling between her thighs, he lingered on her breasts, then moved to her stomach. Instead of drawing the towel down between her thighs, he leaned over and blew against the damp, dark curls.

Jax bent her knees, allowing him access to her body. Ian gave her a sexy grin as he touched her labia with his fingers, stroking her. When his thumb pressed against her clit, she arched her back off the floor, moaning in response.

"*Tá tú go h-áileann,*" he rasped out. "You're so beautiful, so responsive, made just for me." His territorial words and tone made her juices flood her sex, bathing the swollen tissue that throbbed in heated waves. Jax lifted her hips, silently inviting him in.

Ian smiled and slid a finger inside her body. Jax closed her eyes and sighed in pleasure. Her skin stretched with delicious sensation after sensation as he added another finger. His hand stilled when a cell phone started ringing in the next room.

Jax's eyes flew open as Ian withdrew his hand. He placed both fingers in his mouth, his gaze hungry, ready to devour her before his expression turned to one of regret. "I'm sorry, Jax. I have to get that."

Lifting the discarded towel off the floor, he swiftly wrapped it around his waist and walked out of the bathroom.

"Well, damn!" she uttered under her breath. Sitting up, Jax stood and grabbed the towel from underneath her. Scrubbing it through her hair to get out the excess water, she rubbed in a vigorous manner when she realized what might have just happened if the phone hadn't rang.

Ian had woven a web of seduction about her so well, she'd have agreed to just about anything to have his cock and fangs inside her body again. God, she'd never felt such a rush in her life. It was like being infused with a jolt of pure adrenaline and she didn't have to do a damn thing to get there but tilt her head.

She swiped the towel over the mirror, wiping off the mist. Her hair, now mostly dry, fell around her shoulders in unruly waves. Where'd the straight black strands go? Her cheeks bloomed with color and her jaw showed signs of scratches from Ian's morning stubble. Jax moved closer to the mirror. *Ohmigod! I've got a hickey the size of Texas on my neck! Now why the hell hadn't Ian licked her wound, healing it and the skin underneath?* Jax wrapped the towel around her body, tucking the end in between her breasts before she walked out of the bathroom.

Ian stood by the window, looking out into the woods behind the house. "Glad you're considering joining a group. I'd like to hear more about them once this whole thing with Drace is taken care of." He nodded then chuckled.

"No, I didn't think you'd be able to manage Drace and his followers without some help. It's good to know some of your fellow officers wanted to help out."

"Is the house locked down? Good. Thanks. I owe you one, buddy."

Ian paused then gave a short laugh. "I guess that *does* make that two. Thanks again." He snapped the phone closed and set it on the nightstand as he turned to look at her.

"What was that all about?" Jax said, anger snapping her spine to full attention. How could he use someone's help with Drace when he accused her of doing the very same thing?

"My friend Mark just helped me out, that's all," he said as he walked toward her.

When he stopped near her, Jax backed away, her eyes narrowed. "What do you mean 'Mark' helped you? You gave me pure hell for letting someone help me find Drace," she said, her voice controlled, angry.

Ian took another step toward her. "It's not the same thing."

"Yes it is."

"No, it's not." Ian's jaw tightened and his fists clenched by his side.

Jax tilted her chin in a defiant angle. "Then enlighten me."

"Mark is a police officer. He helped oust Drace and the other vamps out of his brother, Kraid's house."

"Well, his brother's dead, much to my disgust. I would have liked to take him out myself," she snorted, "and since his brother is gone, I don't see how your friend had any jurisdiction over his estate."

Ian folded his arms over his chest. "The estate and all the holdings passed to me upon Kraid's death."

Jax's eyes widened in surprise. "You? Why would it pass to you?" Her gaze narrowed. "Are you related to Kraid and Drace?"

"Hell, no," he shot back before he gave her a satisfied smile. "When Kraid died all his possessions as the leader of the Ruean clan passed on to the new Ruean leader."

Realization dawned. "You're the new Ruean leader?"

He nodded. "So as you can see, I have every right to have Drace removed from *my* property."

Surprised by his revelation about his status among the vampires, Jax refused to be sidetracked. "Though I find this information intriguing, I still don't see how this is any different from what you accused me of doing."

"You need to learn to use your instincts more." He paused then went on, "The man helping you was another vampire."

"You're lying." Her heart jerked in her chest. She couldn't believe she'd been duped so thoroughly.

Ian frowned. "No, I'm not. His name is Sebastian Gauthier. He's the leader of the Norriden clan."

"Why would the leader of the Norriden clan want to help me destroy one of his own?"

"Drace isn't part of the Norriden clan. Remember, Drace is Ruean."

Jax waved her hand. "Ruean, Norriden...who the hell cares? They're all vamps to me."

Ian's expression turned to granite and he said in a low tone, "Yes, we're all of the same Kendrian race, but watch what you say, *Sonuachar*. Soon you'll be a vampire, too."

"Yeah, right!" Jax said, folding her arms underneath her breasts. "In your dreams, buddy."

Ian closed the distance between them and grabbed her arms. "Make no mistake. You will mate with me," he said, his expression angry, his tone possessive and brusque.

She tilted her eyebrow, a wanna-make-a-bet expression forming on her face.

Ian continued, "And I won't have to compel you, Jax. You'll ask of your own free will."

Jax tried to pull out of his hold but Ian held fast, his grip like bands of steel on her arms. He pulled her closer, breathing in the scent of her hair. She opened her mouth to tell him where he could shove his arrogant attitude, but Ian dipped his head and took one long stroke with his tongue along the side of her neck.

The warmth and rasp of his tongue skidded through her body all the way down to her toes. Jax froze, completely entranced by the sensation. God, she wanted more! When he clamped his teeth on her neck, not puncturing her skin, but holding her still, her knees buckled and she would've fallen if he hadn't been holding her up.

You will ask to mate, his voice entered her mind in an assured tone.

Jax's mind fought the tide of lust swirling around in her body. Get a grip! She told herself. She started to tell him how wrong he was, but Ian released her neck only to cover her lips with his. Thrusting his tongue inside her mouth, his rough invasion elicited a primal response—heat surged to the juncture of her thighs, her breasts tingled and her nipples ached as he plundered, dominated, and took possession of her body, her heart, and her mind.

While he continued to kiss her, Ian released her arms to yank the towel from around his waist. When he reached for the towel around her body, reason finally decided to show its nagging little self. Jax pushed him away. Inhaling and exhaling in heavy breaths, she held her arm out to ward him off as she grasped the towel around her like a protective shield.

"No!" she said in a forceful voice.

"Your body wants to mate," he bit out, his expression focused, his stance tense as if ready to pounce on her any second.

"It does not," she countered. When Ian took a step toward her, she stepped back, knowing she wouldn't be able to stop if he kissed her again. "Okay, okay, so my body thinks you're a walking, talking supercharged jumper cable, but my mind isn't ready, Ian."

Ian's expression softened and he stepped near her once more. Cupping her face in his hands, he tilted her head so she looked up at him. "If you ask me to accept your need to wait, I have to know why."

Jax blinked back the tears and her lips trembled. "I can't become the very creature who was responsible for my mother's death and my father's grief."

Ian sighed and wrapped his arms around her. Kissing her temple he said, "Jax, I don't believe that a bite from a vampire could be the cause of the kind of problems your mother had during childbirth. Yes, only a rogue vamp would have taken the blood of a pregnant woman, but you didn't say she'd been viciously attacked, right? She'd just been bitten. Nothing more."

How could he try to downplay what had happened? As nagging doubts gripped her, Jax stiffened in his arms and tried to pull away once more. "I-I don't know how bad it was. You'll have to forgive me for not knowing since I was being born at that point in time."

Ian's arms tightened around her. "I understand you want to be mentally ready, but I won't let you shut me out, Jax." He lifted her chin and his golden gaze searched hers. "The attraction I feel for you is unprecedented for me, and I won't be able to be near you for very long without wanting you. All of you. I won't lie to you. I'll do everything in my power, short of compelling you, to make you my Anima, my vampire mate as soon as possible."

His admission of the depth of his attraction shocked Jax into silence. She just stood there, staring at him, unable to formulate a single smart-ass comment.

Ian gave her a roguish smile. "Unless you want me to start working my magic, you'd better get a move on and put some clothes on that gorgeous body of yours to keep me from temptation."

Jax shoved him away so fast he almost fell over. "It might help if I knew where my clothes were," she said with a half smile, her emerald gaze sparkling.

God, the woman absolutely took his breath away. He swept his arm in a gallant manner and bent at the waist toward the bed. "Your clothes await, Miss."

When she noticed her bag sitting on the bed beside her neatly folded clothes she'd worn from the night before, Jax narrowed her eyes on Ian. "I thought you said those were the only clothes I had," she accused.

Ian folded his arms and let an unrepentant grin tilt the corners of his lips. "Everything in my power, remember?"

"Overbearing, arrogant, tyrannical, underhanded..." Jax continued to mumble as she grabbed her belongings and stomped off to the bathroom. Before she shut the door, she called over her shoulder, "And put some clothes on, you exhibitionist!"

Ian laughed out loud at Jax's disgruntled comment as he walked over and pulled out a pair of boxers and some jeans from the dresser. She may be angry with him but he noted how happy she was to have her weapons back. By the time he'd slipped into his clothes and bent the iron post back into place on the headboard, Jax had exited the bathroom and proceeded to lean against the wall and stretch her legs out one at a time.

He noted she hadn't changed into her regular clothes but had changed into a pair of black cotton drawstring pants with white stripes down the sides and a white tank top.

Flipping her long braid over her back, she looked up as he sat on the bed and leaned back against the headboard. "So, what next?"

"Next?" he asked, raising his eyebrow.

She switched legs and continued to stretch. "Yeah, when do we go after Drace? I'm ready to go when you are."

Why did watching the woman loosen her body up give him a hard-on? 'Cause he really did want to put her limber body into some unique sexual positions, that's why. He kept his face impassive as he responded, "I have other plans."

Jax pushed away from the wall. "Other plans?" Lying down on the floor, she folded her hands behind her head, bent her knees, and began doing sit-ups. "Unless those plans involve finding Drace, you can count me out."

Ian ignored her comment. "Tomorrow Jocelyn and Roderick Beaumont will hold their annual party at their estate." He gave her a pointed look. "We *will* be in attendance."

She stopped midway to her knees. "I don't think you heard me so I'll say it slower this time, "Unless...it...involves...finding...Drace...count...me...out." When she finished, she resumed exercising.

The woman truly knew how to push his level of patience. "Let me ask you a question. Now that Drace has had his home taken away from him, tell me, with all your tracking knowledge, where do you think he'd go?"

His question made her pause for a brief second. "He would go to family or friends for help."

"And since he's been banished and judged for his crime in killing your father?" he prodded.

"Then he more than likely would only go to family since blood," she paused, wrinkling her nose and said, "*Ewww*, that's a whole new twist on the saying isn't it?" before she continued, "is definitely thicker than water."

Ian nodded. "Jocelyn is Drace's cousin."

"And you think she'll just give him up?"

No, he wasn't sure, but Drace had been judged and Ian and Jocelyn's friendship went back decades. He really wouldn't know how much, if any, information she would divulge until he talked to her.

"She may not but there's only one way to find out."

"I supposed it couldn't hurt to try his cousin," she said in a grudging tone that made him smile. Jax's cheeks had turned rosy with her exertions. Damn, she had to have done at least one hundred sit-ups by now.

Jax closed her eyes and thought about Ian's logic while she continued her exercise. It made sense that Drace would try to get help from family. Sudden pressure on her feet caused her to open her eyes.

Ian's hands were on her feet, holding them down for her while she sat up and then laid back.

A sexy grin tilted the corners of his lips as he encircled her ankles with his hands. "You know, if you became a vampire, you wouldn't have to do this everyday."

She frowned at him. "I exercise because I like too, Ian. It helps me think."

Ian yanked her legs straight out and moved in between them.

Her heart thudded in her chest as he slid his hand under her shirt and ran his palm across her abdomen, touching every single muscle. Her stomach contracted with each brush of his skin against hers.

His golden gaze met hers. "Don't get me wrong, I love your body just the way it is, but I want you to be aware of the benefits, *a ghrá.*"

If she let him touch her much longer, she'd be begging for him to take her. Jax swiftly pulled her knees toward her chest and tucked into a backward roll until she squatted on her feet facing him.

"Thanks for the tip. I'll keep it in mind."

Before she could rise, he grabbed her wrist. Holding firm, his heated gaze dipped to the cleavage she revealed in her current position before returning to hers. "I look forward to reaping the benefits of your limber body, Jax."

The sexual undertones in the room caused electricity to arc between them, flowing back and forth, settling in the place where his hand held her wrist. Jax had to literally shake herself to break free from his mesmerizing gaze.

Pulling her arm from his grasp, she stood up grumbling, "Stop that."

"Stop what?" he asked, his tone innocent as he stood.

Jax wanted to grind her teeth as his "oh so innocent" look. "Weren't you supposed to put some clothes on?" she snapped.

Ian chuckled and walked over to the dresser to pull out a black sweater. When he slipped the shirt on and turned to face her, he raised an eyebrow as if to say, "Is that better?"

He'd just managed to look even sexier if that were possible. Grrrr. Jax walked back to the bathroom. When she turned the lock on the door, she clenched her jaw at the low laughter she heard from behind the wood barrier.

Chapter Twelve

Ian sensed Jax's apprehension as he pulled down the driveway to the Beaumont's house. What was going on in that strategic-thinking head of hers? She plucked at her khaki pants and pulled at her thick hunter green cable sweater. Was she nervous? Jax nervous? Granted they left his house later than he wanted, arriving at the Beaumont's at around two in the afternoon.

He looked at the brick mansion ahead, the two huge columns supporting the front entryway, the white double door entrance. Jax's estate rivaled this one. There's no way the home could intimidate her.

She spoke as he parked the car in front of the house. "Um, we're not going to be here long enough for the party, right?"

Ian laughed. "Of course we'll be here for the party. Once a year the vampires get together to par-*tee*," he said with a grin.

"I'm not staying for the party." Jax didn't bother to smile back.

He noted her fidgeting with her clothes again, then understanding dawned on him. "Jax, don't worry about not having the right clothes. I called Jocelyn yesterday and told her your approximate size. She said she'd have a few things ready for you to try on."

Her furrowed brow smoothed out but she still seemed nervous. When she reached up and touched the chopsticks in her hair while she looked back at the house, Ian realized she was worried about her appearance in general. But she looked dynamite in a dress. He shook his head and smiled. Joss would take good care of her.

He got out of the car and came around to her side only to see she'd already exited the car and had her bag slung over her shoulder.

As they walked into the foyer, Jocelyn entered the room from a side hall, Sabryn and Rana trailing behind her.

"Welcome to our home," she said to Jax as she grabbed her hands and spread her arms wide. "Ian, you didn't do her justice. My dear, you are quite a beauty," she gushed.

Jocelyn herself was quite a beauty. A petite brunette, with striking features, Jocelyn might be over two hundred years old, but she didn't look a day over forty and everything about her screamed class. From her friendly bearing to her passionate nature, he'd always enjoyed her company.

If Roderick hadn't claimed her years ago, he might have tossed his hat in the ring. But that was before he met Jax and realized what it meant to meet one's soul mate—to be so caught up in another person everything that had been so important to you before, paled in comparison.

Ian grinned at the two pink spots that flushed Jax's cheeks as she murmured a quiet thank you.

"Come in, come in," Jocelyn said as she led Jax into the formal living room. "You too, ladies," she called behind her.

Jax glanced back at him, an I-have-no-clue-as-to-why-I-am-here look on her face as Jocelyn continued, "Are you hungry? I'll have Renee bring you some food…"

Yeah, he'd done the right thing bringing Jax here. Already Jocelyn had taken her under her wing. Ian gave Jax an encouraging smile before turning to Sabryn and Rana.

"Good to see you, Sabryn," he said as he glanced down at Rana's flat belly and teased, "How's the little Vité doing?"

Rana patted her stomach and smiled. She radiated complete happiness and contentment. She wasn't a classical beauty like Jocelyn or exotic like Jax, but her light brown hair and hazel eyes, coupled with peaches and cream skin and a great smile, made him see why Lucian fell for her. Maybe he could get her to talk to Jax about her experience transitioning from human to vampire, well, minus the whole weird death thing.

"The baby is fine. Thanks for asking. Lucian is in the rec room and asked me to have you meet him there when you arrived."

"Thanks, Rana."

As he turned to walk away, Sabryn asked, "How's Duncan doing, Ian?"

Ian turned back to them. "Fine, but he still keeps to himself." He rubbed his jaw as he considered an idea. "You know, you're one of the few women Duncan trusts. If the right opportunity comes along, would you be willing to help me work on drawing Duncan out?"

Sabryn gave him her trademark mischievous smile as she flipped her long dark hair over her shoulder. "I love a good bait and switch, especially if it's in someone's best interest. Count me in."

"Thanks Sabryn. Guess I'd better go find out what *The Vité* wants."

Sabryn called after him, "He'll always be my brother and your best friend first, Ian. Don't let him get all high and mighty on you." She chuckled as she finished, "He knows better than to try that crap with me."

* * * * *

The *crack* of the pool cue breaking a rack of balls reverberated throughout the room as Ian entered. The new room smell teased his nostrils, making him smile. The Beaumont's were never ones to sit idly by, hence the rec room addition to their home among other interests they shared. He wondered what Jax would think about their home theater room. The thought gave him an instant hard-on.

"Well, well, the long absent Ruean leader returns," Lucian said, looking up from his bent position at the table.

Shifting his thoughts to more neutral ones, Ian ignored his friend's jibe and took down a cue from the wall. Pulling back his sleeves, he chalked the stick and grunted, "It's been a helluva month."

Lucian knocked in a solid ball and rounded the table to set up for another shot. He paused and raised a dark eyebrow as he looked at him, giving him an I-know-you-better-than-anyone look. "I do believe you're slipping, my friend."

Ian couldn't believe his best friend was now Vité, leader over all vampires. He noted Lucian's gray dress slacks and black silk shirt and then his own worn jeans and sweater and grinned at the differences between them. Whereas he preferred direct, blunt tactics, Lucian, refined and cultured, had always known just the right thing to say to get what he wanted. Yes, his friend filled the Vité role well. He was a born leader.

"Several Rueans have helped Drace escape on numerous occasions," Ian said as he met Lucian's pale gray gaze with a serious one. "This clan is truly divided now, old friend."

Lucian's smile disappeared and hard lines set on his face as he straightened. "This dissention will end now —" he commanded.

"No," Ian interrupted in a forceful tone. "I'll handle it my way. They are my clan to lead. I will lead them my way. They can wait another couple of days. I have something else I must address first."

"Ah," Lucian leaned on his stick and cocked his head to the side. "Jocelyn mentioned you planned to bring a woman with you. Is she the cause of your delay?" he asked in an innocent tone.

"Jax is the most infuriating, stubborn, highly sensual, I-can't-get-enough-of-her woman I've ever met," Ian gritted out as he hit the cue ball and two stripes landed in opposite pockets. He waited for the ribbing to begin. He'd sure given Lucian hell over Rana.

"So…"

Yep, here it came.

"Kinda crowded under there, isn't it?"

"Huh?" Ian looked up.

Lucian touched the tip of his cue to Ian's forearm. "You know…under your skin…where this woman, Jax, is?" Lucian finished with a huge grin.

"*Touché*," Ian replied. "I knew that remark would come back to bite me in the ass."

"Didn't stop you from making the comment though, did it?"

"Nope and I'd say it again in a do-over," Ian shot back, a wide grin on his face.

"Me too on the do-over part. I wouldn't change a thing," Lucian finished with a laugh, pride reflected in his expression.

Ian walked around the table and put out his hand. "Congrats, Luc. I'm a little put out that you didn't tell me about the baby the last time I saw you."

Gripping his hand, Lucian snorted. "Considering the fact an angel had just told me I was going to be a father, I was still absorbing the news."

"Fair enough," Ian chuckled as he moved back to his side of the table.

"So you haven't mated with this woman?"

Ian hit another two stripes in a corner pocket, one right after the other. "It's a little more complicated than that, I'm afraid." He looked up from sighting a shot. "Jax is John Markson's vampire-hunting daughter."

Lucian gave him a blank stare for all of two seconds before he threw his head back and laughed, a full-bellied, deep, hearty laugh.

When Ian glared at him, he sobered. "Leave it to you to pick the one woman who would rather kill you than sleep with you. Does she know you're a vampire?"

"She does." Ian sighed and leaned on his pool cue. "And she refuses to become my mate because her mother was bitten by a rogue vampire while she was pregnant with Jax. Her mother died right after giving birth to Jax and her father spent his entire life seeking vengeance against all vampires for his wife's death."

Lucian whistled long and low. "Talk about carrying around a lot of baggage. I'm surprised you've gotten as far as you have with her, in other words, that she came here with you."

Ian met Lucian's gaze with a disgruntled one. "I had to bribe her with hopes of finding Drace through Jocelyn."

At Lucian's raised eyebrow, he continued, "She's my Anima, Luc, or as we say in Irish, *Sonuachar*. We're close to a full mating. I can't let her slip through my fingers." His expression turned hopeful. "Do you think Rana would be willing to talk with her about becoming a vampire?"

"I'm sure Rana would be happy to help out. Though I think I'll tell her to leave out the part about dying…not real sure about that whole scenario myself," he said with a grin as he rubbed his jaw.

* * * * *

After they fed her and made small talk for a while, Jocelyn, Rana, and Sabryn led Jax to her bedroom and proceeded to tell her the things to look out for when being involved with a male vampire. Jax started to tell them she and Ian weren't mated but the ladies chattered on, not letting her get a word in edgewise.

Sabryn pulled the chopsticks out of her hair, her unusual lavender-colored eyes glittering with admiration as she pushed her into a chair and began brushing the black mass of hair that had fallen around her shoulders in long, even strokes. Jocelyn opened the tall cherry wardrobe and withdrew gown after gown while Rana and Sabryn yeah'd or nay'd the different dresses.

"Too bright."

"No, too frufru," Sabryn said, wrinkling her nose. "Here let me help."

As Sabryn walked over to talk to Jocelyn, Rana took the brush from her as she passed and took over brushing Jax's hair. "You have beautiful hair, Jax. Do you know how often I wished I had pitch-black hair?"

Jax met her gaze in the mirror. "Do you know how often I wished I had light brown hair?"

They shared a smile. Rana placed her hand on her shoulder and started to speak, "You know, I sense..." Suddenly Rana blinked and then sucked in her breath as if in pain.

Jax turned in her seat and grabbed Rana's hand. "Are you all right?" When she saw Rana's face grow pale, she jumped up and caught the woman before she fell to the floor.

"Rana!" Sabryn said and flew to Jax's side in a swift blur.

Before Jax knew what the woman intended, Sabryn lifted Rana in her arms, calling over her shoulder in a brisk tone, "Jocelyn, I'm taking Rana to their bedroom. Get Lucian now!"

"But wait," Rana said in a weak voice. "I need to—"

"Shhh, Rana," Sabryn interrupted her as she walked out the door. "We'll get Lucian. You need him by your side."

When everyone left the room, Jax wanted to follow but felt very much like a third wheel. She didn't really know Rana and would have no right to follow them to her bedroom. She'd noticed something different about Rana when left alone with her. Yes, Jax's body vibrated like it always did when vampires were in close proximity, but Rana's presence didn't cause her body to vibrate in the same way as Sabryn and Jocelyn's did. Rana did let off a vibe, a very intense one that Jax couldn't put her finger on. She knew Rana had vampire blood running through her veins but Jax felt something more, something stronger.

She looked over at the rainbow of beautiful dresses strewn across her bed, discarded for one reason or another. Organza and linen, silk and rayon, cotton and satin, the ladies had said. To Jax, the materials started to blend together after a while. Personally, she preferred the soft feel of silk against her skin and would pick something in that material, maybe this red one, she mused as she ran her hand across the material.

She glanced up when a scratching sound near the balcony drew her attention. A black cat, with white tufts of hair on its chest and ears, rubbed back and forth against the French doors.

Meow, meow, it mewed.

Jax grinned and opened the doors. "Hello there," she said as she sat down Indian-style to pet the cat.

Meow, meow, the cat continued its singsong noises as it jumped into her lap.

"Well, why don't you just make yourself right at home, Mr..." she paused and lifted the cat's hindquarters, "...uh, make that Ms. Cat."

As she rubbed the cat's neck, she noticed a piece of paper wrapped around the animal's collar. Unrolling the stiff parchment-like paper from the collar, Jax's heart rate accelerated at she read the note.

My dearest Jax,

I'm most unhappy that you decided to part without saying a proper goodbye. And just when I'd had hoped to get to know you better. Well, no fear, my dear. I have the perfect solution for both of us. You see, I have your uncle James under my care and as you know, I'm not a very caring person, so I believe it would be in your best interest to come home, alone.

I warn you, if I sense another vampire in the vicinity, your uncle dies. I think I've made myself perfectly clear, don't you?

Yours,

Drace

Jax's blood ran cold at the chilling, impersonal tone of Drace's note. He meant what he said. He'd kill her uncle just like he'd killed her father. Spurred into action, Jax jumped up, tossed the note onto the dresser, then turned and ripped open her bag, pulling out her weapons.

Yanking off her khaki pants, she strapped a smaller knife to her inner thigh, then pulled on a pair of loose-fitting cargo pants with a multitude of pockets before she slipped into her hiking boots.

While she dressed she realized her first instinct was to tell Ian, but Ian would insist on coming along and Drace's note had been clear. He'd smell a vamp and she had no doubt in her mind he'd kill her uncle if provoked. Where was Blake? Was he captured too? If Blake knew her uncle was in trouble, he'd drop everything to help. With her family threatened, Jax put aside her need to work alone. She started to reach in her bag for her cell phone to call Blake when she remembered Ian had destroyed it. *Damn vamp!* she thought in frustration. She didn't have time to go searching for a phone.

Grabbing a roll of duct tape out of her bag, she used her teeth to rip off a strip. It took some maneuvering but she managed to tape another knife to her back. Reaching behind her head, she drew the knife from its sheath between her shoulder blades and nodded in satisfaction before replacing the weapon.

Jax pulled on a long sleeved black cotton t-shirt, tucked it in her pants, and threaded her gold-buckled belt into the loops of her pants. After she slipped on her gun's shoulder harness, she double-checked the clip and snapped the gun back in the holster before she pulled on her black denim jacket. Methodical, precise movements, no emotion, she reminded herself as she checked and rechecked the rest of her gear.

Winding her hair back up on her head, she jammed the chopsticks in the thick twist. Jax glanced at her watch and noted the time—five-thirty. Damn, the vamp moved fast, considering he wouldn't have been able to go out in the late afternoon light more than a half hour ago. She needed to leave without being noticed. The balcony would have to do as an exit strategy.

When the cat started to follow her out the French doors, she pushed her back inside saying, "No, little one. Drace may have compelled you to help him, but now you can help me. I can't bring a vamp, so you're going to stay here and help Ian figure out why I left. I just need a head start to get my uncle to safety first. I know Ian will follow."

* * * * *

Lucian straightened, pausing in the middle of his shot, his entire stance tense, his expression focused.

"What is it?" Ian asked, concern causing him to frown. He didn't sense any new vampires at the estate yet since the other guests weren't due until tomorrow.

His friend laid his cue down on the table and turned toward the door. "It's Rana."

Just then Jocelyn entered the room, her cheeks flushed.

"Lucian…"

He interrupted, saying in a brisk tone, "What's wrong. Where's Rana?"

"Come," Jocelyn beckoned. "She almost fainted. Sabryn has taken her to your room."

Ian followed, worry for his friend's mate paramount. Lucian waited so long for Rana to come into his life. He hoped she was all right.

Hovering outside their bedroom door, Ian looked up in surprise when Lucian turned from holding Rana's hand and said, "Ian, come in, Rana has to tell you something."

Ian walked to other side of the bed, curious as to why Rana would request his presence. "Are you okay, Rana?"

Rana looked tired but she managed a smile. "I'm fine. The baby's fine. I almost fainted earlier because when I touched Jax's shoulder I sensed danger surrounding her. But it wasn't until she grabbed my hand that the reality of that sensation settled in my mind. Don't let her out of your sight, Ian. Someone will try to hurt her, someone so evil, I couldn't make out features. He only appeared as a dark shadow."

Fear gripped Ian, tensing his entire body. He glanced at his friend then back at her, hoping she'd somehow overreacted. "Lucian didn't mention your psychic abilities."

She gave her husband a sly smile. "Well, that's because I just recently started experiencing them." Lucian splayed his hand over her belly and she covered his with hers and addressed her husband, "I know what you're thinking, and yes, I wonder if my recent experiences are really our child's abilities channeling through me, too."

Turning her gaze back to Ian, she said, "Go be with Jax, and don't let her out of your sight for a minute. She's in your bedroom..." Rana paused, as a guilty expression crossed her face and she continued, "...and probably feeling a bit left out at the moment since we left her so abruptly."

Ian didn't have to be told twice. He rushed out of the room and sprinted across the house to the hall where his and Jax's room was located. Throwing open the door, the sense of dread that filled him spread into gut-wrenching fear when he noted the empty room, Jax's bag thrown open, and her gear and weapons missing.

A black cat jumped up onto the vanity dresser and swatted at a rolled up piece of paper, meowing over and over again.

Ian frowned at the cat, wondering at its presence, while he bent to pick up the note. Unrolling the paper, he skimmed the note. His stomach clenched and his jaw tightened with each word he read.

Chapter Thirteen

Jax glared at the blond-headed vamp that stood in the foyer of her home as she entered. He grinned, displaying his fangs for effect.

"Ever heard of whitening toothpaste, pal?" she said as she approached. When he quickly covered his teeth with his lips and scowled at her, Jax smirked and sidestepped him as he attempted to grab her arm.

"Ah, ah, ah. I don't think Drace would like you touching the merchandise," she *tsked* and walked into the living room.

"In the office," the vamp ground out in a pissed tone. When she turned, he followed her into her uncle's office.

Her gaze immediately landed on her uncle James tied to his office chair, a strip of duct tape over his mouth.

"Nice of you to join us, Jax," Drace said in a lazy drawl from his leaning position against the office window. Dressed in a black leather vest, a white shirt and black jeans, the vamp looked every bit as dark and evil as she knew him to be.

Jax narrowed her eyes on Drace and started toward her uncle.

"Not so fast," Drace said, stopping her in her tracks. He nodded to the vamp behind her. "Search her for weapons."

The blond vamp grabbed her so fast, Jax didn't have time to move away. She tried to appear nonchalant when the vamp pulled her two wrists together behind her head with one hand. He reached under her jacket and pulled her gun out of its holster, then slid his hand over waist and stomach. While he searched her body, he brushed his crotch against her backside on purpose. Jax bit back a sarcastic comment, not wanting to prolong her search any more than necessary.

She tensed when he reached for her thigh, concerned he'd discover her hidden weapon. At the same time she noted the look of jealousy that flashed in Drace's gaze and decided to use the vamp's selfish nature to her advantage. "He's groping me, Drace. I figured you for the type of guy who wouldn't want damaged goods."

As if on cue, the vamp behind her grunted and let her go as his body slammed against the bookcase. "Enough, Neil. Go back to your station at the front of the house," Drace said in a deadly voice.

Once Neil walked out, Jax approached her uncle. "Why do you even pretend to be civilized, Drace? You and I both know you're pond scum."

When she started to unwind the tape holding her uncle's wrist to the chair arm, Drace said, "Leave him."

She looked up, glaring at the vamp. "I will not! You've bound his arms too tight. My uncle's an old man."

"That *old* man almost fried my ass, twice," he ground out. "I think I'll pass on you untying him."

Jax gritted her teeth as she reached for the duct tape over her uncle's mouth. "I'm removing the tape from his mouth at least."

When she pulled the tape off, her uncle yowled in pain and then spat out, "Sonofabitch."

"Sorry, Unc," she said, giving him an apologetic smile.

"I believe he referred to me with that nasty comment," Drace said in a droll tone. His black eyes narrowed on her uncle. "Hence the reason for the duct tape. If I had to hear one more time how my mother was a bitch, I think I would have killed him where he stood."

"Son-of-a-bit—"

Clamping her hand over her uncle's mouth, Jax said in a clipped tone, "You've got what you wanted. I'm here."

Drace gave her a satisfied smile. "Yes, you are." Straightening, he walked over to the doorway and called out, "Get the car ready. We're leaving in one minute."

Neil entered the doorway, questioning their destination. Drace approached Neil and while they discussed the location, Jax whispered to her uncle, "Where's Blake?"

He gave her a disapproving frown. "Looking for you."

Guilt washed over her. Because of her, her uncle had been left without a strong hunter to back him up.

"I'm sorry, Uncle James."

"Sorry Blake had to go looking for you or sorry you've taken up with a vamp," he said, his voice harsh.

"Ian's a hunter and a good man," she defended Ian without a second thought. Too late she realized the conclusion her uncle would draw.

"We're all one in the same, my dear. A vamp's a vamp," Drace said from the doorway.

She cut her gaze to Drace. "Ian is way above you. Don't even begin to compare yourself."

Drace's eyes lit up. "Ah, so that's the way the wind blows. You really *have* fallen for a vampire. That'll make my revenge so much sweeter," he finished with a hearty laugh.

Jax's skin crawled at the sheer malevolence that emanated from the man.

"Go fuck yourself," she snapped, fear finally taking hold. She could only imagine the pain the man had in store for her.

"Oh, I plan the fuck part, but I won't be doing it alone." His expression sobered into a cruel twist of his lips as he walked across the room toward them.

"No!" her uncle yelled and let off a string of curses as he struggled against the bindings around his arms.

Jax turned to her uncle and said in a low voice, "Don't worry about me. I can take care of myself, but I need to know something before I leave. When my mother was bitten, was she also brutally attacked? Or was it just a bite and nothing more?"

Her uncle stopped his frantic movements, his brows drawing together in puzzlement as Drace reached them and clamped a hand on her arm.

As Drace pulled her away, James called after them, "Don't worry, Jax. Blake will track you down."

"Answer me," she said in a raised voice, desperate to know the answer. This might be her last chance to know the truth.

"Just a bite from what I remember," her uncle answered in a grudging tone.

Jax sent up a silent prayer that her mother had not suffered. Before Drace dragged her out of the room, he looked back, addressing her uncle, "I know Ian Mordoor. He'll track Jax here. When he does come, tell him to meet us at the old lumber yard off Route 250."

While her uncle strained to get loose from the chair, Jax called out, worry for him at the forefront of her mind, "Uncle James, please calm down. Remember your heart..." That's all she got out before Drace yanked her out of hearing range.

* * * * *

Ian slammed on the breaks in his Hummer and cut the engine. Once he climbed out of the vehicle, he didn't bother walking. He took one long leap and landed on the front porch of Jax's house, ready to battle. Nothing. He didn't sense a single vampire, but he certainly heard yelling.

He opened the front door and called out, "James?"

"Back here. In the office," the old man yelled back.

As soon as he entered the office, James griped, "Get this damn tape off of me. I can't feel my damn hands anymore."

Ian pulled the knife from the sheath on his leg and cut the bindings. "Where'd he take her?" he asked, not bothering with pleasantries as he slid the knife back in the sheath.

"To an old lumber yard off of Route 250," James answered while rubbing his wrists. "He's expecting you."

Ian's stomach clenched at the fact the vamp expected him to follow. That meant he had plans for him. When he turned to leave, he paused at James' words, "No, wait. I'll call Blake and you can go together."

Ian shook his head. "No. I don't have time to wait. Who knows what that bastard has planned for Jax?"

James' face blanched. "Get to her as fast as you can. That vamp is pure evil."

He gave James a curt nod and started to walk out of the room. Turning back to Jax's uncle once more, he met the old man's gaze. "Know this. I love Jax, and I'll do everything in my power to convince her to become my vampire mate."

James stood and clenched his fists by his sides. "You might have shown me there are some good vamps in this world, but I won't accept Jax becoming a vampire."

Anger flared through him at the man's prejudice against all vampires. Ian stared James down. "You don't have a choice in the matter. It's up to Jax to make that decision."

* * * * *

Ian crawled on his belly to peer over the edge of the abandoned lumber building. Down below, he noted Drace and Jax's location as they stood in the middle of bundled stacks of old plywood and two-by-fours. He heard Drace say, "Mordoor's here. I sense his presence."

Sliding a bolt into Jax's crossbow pistol, he sent her a silent thank you for leaving the weapon behind. Before the vamps could spread out, he had to silently take a few out. He sighted the first vamp and pulled the trigger. He had already reloaded as the bolt slammed right into the vampire's heart. Dead on target, just as he intended. As the second vamp went down, he gave a humorless smile when he heard Drace losing it.

"Sonofabitch!" Drace howled out, looking everywhere for Ian while he waved his gun. "Spread out and find the bastard." But before the other vampires had taken more than a few steps, Ian took down another man.

When the third vampire fell, Drace grabbed Jax around her neck. Ian's stomach tensed as he watched Jax struggle.

"What's this?" Drace asked as he reached down the back of Jax's jacket and pulled out her Bowie knife. Clasping the back of her neck in his hand once more, he yanked Jax back against his chest and held the Bowie knife up to her neck.

Ian shut his eyes for a brief second to gain control over the blind rage that raced through his veins. He fought the primal instincts that kicked in, telling him to attack Drace head on.

"Get down here now, Mordoor, or I'll slice Jax's lovely throat. You see...you need to give me a reason not to."

Ian jumped down from the building, the sawdust stirring up underneath his feet as he landed fifteen feet away from Drace and Jax. "Enough threats. I'm here," he said, his voice confident and steady as he stared Drace down.

"Take his weapons," Drace ordered. A blond vamp, he'd heard Drace call Neil, held his automatic gun on him while the other, a dark-haired vamp, divested him of all his weapons, including the knife strapped to his leg.

Ian narrowed his gaze on Drace as they removed the last of his weapons. Drace's men then moved on either side of him and pointed their guns toward him, ready to kill.

Drace wrapped his arm around Jax's neck and pulled her back. Stabbing her knife into the wall of wood stacked behind him, his lips curved into an evil smile as he slid his palm down her chest and clasped his hand fully over her breast.

Ian barely heard Jax's gasp of outrage over the train roaring in his ears. Pure hatred for Drace slammed through him. He took a step and pain sliced through his leg. Looking down, he noted the blood gushing from his leg, but his brain didn't really register what had happened. He clenched his fists by his sides and started to take a flying leap toward Drace when Jax's voice entered his rage-filled mind.

No, Ian, they'll kill you!

Her voice and imploring gaze brought him out of the haze of fury that had gripped him enough for Ian to realize he'd been shot. When he looked at the vamps beside him, he noted they now had their guns pointed toward his skull.

"Yes, do be a good vamp and don't move, Ian," Drace drawled as he pulled Jax's jacket off and dropped it on the ground. He slid his hands over her arms and then down the sides of her body. "Got any more weapons hidden on you, hmmm?" he asked as he continued to skim his hands around her hips and down her thighs.

When his hand brushed against her inner thigh, Drace made a *tsking* sound. "What's this?" He ripped her pants near her upper thigh and withdrew another knife she'd strapped to her leg. "Always ready for a battle, aren't you, my dear?" He gave an evil chuckle and brushed his lips against her neck then glanced at Ian for a reaction.

Ian kept his expression impassive and set his jaw as his stomach churned. He'd never felt so helpless and out-of-control in his life. He met Jax's gaze but she just bit her lip and shook her head, her actions telling him not to interfere.

When Drace wrapped his arms around her waist from behind and tried to remove her belt, Ian's chest contracted. She gave Ian a secret smile as Drace growled in frustration, failing at his task.

"Remove it," he ordered.

"Kiss my ass," Jax retorted.

"Have it your way," he gritted out. Grabbing the material in her pants where he'd ripped a hole earlier, he pulled hard, rending a much larger tear in the fabric.

When Drace shoved his hand inside the rip, Ian's entire body shook in fury. He didn't give a shit if he lived or died. He'd kill Drace before he had a chance to touch Jax.

Jax's body jerked when the gun popped off so close to her. Ian's body slammed to the ground, blood seeping into the sawdust underneath him. She'd forgotten Drace had a gun since he'd tucked in it his pants when he'd found her Bowie knife. Drace had fired twice. Where had Ian been hit? Panic gripped her. She couldn't see from where she stood.

"Ian!" she screamed and tried to run to him, but Drace grabbed the back of her shirt and yanked her against his chest once more.

"Pick him up," Drace said to the two vamps. "I want him to watch," he finished, his voice excited, almost gleeful.

"Fucking sonofabitch," Ian ground out, shooting a murderous glance at Drace as the two vampires yanked him to his feet, heedless of his wounds.

Jax's heart thudded against her chest. There was so much blood on his upper body it was hard to tell where he'd been hit. The shoulder? Closer to his heart? She had no clue.

"Yes, I guess I *will* be a 'fucking sonofabitch' very soon," Drace responded with a laugh as he nipped at her neck.

"Not so tough now that you've been stripped of all your weapons, huh?" Drace taunted in her ear as he slid his hand up the exposed flesh of her thigh.

Jax closed her eyes as Drace's fingers skimmed inside her underwear. Pure revulsion bubbled up inside her. Self-preservation kicked in and she tried to close her legs, but Drace spoke in her mind, *Accept my touch or Ian dies.*

The need to fight him warred within her now that Ian's life was held by such a tenuous thread. He'd be no match for Drace in his current condition. Jax tried to think of other things, not what this evil vampire had planned for her. But she'd never been a wilting flower and she sure as hell didn't plan to start now.

She laid her hand over Drace's as he slid his finger into her curls and down her labia, stopping his descent. "I'll remove my belt now."

"No!" Ian lifted his head, his expression filled with pain, yet thunderous nonetheless.

"Silence, Mordoor," Drace bit out.

Ian suddenly doubled over, gasping for breath, as if Drace had used his mental powers to punch him in the stomach. Jax's insides jerked and her hatred for Drace spiked.

Drace removed his hand and turned her around to face him saying, "By all means, remove your belt and then your clothes."

Jax's heart rammed against her ribs, adrenaline and fear for Ian clamoring within her as she pressed on the secret release button on her belt buckle. She forced herself to meet Drace's hooded gaze. Noting the sexual hunger burning in their dark depths, she decided to use his desire against him.

Stepping close to him, she said in a low voice, "Will you take my blood when you fuck me, pureblood?"

When Drace's eyes lit in lustful excitement, she stepped even closer. "There's one thing you need to know about me first."

"What's that?" Drace's eyebrow rose in interest.

In a swift, smooth movement, she gripped her belt buckle, withdrew the dagger, and slammed it all the way to the hilt into Drace's stomach saying, "A good vampire hunter always carries an extra weapon."

With swift movements, she withdrew the knife, gripped Drace's shirt and pulled him in front of her while he held his stomach and groaned in agony. Jax shoved the dagger's sharp edge against Drace's neck and looked at the two vamps holding Ian.

"I suggest a trade. Drace for Ian."

When Neil narrowed his gaze on her and she felt her throat began to close as if an invisible hand squeezed, she jammed the knife tighter against Drace's skin, drawing blood. Unable to speak, she narrowed her gaze, letting him know she'd kill Drace before the vamp cut off all her air.

"Let him go," Drace moaned out, his pain evident in his expression as his knees buckled. His shirt pulled from her grasp and he fell to his knees. The two vamps dropped Ian and rushed to lift Drace to his feet. Jax ran to Ian's side as he crumpled to the ground. Drace's gun, lying on the ground, caught her attention. She looked up at the retreating figures moving to their car. It would be so easy to pick up the gun and shoot them all.

Ian called her name, his voice low and pained, "Get me back to the Beaumont's house, Jax. Mora should be there by now and she'll be able to help me...I hope."

Revenge forgotten, Jax turned her full attention to Ian as the vamps got in their car and left. "Where's your car?" she grunted as she tried to lift him to his feet. Ian leaned on her, his weight heavy. Blood coated her shirt from his wounds. God, there was so much blood. Her body shook in fear for his life. On closer inspection she noted that his shoulder appeared to be hit as well as his side, but the amount of blood loss was tremendous.

"A half block away toward town," he said, his voice fading.

"Don't pass out on me, Ian. I won't be able to get you to your car."

"Well, if you had become my vampire mate you wouldn't be such a wuss," he said with a pained half-smile.

"Very funny," Jax retorted. What an idiot, joking, when he could very well be dying. She set him back on the ground. "Where are your keys? I'll go get the car and bring it to you."

"They're in the car."

"In the car..." she started to exclaim, but just turned and ran away. *He leaves his keys in a seventy-thousand dollar vehicle?* She shook her head as she sprinted off.

* * * * *

Jax kept the pedal to the floor all the way back to the Beaumont's house. Ian had passed out right before they got there, freaking her out even further. Her heart raced as she hit the brakes, cut the engine, and dashed out of the car. Throwing open the front door, she ran inside.

"Sabryn!" she called out to the first person she saw. "Ian needs help. He said to get Mora. Is she here?"

Sabryn turned concerned eyes her way, noted the blood on her clothes and said, "Where's Ian?"

Jax rubbed her temples. "He's in the car, passed out. Oh God, he's lost so much blood."

Sabryn visibly paled. "Yes, Mora's here. Lucian will want to help. I'll get him."

Jax ran back to the car, her entire body shaking as she opened the passenger side door. A tall, dark-headed man with silver eyes suddenly appeared by her side. Man, she'd never get used to vampire speed.

"I'll carry him inside," he said in a gruff voice as he pulled Ian's limp body from the car.

Jax followed behind him, her insides churning. Ian couldn't die. No. He couldn't die.

A tall, older woman, her dark hair pulled away from her face, joined them in the foyer along with Sabryn.

"What happened?" she asked Jax.

"He's been shot in the leg, the shoulder and his side," Jax answered, her voice quivering.

Mora put two fingers on Ian's throat and looked at Lucian. Her brow furrowed. "Let's get him to his room." She gave Sabryn a pointed look. "He'll need blood, a good deal of it."

Mora started up the stairs and Lucian followed. Jax stepped beside him. "I'll give him my blood," she said, eager to help in any way she could.

"No," Lucian said, his tone firm.

Surprised by his clipped answer, Jax wasn't about to back down. "But he needs blood and I'm here."

Lucian paused on the stairs and met her gaze. "Don't worry, we'll get blood for him," he said, his tone dismissive as he started up the stairs again.

Jax stared after him, tears stinging her eyes. Sabryn touched her shoulder. "Jax, Lucian is Ian's best friend. He's just worried right now. Please don't take what he said the wrong way."

She blinked back the tears and mumbled, "I know. I just feel so helpless."

Sabryn gave her an encouraging smile. "Go on. Do what you can to help Mora."

Jax nodded, straightened her shoulders, and ran up the stairs after Lucian.

Once Lucian set Ian on the bed, he ripped Ian's shirt open to expose his upper body for Mora's inspection.

"Get me some towels to soak up all this blood," Mora said to no one in particular as she gently lifted Ian's body and looked at his back. Laying him down carefully, she then ripped his pants and inspected his leg.

Jax ran to the bathroom and looked around. Spotting a linen closet, she opened the door and pulled down some towels.

"Here," she said, handing the towels to Mora, her heart thudding in fear.

Mora set a towel behind Ian's shoulder and one under his side, saying to Lucian who stood on the other side of the bed, "He has exit wounds on his shoulder, side, and leg. So we don't have to worry about digging out the bullets." Sighing, she continued, "All we can do now is replenish the blood he lost and hope his body hasn't lost too much to heal on its own."

"I—" Jax started to speak.

"No," Lucian interrupted as his gaze narrowed on her.

"Listen, Lucian. I don't know you..." Jax paused when Rana walked into the room.

Lucian's fierce expression faded as he smiled at his wife. "Rana love, please take Jax to our room where she can shower and be ready when Ian awakes."

"Shouldn't you be resting or something?" Jax asked Rana, remembering how she'd left Lucian's wife just a few short hours ago.

Rana smiled. "No. I'm fine. But I'm so glad to see you're okay. If you'll come with me, I'll tell you all about it."

"I can't leave Ian," Jax insisted.

Mona put her hand on Jax's arm, her gaze kind and wise. "Go with Rana, dear. Ian's got a strong will. Always was a scrapper. He's too stubborn to die anytime soon."

With everyone wanting her out of the way, what was she to do? Jax had never felt so out of place. Reluctant to leave Ian, she picked up her bag and followed Rana down the hall to her bedroom.

Chapter Fourteen

After her shower, Jax pulled on a white zip-up sweater and a pair of blue jeans. Running her hairbrush through her hair, she walked into the bedroom.

"Thanks for helping me get through this, Rana."

Rana sat on the edge of her bed, a friendly smile on her face. "You're welcome." She patted a space on the bed beside. "Sit for a bit."

Jax smiled and sat on the bed. There was just something warm about Rana. With her dad's unusual occupation, she'd never really had any girlfriends growing up.

Rana touched her hand and inhaled, her smile broadening. "Good," she said, her hazel gaze locking with Jax's. "I don't feel anything. Well, other than your low vampire vibe."

Jax chuckled. "Uh, I'm not a vampire, Rana." She drew her eyebrows together and continued, "But we'll get to that in a minute. What did you mean, you don't feel anything?"

Rana took her hairbrush from her hand and waved her hand in a shooing motion to indicate she wanted Jax to turn around. Jax shrugged and turned her back to Rana. No one in her life had ever pampered her. *This she could get used to.*

When Rana pulled the brush through her hair from her crown all the way to the ends, Jax closed her eyes and imagined that this was what it would have felt like if her mom had done this for her as a child. Her heart melted at the thought. She'd like to have children one day…little hearts and minds to mold and influence as best she could.

"When I touched you earlier today, I almost fainted, not because of the baby, but because I had a premonition someone was going to try and hurt you."

Her comment surprised Jax. "I wasn't aware that vampires had the gift of seeing into the future."

Rana laughed. "They don't. We'll, not that I'm aware of. But what do I know? I've only been a vampire for a little over a month."

"What?" Jax turned around and stared at her. "But your vibe is so strong, stronger than most vampires I'm been around."

Rana rubbed her hand over her stomach. "I guess it's the little Vité I have growing inside me that's making my vibe so strong to you." She winked. "I think he's also the reason I had the premonition about you."

Here was the perfect opportunity to ask a person who'd only recently become a vampire how much it had changed her life. "Did it hurt?" Jax asked. "Becoming a vampire, I mean."

Rana nodded. "According to Lucian the transition is painful, yes." Her smile broadened and her eyes lit up when she spoke of her husband. "But he made sure I slept through the whole process." When she finished speaking, Rana flipped her hand again and Jax turned back around once more.

As she ran the brush through her hair, Rana said, "But you're already part vampire, so your transition shouldn't be as bad, I would imagine."

Jax turned her head, facing Rana again, her brow furrowed. "What? You keep saying that. I'm not a vampire, Rana."

Rana gave her a patient smile. "I know you and Ian haven't mated, but I was referring to you as an individual, Jax. You have vampire blood in your veins."

Jax's eyes widened in surprise as Rana's statement. "No, I don't."

"Yes, you do. How else can you explain your ability to sense vampires when other humans can't?"

"How did you know that?" Jax started to ask, but stopped when Rana gave her a knowing smile. "Well, my friend Blake can, too," Jax defended.

Rana raised a brow. "Oh, your friend can sense vampires just like you?"

Jax slowly shook her head. "Well, no. He can't sense them. He has this strange ability to be able to smell the difference." She gave a hollow laugh. "Even he can't explain his capability to do so."

"Lucian told me that your mother had been bitten by a vampire while she was pregnant with you, correct?"

Jax nodded.

"You were a baby at the time, Jax." Mora said, standing in the doorway. She walked over to the bed and continued, "Your body was small and therefore affected in a much stronger way by the vampire's bite."

She looked at Rana and smiled. "Well done, Rana. You could sense her diluted vampire blood when we couldn't."

Rana laughed and patted her belly. "He's helping me discover all kinds of things."

Jax looked away and shook her head. She couldn't be vampire. Her heart raced and her stomach knotted. What would her uncle think? But having some vampire blood running through her veins would explain her ability to sense vampires and maybe even her recently discovered talent to speak mentally with Ian.

Rana put a hand on her shoulder. "Jax, Ian is a good man. I know you have doubts, but if you love him, becoming his vampire mate is truly a beautiful experience. I treasure every moment with Lucian and now that I'm his vampire mate, I'll be able to live out my days with him."

Jax noted the love Rana felt for her mate in her eyes. She hadn't thought about the fact Ian would outlive her. For that matter, until an hour ago, she hadn't thought beyond tomorrow as far as their relationship was concerned. All she did know was that she cared for Ian very much. "Thanks for your support, Rana. I appreciate it."

"Ian should be ready to see you soon," Mora said. "But first before you go to him, I want you to stop by the kitchen. Renee has a plate of food ready for you."

Jax's heart soared to know Ian seemed to be recovering. She needed to see him right way. Forget the food. Her expression must've shown her intent, for Mora said, "Uh, uh, doctor's orders."

✳ ✳ ✳ ✳ ✳

Jax passed a set of tall blonde-headed twins in the hall as they came out of her bedroom. She didn't sense a thing. They were human, not vampires. Her blood pressure shot up. That could only mean they were here for one thing. As she entered the room, Lucian clasped her arm and pulled her back outside into the hall, speaking in her mind, *He's asking for you. Ian needs to sleep to heal properly, Jax, but he won't until he knows you're safe.*

Jax nodded to the two shapely, well-endowed blondes retreating down the hall. "Were the Booby twins here for what I think they were here for?" she bit out in a low voice.

Lucian's silver gaze met hers. He said in a patient tone, "Yes. They saved his life, Jax."

Angry, Jax jerked her arm from his grip.

"I did what was best for Ian and *you*."

At Jax's "Yeah, right" look, he continued, "Are you ready to become his mate? Because if you aren't, I'm aware you two were at the point that a final giving of your blood would have bound you to him, regardless of your wishes."

Jax looked away, some of her anger dissipating at the truth of his words. Even acknowledging the truth, jealousy still nagged at her. She didn't want Ian taking blood from other women. How could they not want him, like she did? The idea of Ian making love to another made her sick to her stomach.

"Go to Ian, Jax. He needs you right now."

She nodded and walked into the bedroom.

"Jax," Ian called out, his voice low.

Jax walked over to the bed. He didn't look as pale as he did earlier, but he still appeared to be in pain. Ian lifted her hand and twined his fingers with hers.

"Hey," he said as his gaze roamed over her, slow and sensual. Even in his incapacitated state, he made her tingle.

"Hey, yourself," she answered. Her gaze landed on the bandage wrapped around his waist and shoulder, the white material a stark contrast to his tanned skin.

"Come lay with me," he asked, his hooded golden gaze regarding her.

Jax climbed into bed, trying not to shake it too much. Ian slowly rolled over and faced her as she laid her head on the pillow.

Before she could ask how he felt, he reached over and speared his fingers through her hair, cupping the back of her head. Rubbing his thumb along the soft spot behind her ear he asked, "Are you okay?"

She knew what he meant by his question, but she didn't want to acknowledge her feelings on what Drace had almost done to her. "You're asking about me? I'm not the one who lost buckets of blood and took three bullets."

"Jax."

"And what person in his right mind leaves his keys in a seventy thousand dollar vehicle—"

"Jax," he repeated in a gentle, but firm tone.

"May as well put a sign on your car 'take me, I'm free and ready to go,'" she babbled on.

"I love you."

Jax stopped her nervous chatter and stared at Ian, shocked by his declaration.

"No matter what you decide, to become my vampire mate or not, I love you, Jax. I'm not saying I'll accept your decision not to mate. Hell, if anything, I'll double my efforts to convince you otherwise, but I just wanted you to know how I feel."

Jax closed her eyes and willed the tears away, but try as she might they seeped out anyway.

When Ian brushed the wetness away with a gentle touch, she opened her eyes. Noting the tenderness in his gaze, she snuggled as close as she could without hurting him. Burying her face in his neck, she inhaled his masculine scent and said, "I care very much for you, Ian. I don't know what I would have done if you had died. I've never felt this way about anyone and I'm not at all sure if I'm equipped to handle the strong emotions I feel when I'm with you."

When his hold on her tightened, she continued, "I do know that I don't like the idea of you with another woman, and I sure as hell won't let another man touch me." She shuddered at the near miss with Drace.

She lifted her head and kissed his jaw. "Does that count for something?"

Ian smiled down at her. "Yes, *a ghrá*. It means a great deal."

When Jax looked up at him, the tears in her luminescent eyes turned them a beautiful shade of deep emerald green. He loved her with such fierceness the emotions took his breath away. He admired her strength and her ability to disconnect from her emotions, a skill that was so very important in battle, but that admirable quality about Jax also frustrated him. He wanted her to share with him, to allow herself to cry, to laugh, and most of all to love him.

Ian kissed her temple and hugged her close, ignoring the pain his movements caused. How would he keep from taking her blood if Jax decided not to become his vampire mate? He hoped he wouldn't have to find out, because he wasn't sure he'd be able to not take her blood—what he felt was rightly his—whenever he made love to Jax.

Jax pulled back. "I'm crowding you. You need your rest."

Ian gathered her body close to him once more. "Yes, I do and I'll rest better knowing you're safe here with me."

"Ian—" she started to object.

"Sleep, *a thaisce*," Ian said, his tone more fierce than he meant it to be, but damn it she was so stubborn and he ached all over.

"When you're well, I'm going to make you pay for compelling me to sleep," she yawned out her complaint. Ian watched her eyes droop and his lips twitched in humor to see just how much she fought him. He didn't care. He wanted her close and safe. When her eyes finally closed and her breathing evened out, Ian pulled the covers around them and succumbed to the deep sleep his body needed to heal.

* * * * *

Jax awoke feeling groggy and very tired. Lifting her wrist, she squinted to make out the time on her watch. What! She tapped her watch to make sure it was working. Yep, the date was right. She'd slept almost eighteen hours!

She looked at Ian who lay resting on his back, his dark lashes closed in sleep. He seemed to be breathing well. Easing off the bed, the heavy weight from being compelled to sleep still clung to her. Jax rolled her shoulders and then her neck. *Ugh, I need to shake this! I feel like all my muscles have taken the weekend off.*

Pulling out her exercise clothes, she dressed and secured her hair with the chopsticks. Exiting their room, she was thankful she made it to the front door without meeting anybody. She didn't want or need anyone telling her not to venture out. Surely Drace wouldn't be so stupid.

Once outside, Jax stretched her muscles, preparing to run. While she went through her exercises, she wondered about her uncle. Had Blake gone back to watch over him? She hoped so. She really owed Blake big time for keeping an eye out for James during this whole ordeal. She'd be so glad to finally get Drace, if nothing else so she could move on with her life.

Jax took off running until she reached the outer perimeter of the Beaumont gated property. Following the edge of the tall, wrought iron fence, she thought about where she wanted to go with her life. Ian affected her like no other man had. She loved him with all her heart. Even though she couldn't say it to him yet, she did. But was she ready to take the next step? To become a vampire when all her life she'd fought against them? The last few days had taught her a valuable lesson. Not all vampires were evil.

Her heart raced as she climbed a steep hill, running with all her might, her calf muscles straining, her chest heaving. Noting an old barn down the hill that backed up against the woods on the far side of the property, Jax started to take off toward it, curious to discover what the Beaumont's would use it for since she hadn't seen any horses on the property. Storage maybe?

Before she'd taken more than a couple of steps, a wall of muscle landed right in front of her. Jax bounced back off the man's body and fell hard on her ass. Looking up, she glowered at Blake.

"Holy shit, Blake! What the hell you'd do that for?"

Blake leaned over hand and grabbed her hand, pulling her to her feet.

"I'm getting you the fuck outta here, Jax," he said, a scowl on his handsome face.

Jax let go of Blake's hand. "I'm not going anywhere."

Blake grabbed her upper arms and said in a low voice, "What has Mordoor done to you? Why would you want to hang out with bloodsucking vampires?"

Jax shrugged out of his hold and faced Blake head on. "Not all vampires are evil. Ian helped Uncle James and he has saved my life several times over the last few days."

"God bless!" Blake exclaimed, realization dawning in his expression. "I didn't believe James, but after talking to you…" he paused and ran his hands through his hair as he paced away and then paced back. "You're fucking in love with him, aren't you?"

At Jax's silence, Blake put his hands on her shoulders and pulled her close. He kissed her temple and said, "Think long and hard about a life with Ian, Jax. I care very much what happens to you."

Jax hugged Blake. She hoped he found someone to love as much as she did Ian. He had so much to offer her. Stepping back, she smiled. "I know you care, Blake. I appreciate you looking out for me."

"Did Ian kill Drace?" he asked, his brows slashing downward.

"No, Ian almost died saving my life. We still have to get Drace."

Blake's fierce expression softened as he clasped her chin in his hand. "I'll be there for you, Jax. This time you're not doing this alone."

Jax nodded and smiled. "I'm ready to move on, Blake. I'd appreciate all the help I can get."

He cocked his head to the side and gave her assessing look. "You have changed. I may just have to let Mordoor live when all this is over."

"Blake!"

He grinned. "How much longer will you be here?" he asked looking around. "This place is infested with vampires. I smell them."

Jax met his steady gaze. "There's a party for the vampires tonight. I'll be here through tomorrow."

Blake's eyes lit up. "You mean I could get a bunch of them in one fell swoop?"

Jax crossed her arms over her chest saying, "And me, too, buddy. Just remember that."

Blake laughed as he touched a chopstick in her hair. "Glad to see you wearing my gift." Moving away, he started to climb the fence, but then he turned back to her for a brief moment. "I'll be around."

Jax nodded and watched him climb the fence like a monkey. In two seconds flat, he'd vaulted over and landed on his feet.

Facing her through the bars, he warned, "Keep your eyes peeled. I smell trouble."

"Will do, *Herr Commandant*." She grinned at him.

Blake scowled at her before taking off into the woods.

Jax checked her watch. She'd been gone almost an hour. She wanted to get back before Ian awoke.

As she neared the house, men and women were climbing out of their cars wearing the most beautiful clothes—the men in tuxes and the ladies in elegant gowns and jewels. Jax's body vibrated in high intensity. She'd never been in the presence of so many pureblood vampires at once—her entire body hummed to life. Nor had she ever felt so blah either compared to their exquisite finery. She decided to find another way to get back inside.

Walking along the side of the house, Jax spotted a door. Opening it, she walked in and ran right into Renee, the cook.

"Hi," she said, feeling like a heel for coming in through the kitchen.

"Ooh, a guest." The older woman smiled. "I was just getting ready to leave." She grinned and continued, "Since I'm not really needed for this event. Are you hungry dear?"

Jax smiled at the only other human she'd met at the Beaumont's house…well, other than the two blondie toothpicks with olives stuck on them, but she didn't want to think about Ian's blood donors. She nodded. "Can I have a glass of water?"

As Renee turned and opened the stainless steel fridge, Jocelyn walked into the kitchen.

"Here you go," Renee said in a bright tone as she handed Jax a glass of water and a plate of fruit, her eyes twinkling. "You need to eat, dear. You'll need your energy to keep up with the guests tonight."

"Yes, you will," Jocelyn grinned as she entered the kitchen. "So eat up and then I want you to come with me."

Jax sat down at the contemporary tile covered table and plopped a strawberry in her mouth. "I need to check on Ian first."

Jocelyn flipped her hand in a dismissive gesture. "He'll be fine. Don't worry. You'll see him in an hour."

When Jax finished off the last piece of fruit, Jocelyn grabbed her hand and said with an excited look in her eyes. "Come on, we have less than an hour to get you showered and dressed."

"But…but…we never even picked out a dress," Jax pointed out as Jocelyn dragged her up the stairs behind her.

Jocelyn didn't slow her pace as she responded with a laugh, "Don't worry, dear. I've got the perfect dress for you."

Chapter Fifteen

Jax stood in front of the full-length mirror in Jocelyn's room staring in total shock at the woman reflected back at her. Her gown, a blood red silk creation, clung to her curves. From the long sleeves to the floor length straight skirt, the entire dress hugged her body to perfection. She smiled, knowing Ian wouldn't be looking at her curves in this dress once his gaze landed on the neckline—a deep vee that plunged all the way to her navel. Only a couple of thin spaghetti strap ties strategically placed held the dress together, the effect displaying ample toned flesh and the full curves of her breasts.

Thankful for the thigh-high slits in either side of the dress' skirt, Jax bent down as Jocelyn reached around to clasp a diamond and ruby necklace around her neck.

Clapping her hands together, Jocelyn smiled in delight as Jax met her gaze in the mirror. "You're perfection, Jax."

Jax smiled at the overall effect, her heart soaring. She *did* have it in her to be sexy and beautiful. With Jocelyn's help, her makeup accentuated her wide eyes and full lips and her hair glistened in a curtain of dark waves behind her. She turned to Jocelyn and hugged her tight, whispering, "Thank you, Jocelyn."

Jocelyn pulled back. "No, thank *you* for being such a beautiful woman to dress up, Jacqueline."

Jax's eyes widened in surprise at the compliment and the fact Jocelyn knew her name.

"Ian told me your given name." Jocelyn kissed her on each cheek and smiled saying, "Tonight, my dear, you *are* Jacqueline."

Waving her toward the doorway, she said, "Go and knock Ian's socks off and everything else for that matter," she finished with a sly smile.

"What about you?" Jax asked, feeling guilty for taking up so much of Jocelyn's time when her guests awaited her downstairs.

Jocelyn grinned. "Don't worry about me. I'll be down shortly."

Jax descended the stairs, her stomach tightening in nervous knots as several people on the main level stopped talking and looked up at her. *Keep your smile pasted on your face, Jax,* she told herself. *Don't let them know you feel like you've just stepped into another dimension.* It was true. Even though they had the money, her father had never entertained on this kind of scale and even when he did, the guests were all men there to discuss the latest weapons or strategy.

As her shoe hit the bottom step, she breathed a sigh of relief when she saw Ian, dressed in all black, leaning against one of the wide floor-to-ceiling columns. He wasn't wearing a tuxedo, but the effect of the expensive suit and black silk shirt was sexy nonetheless. The guests had finally stopped staring and since Ian hadn't seen her descend the stairs, she decided to surprise him.

Walking up beside him, she slid her hands around his waist saying, "Hi there."

Ian turned in her arms, his eyebrow raised, a cocky half smile on his lips.

Jax wasn't waiting for an invitation. She wound her arms around his neck and pressed her lips to his. Ian placed his hands on her hips and pulled her close, thrusting his tongue deep in her mouth, tasting her thoroughly.

As he kissed her Ian seemed to walk right inside her mind. She couldn't explain it but she sensed his mental presence: aggressive, dominant, seductive and...dangerous. She'd never sensed such dark intensity in him before. Ian ran an invisible tongue across her nipple, then sucked hard on the tip, making her gasp against his mouth as his hands tightened around her waist. Lifting her off the ground, he pressed his erection against her, letting her know just how much he wanted her.

Jax knew he was exploring her mind as well as her body, and though it was exciting, something seemed different. She couldn't put her finger on it...suddenly Jax felt warmth behind her as a hard chest pressed against her back and a man rasped in her ear in a low, warning voice, "I do hope you can tell the difference, *a ghrá.*"

Jax sucked in her breath as Ian clasped her hips. She tried to pull away from the man holding her, but Ian pressed his erection against her rear end, forcing her mons to rub against the man in front of her. As her heart rate quadrupled and her sex flooded with liquid heat, his words entered her head.

Do you like that? I hear your heart racing, Jax. One day I'll take you this way, but it'll be me and me alone filling your body in every place possible.

Ian's words made her body hum to life. Jax felt a shift in her mind and suddenly the other man's mental presence disappeared as if he'd been forcefully shoved out.

Ian pulled her against his chest as the man released her, a reluctant expression on his face.

The stranger gave her a sexy smile and his gaze never left hers as he said to Ian, "I see you've been brushing up on your mental skills. *Bheinn sásta an bhean bhreá seo a roinnt leat, a dheartháir.*"

"Not this time, Duncan. *Is liomsa í,*" Ian said in a possessive tone as he kissed her neck.

"You...you're twins?" she managed to get out, still reeling from the knowledge she'd just been intimately kissed and mentally fondled by a complete stranger and her lover's brother to boot.

Duncan's amber gaze, so like his brother's, slid down her body and back up. "'Tis a shame, too. For once, I would've loved to step into Ian's shoes." He raised an eyebrow when he looked at his brother. "But apparently, Ian wasn't as hurt as Sabryn led me to believe."

Ian's laughter rumbled against her back. "Well, now that you're here, you may as well stay awhile and mingle."

Duncan's jaw tightened and he gave his twin a steely look. "I'm staying, but only because I need to have a little chat with Sabryn Trevane."

Just then Sabryn walked past, a glass of champagne in hand. She said with a sly smile, "Glad to see you out and about, Duncan."

Duncan grabbed her arm as she passed, saying in a low tone, "I believe we need to talk, Sabryn."

Sabryn laughed, her violet eyes twinkling. "If you want to talk to me, you'll have to do so while we dance, because that's where I'm going."

Duncan pulled her glass from her hand and set it on the tray of a passing waiter. "Then by all means, let's dance."

As they walked off, Sabryn cast a glance back at Ian and winked. Ian chuckled and hugged Jax close saying, "I feel sorry for the vamp Sabryn reels in. Even when he thinks he knows what he's getting into, she'll throw him for another loop just to keep it interesting."

Jax heard the music start up in the large ballroom and smiled as Sabryn and Duncan followed the other guests into the room. Sabryn was such a beautiful woman with her tall, willowy form in her exquisite periwinkle gown. Why wasn't she mated?

"Why do you think it'll be a vamp?" she mused aloud.

Ian laughed outright. "Because no human male would be strong enough to keep up with Sabryn."

She noted what a striking couple Sabryn and Duncan made. "What about Duncan?"

"There's always that possibility, but Duncan's a loner. He has known Sabryn for decades. And Sabryn has her own ghosts from the past to deal with." Sighing, he continued, "Leave it to Duncan to finally show interest in another and she would be *my* woman."

"Is that what he said in Irish?" she asked.

Ian growled close to her ear, "Actually, he said he'd be willing to share you."

Jax chuckled saying, "You don't have to tell me your response."

His hold on her tightened. "I told him you're *mine*. You don't know how much restraint it took not to deck my brother when I saw his arms around you and his tongue down your throat." He bit her neck with a light nip. "I'll kill any man who tries to put his hands on you."

His intense tone caused a shiver to slide all the way down her spine — a shiver that settled into a fierce, raging need to be as close to Ian as possible. Right now he sounded pretty damn dark and intense, she thought as she turned and faced him, sliding her arms around his waist. She'd never been more turned on. His golden gaze blazed at the sight of the exposed flesh all the way to her navel, then focused on the curves of her breasts the dress revealed.

"*Tá tú go h-áileann,*" he said and whispered in her head, *You're beautiful.* When his eyes met hers once more, he pulled her close and pressed his erection against her mound saying, "I want to make love to you, Jacqueline Markson. I want to taste your blood while I move within you." He paused then said, "I want to make you my vampire mate."

Jax's heart rate sped up so hard and fast that her entire body felt as if it jerked to the rapid beat. She wanted to feel his fangs slide into her skin again. She wanted to give him her blood, her body, and her love. Was it so wrong to want to be with him always and forever?

"Ian, I—" she started to say, when Rana, Lucian, Jocelyn and a striking man with salt and pepper hair started down the stairs.

"Ian, I need to speak with you a moment," Lucian called out.

Ian held her gaze. *Hold that thought*, he said to her mentally and turned to the group as they approached.

As Ian walked off with Lucian toward the living room, Rana said, "You've made up your mind then." Her comment was more a statement than a question.

Jax smiled not ready to voice her thoughts or analyze her emotions just yet.

"Ian is quite a man," Jocelyn chimed in.

"But he's not half the man your husband is," the man beside Jocelyn said as he wrapped an arm around her waist and pulled her close, kissing her mouth before she could respond.

Jax grinned when he pulled away and Jocelyn's cheeks had a rose tint to them. The complete devotion she saw in Jocelyn's eyes when she gazed at her husband made Jax ache for a deeper connection with Ian.

He put out his hand and said with a smile, "Roderick Beaumont, Miss Markson. Sorry I haven't had a chance to meet you before now."

Jax shook his hand. "Call me Jax."

Once she released Roderick's hand, Rana grabbed hers and said, "Come on. Let's go into the ballroom. The men will meet us in there."

When they entered the ballroom, Jocelyn and Roderick went off to play host and hostess, mingling among the guests. Jax scanned the room, noting the live band on a raised stage off to the left. A few people sat at the tables that were adorned with fancy white tablecloths, but most of the guests danced in the center of the room to an upbeat reggae tune.

"Oh, I see Mora," Rana said in an excited voice. "I need to ask her a question about my pregnancy. I'll be right back."

As Rana walked way, Jax felt a warm hand clasp hers. She turned, smiling. When her gaze landed on a tall, sexy man with long dark hair tied back from his face, she tensed. Where'd he come from? She wondered. She met his dark, probing gaze and started to pull her hand away, but he held firm, a seductive smile on his lips.

Come dance with me, he whispered in her mind.

His self-assured voice lured her and she followed him like a child seeking a piece of candy. *Why the hell are my feet moving when my mind is screaming no?*

The music changed and a slow song filled the room. The stranger placed his hand on her waist and held her other hand out in a formal fashion as his feet literally glided across the floor, in perfect, fluid movement to the music.

His gaze traveled the length of her body, lingering on the deep vee in her dress. Finally his black eyes met hers once more. "You are very beautiful, Jax Markson." His seductive voice held an air of total confidence as if he'd had years, possibly even decades to perfect his finesse with the ladies. "You make me wish I had delivered my messages personally."

Jax's eyes widened at the familiar deep, cultured voice. She took in the man's darker, olive-toned skin, his chiseled face and black, bottomless eyes—eyes that seemed wise and cynical beyond his years for someone who appeared to be in his late thirties.

"You're Sebastian Gauthier?"

He nodded, a roguish grin on his face. "In the flesh."

"Why did you help me?" she asked the question she'd been dying to know from the first time the man called her.

Sebastian gave a nonchalant shrug, his movement accenting the perfect cut of his tux against his well-built body. "I didn't agree with what Drace had done and I thought it fitting that the vampire hunter's child be the one to exact revenge."

She raised a doubtful eyebrow. "But Ian Mordoor was already on the job. Why wouldn't you want one of your own to take out Drace? Why would you encourage a human, an outsider?"

Before Sebastian had a chance to reply, the music abruptly trailed off and everyone in the room turned to look at the stage. Lucian stepped up on the front of the stage, his expression hard and focused. Where was Ian? Jax wondered until her gaze found him across the room. He stood in the doorway, looking very handsome in his tux. She liked the fact he'd opted for a stand up collar and black vest. The look suited his personality very well. She noted his attention was focused on Lucian, his expression angry, disgruntled.

"I'm sorry to interrupt the festivities tonight, but I feel an issue needs to be clarified before we can go on with the party," Lucian said.

As if he felt her eyes on him, Ian met Jax's gaze. His gaze flicked to Sebastian's arms around her and then narrowed. Jax sensed the rage that radiated through him, replacing the irritation he seemed to have with Lucian. *Am I going to have to kill Sebastian now?* he spoke in her mind, his voice barely controlled.

Jax started to pull away, but Sebastian tensed and held fast, pulling her flush against his chest. She jerked her gaze up to his and saw the devilish grin on his face as he met Ian's challenging gaze.

Her own anger rising, she realized she'd played right into Sebastian's game. "This is why you helped me to find Drace each time," Jax said. "You wanted me to beat out Ian, didn't you?"

"In light of recent events, I'm going to reiterate that as Vité..." Lucian continued.

Sebastian met her gaze, regarding her for a moment. "And you still can, Jax. I happen to know —"

"No," she interrupted. "Don't tell me. *We* will find Drace on our own," she finished and turned her attention to Lucian.

" —I chose Ian to lead the Ruean clan. If any of you don't like it —"

"You're welcome to leave the clan," Ian finished for Lucian as he stepped up on stage beside his friend and faced the group.

A murmur broke out among the crowd, making Jax's stomach tense. Ian had a stony look on his face as he said, "Make your decision. If you support Drace, it would be best for you to leave the clan, effective immediately. Be warned, if I discover you've helped Drace in any way once you leave here, I will hunt you down. Guaranteed."

Ian's steely gaze zeroed in on the four men that suddenly separated from the crowd and walked out of the room. "Anyone else?" he said, turning back to the crowd, his voice commanding, his expression resolute.

Ian met Sebastian's gaze as the last words died on his lips. *Get your hands off my mate, Sebastian.*

"Well, now that we have settled this issue, let's get back to enjoying our evening," Lucian's voice held a lighter tone as he clapped Ian on the shoulder.

Sebastian's lips curved upward. He answered in an amused tone, *She's not mated to you yet, Mordoor. I don't sense a vampire vibration in her.*

Ian clenched his fists. *She's mine. Make no mistake.*

Sebastian continued in a droll tone, *Is that any way to treat the man who helped save your life? I would think you'd be more grateful.*

Ian stiffened at his words and followed Sebastian's gaze as the vamp glanced across the room to the two blondes sitting at one of the tables.

Clamping his jaw tight, Ian met the Norriden leader's gaze once more. He didn't like owing anyone, ever. He acknowledged his thanks with a curt nod as he spoke in Sebastian's mind, *Noted. Now remove your hands before I have to remove them for you.*

With a lift of his eyebrow, Sebastian pulled Jax close and kissed her forehead before he released her. To her credit, Jax scowled up at Sebastian and spoke. Ian smirked, knowing the man had just received an earful from her.

As the music started back up, he stepped off the stage, intending to go straight to Jax, but several of the Rueans approached. Ian met her gaze over the crowd surrounding him. She gave him a sexy smile and walked toward the doorway, her hips swaying their own seductive dance. Hot damn, she looked dynamite in that dress. He couldn't wait to peel the material away and taste every single inch of her body.

Edward, an older vampire, asked him a question, distracting his attention. Now for the part he loved the most—freakin' politics. Ian inwardly cringed and shook the vamp's hand, thanking him for his support.

* * * * *

Jax walked out into the main hall, away from the crowd. She hadn't really had a chance to explore the Beaumont's home, so she decided to do so while she waited for Ian. She smiled, knowing Ian would find her no matter where she wandered.

Turning down a hall, Jax passed a recreation room with a pool table, a bar, and a large screen TV. The Beaumonts had thought of everything, she mused as a house-wide sound system carried the music from the dance throughout the rooms in the rest of the downstairs. At the end of the hall, Jax opened the wide double doors in front of her. As she peered into the darkness, she could barely make out several rows of seats. Fumbling along the sidewall for a light switch, her fingers landed on several buttons.

Pushing a couple of the buttons, she frowned when no lights came on. A whirring sound resonated from the front of the room and she turned to see a wide screen lowering from the ceiling.

Intrigued, Jax touched a couple more buttons and waited in anticipation. A striking couple appeared on the screen. She couldn't hear what they were saying above the sound of the music, but the engrossed look on their faces left her little doubt as to their intent.

The man's fingers plucked at the buttons on the woman's blouse as his lips curved into a sexy smile. Jax smiled too at the seductive look on his face. The woman ran her fingers through his thick, black hair and leaned her head back as he kissed her neck.

Her blouse dropped to the floor along with her bra. The man's hungry gaze skimmed over her naked flesh as he grasped her around her upper back and pulled her toward him, closing his mouth over her exposed nipple.

Jax's heart raced at the sight and her own nipples tingled in response to the stimuli.

The woman pushed away playfully and her hands made fast work of removing his shirt and pants. Standing before her completely naked, the man hooked his fingers inside the waistband of her skirt and slid her clothes off her body.

Jax sucked in her breath at the sheer perfection of their bodies. His bronzed skin, muscular body, and broad shoulders stood in complete contrast to her fair skin and soft, curvaceous form.

When the man cupped his hands over the woman's buttocks and effortlessly lifted her body against him, Jax swallowed, her insides jangling as she awaited their inevitable joining.

The woman wrapped her legs around his trim waist and let her head fall back. She clasped his shoulders and her long, wavy red hair brushed the backs of his hands as he slid his impressive erection inside her. Their sensual coupling completely mesmerized Jax.

The man spoke to the woman, grabbing her attention. She opened her eyes and met his intense gaze. His biceps flexed as he held her while he rocked his hips, driving deeper inside her. The woman pulled close to him, her expression one of sheer ecstasy as she plunged her teeth into his throat. The man's body tensed and he stumbled back at the sheer force of their passion.

Jax grasped the back of one of the cushioned chairs and held her breath at the seductive, carnal nature the couple displayed on the screen. She felt her own juices gather and her sex begin to throb at the sight before her. She wanted passion to make Ian shudder like that when she bit his neck.

But that level of passion came with a price. Was she willing to pay it? She wondered. All her life she'd been raised to believe vampires were evil beings and it was her job to rid the world of their presence. In the past few days, she'd discovered that not only was her mother's death unrelated to a vampire bite, but she'd also learned that not every vampire was a depraved, heartless, bloodsucking fiend bent on destroying humans.

Her father had spent so much of his time hunting vampires, he hadn't thought of the price he'd paid. Jax didn't resent her father, but she had come to realize how wrong he was. It saddened her to think of the time she lost with her father while he was out seeking his revenge. How ironic that a vampire had shown her more love, understanding and level-headed guidance in these past few days than her own father had all her life.

Ian was truly a man to admire…and love. She couldn't imagine aging faster than Ian, that he would outlive her by decades. She wanted his love, wanted to share a life with him and if that meant becoming a vampire she would.

Strong arms surrounded her waist, pulling her against a hard chest. Ian whispered in her ear as he pressed his erection against her backside, "I can't wait for you to sink your fangs into my skin while I come inside you, Jax. The thought has never left my mind since the first time we made love." Jax shivered as he turned her around to face him and nipped at her neck.

As Ian regarded her, the light from the screen behind them reflected off his intense amber gaze. He slowly drew a finger down the vee in her dress all the way to her navel, his touch leaving a burning trail on her flesh. His hungry gaze followed the path his finger took as he skimmed his fingers back up and brushed them across a taut nipple through the thin material covering her breast.

Tilting her chin so she had to meet his gaze, he said, his voice husky and full of desire, "I hope your answer is yes, *a ghrá*, because I don't think I can be around you much longer without making you mine in every sense of the word."

Chapter Sixteen

Jax reached up and unbuttoned the top button on his shirt. Moving to the next one she said, "I want to know what you taste like, Ian."

He clasped her arms, holding her still. A muscle in his jaw ticked before he rasped out, "Be sure, Jax. Be very sure. You will be mated to me for life — my vampire wife."

She gave him a siren's smile and answered him mentally as she slid her hands inside the opening in his shirt and across his bare chest, *Yes, I know. I want you very much.*

Ian let go of her arms and said in a gruff voice, "'Bout damn time."

"Ian!" she screamed out in surprise as lifted her over his shoulder and turned, exiting the home theater.

"I want privacy, Jax. I don't want to be interrupted."

As he quickly moved down the hall toward the stairs Jax said, frustrated at his highhanded manner, "I can walk on my own."

"At your human's pace?" He snorted as he mounted the stairs. "Way too slow."

Before she knew it, Ian set her down inside their bedroom and shut the door. With an inward chuckle, she had to admit to herself, he got them upstairs pretty damn fast.

Ian turned to face her, a roguish grin on his face as he pulled one of the ties, the only material holding the vee of her dress closed. The knot gave way and her breasts spilled out, her nipples hardening at his hungry stare. He made a low growling sound in his throat and reached for the next tie.

Jax's heart seemed to skip several beats before it sped up to a staccato rhythm while Ian eased her dress down her body. As he revealed more and more of her flesh, her legs turned to rubber at the heated look in his eyes. When her dress slid to the floor and he saw she not only had nothing on underneath but had shaved her mons completely, he raised an eyebrow and gave her a devilish grin.

Ian stepped closer, backing her up. The rasp of his jacket as it rubbed against her sensitized nipples made Jax moan in anticipation. When the back of her knees bumped against the end of the cushioned chaise lounge chair, Jax's wobbly legs gave out. She sat down quickly and leaned over to undo the straps on her sexy high heeled shoes. Ian squatted in front of her and encircled her ankles with his warm fingers. "No, don't, *a ghrá*. Leave them on."

Jax met his steady gaze and leaned back on her hands as Ian lifted her foot and set it on the cushion, bending her knee in front of her. He then did the same with the other foot and slowly slid his hands down the insides of her thighs, directing her to open her legs for him. Desire coiled within her lower belly, raging like wildfire at the look in Ian's eyes when he gazed at her exposed flesh.

Ian put one knee down on the floor and slid his fingers along her outer skin. Jax bit her lip at the foreign sensations coursing through her. The newly shaved skin had never been touched and was very sensitive. His fingers found her crease and slid down her slit, gathering her moisture. Jax closed her eyes and moaned at the brief brush of his fingers against her labia. When she opened her eyes, blood rushed to her sex to see Ian slide his fingers, wet with her moisture, inside his mouth.

"I want to taste everything your body has to offer," he rasped before he leaned close and captured her lips at the same time he guided two fingers inside her warm sheath. Jax's hips canted, rocking with the seductive movement of his hand in and out of her body while Ian's tongue danced with hers in the same slow, measured pace of his fingers.

As her body heat ignited, her arms began to tremble and if it weren't for her high heels digging into the cushions underneath her, she knew for sure her legs would have unfolded on their own. Ian kissed her chin and then the curve of her breast before he captured a pebbled nipple in his mouth, sucking hard.

Jax cried out in sheer pleasure, pushing closer when he nipped at the pink tip with his teeth. As Ian kissed a blazing path down her body toward her sex, Jax's stomach muscles tensed in sweet agony. She clenched her inner muscles around his fingers, wanting him to continue the onslaught on her body until his mouth could take over.

Ian rubbed his thumb over her swollen clitoris right before he sucked on the tiny bud, causing Jax to keen out her pleasure.

"I want to hear you scream when you come, Jax. Loud and long. Got it?" he demanded as he glanced up at her.

Jax worried her bottom lip with her teeth and nodded as she waited for him to taste her again. Ian withdrew his fingers and slid his hands behind her. Cupping her buttocks, he pulled her closer to the cushion's edge as his tongue slid in a seductive path around her folds. When he plunged his tongue inside her core, Jax gasped. Her breathing turned shallow and she arched her back, wanting him to take her over the edge.

Ian stopped his exploration of her sex and slid two fingers in and out of her body once more as he looked at her, his gaze focused and intense. "Tell me how much you want this. I have to hear the words."

"I want you, Ian," she panted and rocked her hips, seeking release from the sensations curling within her body.

Ian pressed on her clit, his tone fierce, "Tell me everything."

Wave after wave of desire slammed through her at the pressure on her clitoris, making it difficult to form a coherent word. Jax forced herself to meet his gaze as she breathed out through ragged breaths, "I love you, Ian. I want to be your vampire wife."

A look of unadulterated triumph crossed his face before he gave her a broad smile. The sight of his fangs extended to their full length caused Jax's heart to ram in her chest. She had never seen a more seductive sight in her life as she watched him lower his head to her body. Her breath hitched as Ian licked a path along her inner thigh until he reached her sex. She felt his hot breath on her leg and the mere thought of what he had planned caused her body to clench in gut-wrenching suspense.

He guided his fingers into her sheath once again, finding and pushing on her sensitive spot inside as his thumb teased her clit. *Tell me you love me again, a chroí,* he whispered in her mind.

Jax felt her body begin to spasm around his fingers and she clenched her jaw, holding back her orgasm so she could answer him. "I love you with all my heart—"

Her words ended in a high-pitched scream when Ian clamped his teeth on the juncture of her leg, his fangs piercing her skin as he drove his fingers deep within her while he pressed his thumb hard on her clit.

The erotic sensation of being bitten in such a sensitive area as she came caused Jax's trembling arms to collapse. She landed on her elbows before falling on her back in total submission. Reveling in the erotic sensation after delicious sensation that slammed through her body, Jax did exactly as Ian requested. She screamed long and loud throughout her entire mind-blowing climax.

As Jax's heart rate slowed, Ian laved at the place where he'd taken her blood. When she opened her eyes, it was to see Ian stand up, yank off his jacket and rip open his vest and shirt, his expression primal and territorial as he stared at her body. Her chest began to pound once more as he unbuckled his belt and then unzipped the zipper, stepping out of his clothes and shoes with quick, jerky movements.

Jax scooted back on the lounge chair to allow him room, her breathing erratic. Ian set one knee on the cushion between her legs as his strong fingers encircled her ankles.

He lifted her legs, and laid her knees over his shoulders, saying as he pressed his erection against her entrance, "I want to find out just how limber you can be, *a thaisce*. To bury myself in you as hard and as deep as I can get."

She'd barely gotten out the word, "Yes," when he rammed to the hilt inside her.

"Ian!" she screamed out at the all-consuming satisfaction she experienced as his erection filled her, stretching her to accommodate his hard shaft.

Ian clenched his jaw and held his body perfectly still. "It's going to be hard, Jax. I've wanted this too damn long and too damn much to be gentle right now."

Her insides jangled with nervous eagerness at his feral words, but before she could speak he clasped her hips, withdrew and slammed back inside, his voice gruff, "I'm not asking your permission, *a chroí*. I'm asking your forgiveness."

Jax drew in her breath as Ian's hard shaft hit her cervix. He was right, their current position allowed him the deepest penetration she'd ever felt, and damn, it felt so good. She dug her nails into his biceps and said with a throaty laugh, "It's not hard enough, lover."

Ian stopped moving and glanced at her in surprise. A challenging glint sparkled in his eyes as he lowered her legs around his waist and lifted her against him saying, "Why don't we let gravity help a bit with your need for friction, hmmm?"

Jax had just enough time to wrap her arms around his neck as Ian pulled her against him and took the few steps to the door. Using his chest and hips, he pressed her back against the wood surface. Clasping her buttocks in his hands, he withdrew and pistoned into her once, twice, three times, each thrust rougher and harder than the last.

As her desire rebuilt with each heart-stopping grind against and within her body, Jax dug her nails deeper into his shoulders. Ian groaned against her neck, "My little wildcat. All *mine*."

When his teeth clamped onto her neck, Jax went right over the edge. She let her head fall back against the door and relished in all the sensations bombarding her body: the rush of adrenaline, the clench of her muscles around Ian as his body hit her clitoris with just enough pressure, the fullness with which he filled her channel—everything made her body respond to Ian's like a fine tuned instrument.

You're an elixir. Exotic and spicy. You make me dizzy with need to taste you again and again, Ian spoke in her mind as his fangs pierced her skin. He made a primal sound deep in his throat and jerked her closer, taking her blood again while he rocked his hips against her and buried himself as deep as he could get. Jax's body clenched and spasmed around him as she climaxed, keening her pleasure.

Ian's body tensed and he groaned against her neck while he came. Jax smoothed her hands over his shoulders until he stopped moving within her and withdrew his fangs from her throat. Why did she feel so damn tired? Her arms dropped from Ian's shoulders and hung like limp noodles. When her legs slid down his hips, he caught her in his arms before she collapsed to the floor.

Ian kissed her forehead and carried her to the bed. As he set her down and proceeded to unbuckle the straps on her shoes, a look of concern crossed his face.

"Your body will start to transform very soon."

"Will I be like you? Able to tolerate daylight?"

Ian nodded. "Each vampri made has the same limitations as the vampire who made him or her. In your case, you'll have my ability to walk in the daylight as well as my need for blood to survive, but as my Anima you'll have an advantage over a regular vampri. You'll have the same powers I do."

"Anima? You mentioned that before. What does it mean?"

He smiled. "Anima means you're my vampire mate. But even if you hadn't chosen to become my Anima, Jax, you'll always be my *Sonuachar*, my soul mate."

He rubbed his thumbs over her ankles and finished, "I'll send you to sleep so you won't have to experience the pain of transition."

"No," she managed to wrangle out. Already her body ached all over as if she were getting the flu.

Ian jerked his gaze back to hers. "What?"

"I don't want you to compel me to sleep, Ian. I'm tough. I can handle it." When he removed her shoes and sat down on the bed to pull her in his arms, Jax backed away. She needed to hear his answer first.

He narrowed his gaze on her. "Jax, this isn't up for debate. You will *not* suffer through this. Your martyrdom is unnecessary. I won't allow it."

While he spoke, Jax's chest had started to burn as if she couldn't get enough air. Grasping her chest she took deep breaths. "This is my decision, Ian. Not yours. Now promise."

A sudden wave of pain shot through her arms and legs, causing her to wince. Ian clasped her hand. "No fuckin' way will I agree to that," he ground out, his expression resolute and hard as granite.

Jax tried to meet his gaze but her stomach cramped and she doubled over in pain as sweat broke out all over her body.

Ian brushed her damp hair off her forehead, his touch tender. "Jax—"

"Promise." She forced herself to look up at him. She needed to prove to Ian how strong she was. Otherwise, as her mate, he would try his best to overrule her any chance he could.

The effort to look up caused her to scream out in pain. Ian crawled into bed and pulled her into his arms, saying quickly, "I promise I won't send you to sleep without good reason."

"Ian," she squeaked out her warning.

"That's the best you're going to get, *a ghrá mo chroí*," he said in a disgruntled tone.

That was something, she thought. Jax let herself relax against him as best she could considering the unforgiving fire licking through her body. "Talk to me, Ian. I-I need a distraction. Tell me where you learned to speak Irish."

Ian pulled her back against his chest. Placing his hand over her abdomen, he kissed her neck, then her temple. "Me ma is Irish. Throughout our youth she spoke Irish to both Duncan and me, saying, "'Tis a part of yere heritage, lads. Speak Irish whenever ye get the chance. Living for centuries just means ye've longer to perfect yere horrid pronunciation.'" He finished the last sentence with a chuckle.

Jax could tell by his tone and the easy way Ian slipped into talking like a true Irishman when he spoke of his mother, just how much he loved and respected her. '*Me ma*', *how charming*, she thought.

She started to reply, but her body's temperature shifting from hot to immediate cold caused her to shiver all over. She forced herself to concentrate. "I've got to hear your mother speak then, because I think you sound magical."

Ian whispered in her ear, "I've had a couple of lifetimes to improve, *a ghrá*."

She tried to laugh and he must've realized the effort it took, because Ian began to speak in Irish in a soothing tone as if he were telling her a story.

When a nasty pain spiraled down her chest and into her lower belly, Jax sucked in her breath and dug her fingers into Ian's thigh.

"Fuckin' hell," he gritted out at her obvious pain. Ian rolled her over and kissed her, his lips moving over hers in a tender caress. As their kiss deepened, he continued to whisper his sexy Irish words in her head. The last thing she heard before she lost consciousness was Ian saying in her mind, *Forgive me.*

* * * * *

Jax awoke with a quick intake of breath as if she'd just surfaced from being underwater and unable to breathe. Even though it was pitch black in the room, she could see Ian as clear as if it were daytime. Jax blinked, trying to reconcile the new ability of night vision in her mind.

Ian leaned over her, his golden gaze searching her face. "How do you feel?"

Everything came back to her: Ian making her his vampire mate, her refusal to let him compel her to sleep, his anger, Ian finally relenting and then blackness, blissful, pain-free blackness.

Jax put her hands on his chest and said, "Betrayed," as she shoved him away. She watched in shock as Ian flew across the room and slammed against the far wall before he fell to the floor.

Sitting up on her knees, she turned her hands over and looked at her palms in amazement. *Man, I could get used to this kind of strength.*

Ian stood up and walked back toward the bed, his expression impatient. "Lesson number one. Learn your own strength, Jax."

Before he could reach for her, Jax leapt from the bed, landing near the bathroom, a good fifteen feet away. "Don't think for one minute you're going to touch me, Ian Mordoor."

Ian started toward her once more, a look of sheer determination on his face, but Jax darted to the other side of the room in a matter of a millisecond. Even though she was angry with him, she couldn't help but spend a moment appreciating her newly acquired powers. *Ooh, this is so cool. I feel like a superhero...well, a naked super hero, but still, these powers are awesome. No wonder vampires are so freakin' arrogant.*

Jax waited until he had almost reached her before making a dash toward the balcony. Ripping open the door, she almost tripped over the black cat as she took a flying leap over the railing, landing on her feet in the soft grass below.

"Jax!" Ian thundered from above her. Jax didn't even spare a glance back. She needed space to think and took off running as fast as her body would let her.

The cool wind batted at her hair, filling the air with scents — scents she'd never had the ability to appreciate before. The obvious scent of burning fall fires accented the wet, rich earth and the smell of fresh cut grass brought on by her bare feet crushing blades of grass while she ran. A sudden shift in the wind around her warned Jax a split second before she heard Ian's footfalls behind her, gaining fast.

Her heart didn't race like it did before she turned vampire, but its steady thud within her chest jerked her body in its intensity. She turned in the direction of the barn at the back of the Beaumont property.

Before she made it more than a few feet, Ian grabbed her arm. Losing her balance, she stumbled and Ian fell with her, cushioning her fall as they rolled down the steep slope. Once they reached the bottom, they stopped, and Ian's full weight landed on her, causing her breath to escape in a loud *whoosh*.

Ian quickly pulled her hands over her head. "Stop screwing around, Jax. You haven't fed and overexertion and unnecessary use of your powers will only weaken you further."

The crisp grass underneath tickled her shoulders, back and buttocks. She didn't care if Ian's sexy, exotic scent tantalized her senses or that the heat of his body made her sex throb in memory of their lovemaking. The feeling of betrayal was just too great.

"Get off me," she said, anger simmering. He'd compelled her to sleep against her will even when he'd said he wouldn't. How could she forgive him for that?

"No, I won't," he said, his tone forceful. "I know you're angry with me for compelling you to sleep—"

"Ya think?" she shot back, her voice full of sarcasm as she looked away from him. Her stomach knotted and her chest tightened upon hearing him confirm his betrayal. She struggled to get up.

Ian pressed her hips back to the ground with the weight of his body and demanded, "Look at me, Jax."

She kept her gaze averted, refusing to meet his bold stare.

His grip on her hands tightened. "Look at me," he said in a harsh, commanding voice, a voice he'd never used with her before.

Jax met his gaze with a defiant one. She noted the downward turn of his eyebrows along with the scowl on his face.

"I know you think I compelled you to sleep because I thought you weren't strong enough to handle the transformation." He shook his head and gave a wry laugh as his fierce expression gentled. "No, *a thuisce*, I sent you to sleep because I knew *I* wasn't strong enough to handle it."

Jax's heart melted at his admission and her anger dissipated, replaced by sheer elation. She was so choked up with emotion, she couldn't speak. Instead she conveyed her thoughts mentally. *Thank you for loving me so much and believing enough for both of us.*

A sexy smile canted the corners of his lips as Ian bent and kissed her jaw. "I don't think I've said it yet today, so I'll say it now, I love you, Jax Mordoor, more than I thought I could ever love another."

Jax Mordoor. That had a nice ring to it, she thought.

All coherent thoughts fled as Ian kissed a fiery path down her neck. When his mouth clamped over her nipple, sucking hard on the distended bud, Jax gasped in delight at the tingling sensations that started in her breast and radiated throughout her body. She arched closer and Ian released her arms to run a hand down her chest, fondling one breast while he teased the other with his tongue and teeth.

Jax shivered at his touch. The combination of the heat on her front and the cold ground beneath her made goose bumps surface on her skin. What was she thinking, running outside in fifty degree weather without a stitch of clothes on?

Ian looked up and asked, "Cold?"

When Jax nodded he lifted himself off of her on his hands and knees. Spreading her legs, he moved between then and kissed her thigh as he met her gaze with his heated one. Ian placed his hands on her thighs and slowly slid them up her hips and across her abdomen. A surge of warmth followed the path his hands took, radiating throughout her body.

Jax moaned as he touched every part of her body, leaving a swath of heat behind to chase away the chill.

"Vampire power?" she asked, raising an eyebrow as she placed her hands on his muscular shoulders.

"Even us hybrids have a trick or two up our sleeves." Ian gave her a devilish smile before he bent his head to kiss the curve of her breast near her nipple. At the same time, she felt a tongue take a mental swipe across her labia.

Jax's breath hitched in her throat at the unexpected dual sensation. With the heat spreading throughout her body and Ian's mental stimulation, she tingled all over. He made her feel hot, and achy, and cherished and…"Ow," she cried out, stiffening at the jolting, yet erotic sensation of Ian's teeth puncturing the soft skin in her breast while he slid his hand between her thighs.

"Mine," he said, his tone possessive and forceful as he massaged her clit before he plunged a finger inside her.

Jax involuntarily bucked against his hand. When he trailed his tongue down the curve of her breast and slowly lapped up the droplets of blood that escaped her wounds, liquid heat surged through her body. It was more than warmth this time. Raging waves of hot mercury boiled through her blood, changing her sluggish heart- beat to a thumping rhythm.

The sensual sight of Ian tasting her blood, coupled with the seductive strokes of his finger moving inside her, took her breath away.

"Smell your arousal, *a ghrá*," Ian urged as he met her gaze, his own hungry, intense, and aggressive.

She smelled her own scent, but more than that she smelled the true depth of his for the first time—musky, spicy, and all male. Jax's own incisors lengthened as her arousal spiked at his words and his alluring scent. She pushed Ian on his back and leaning over him grasped his impressive erection in her hand. Ian rocked his hips and groaned when she slid her hand up and down his hard shaft.

Jax released him and licked a deliberate path from his sac to the tip of his cock. When she finished, she met his gaze, careful to keep her upper lip covering her extended teeth. Right before she closed her mouth over his cock, she smiled, showing him her fangs. His low growl of approval made her completely aware of her own sexual power.

Sliding her mouth over his cock, she twirled her tongue around the soft, rigid flesh, inwardly smiling as his breathing changed to ragged, deep breaths. When she lightly bit down on his erection, putting two perfect puncture wounds along the side of his hard cock, Ian jerked his head up and grated out, "Holy shit, Jax!"

Jax smiled and lapped up the blood that welled to the surface. Ian let his head fall to the ground while he groaned in ecstasy. She projected a husky mental laugh and spoke in his mind, *What's good for the goose...a ghrá.*

Ian shoved his fingers through her hair, grasped her head and rasped, "Take all of me, Jax."

The sample she'd tasted of his blood rolled over her tongue and down her throat, fueling her desire for more. But Jax intended to drive Ian to the edge first. How many times he had done that to her? she thought with an inward chuckle. Now it was her turn.

Suppressing her own arousal, she was able to retract her fangs as she lifted her leg and straddled him, facing his erection. She rose up on her hands and knees and took his hard shaft into her mouth, tasting him to the fullest. Ian pushed his erection deeper into her mouth and groaned. Clasping her thighs, he pulled her close and lifted his head, intending to taste her as well.

Jax let him pull her close, but before he could touch his mouth to her body she quickly stood. If he had connected, she'd be a goner. Ian encircled her ankles and called her name in a warning tone.

Jax jumped out of his loose grasp and took off running toward the woods, laughing and calling out behind her, "Gotta catch me first, Ian the Enforcer." When she heard his roar of frustration, she glanced back to see him stand and start to pursue her.

I'm more of a match for you now, she said, using their mental connection.

As she ran, she dodged low tree limbs and hopped over exposed roots and rotten logs. The smell of the damp forest heightened her senses, causing her heart to pound in her chest. She grinned, feeling almost human again.

Adrenaline thrummed through her veins and her lungs burned with the need for oxygen. But the sensation that thrilled her most was her inability to keep her fangs from extending on their own. The mere thought of what Ian would do with her when he caught her made her shiver in anticipation.

Chapter Seventeen

Ian's cock ached with the need for release, but the naked nymph running in front of him only managed to fuel his desire even more. He smiled as he chased Jax into the woods, reveling in this playful side to his *Sonuachar* he'd never seen. Just when he thought he had her figured out, she managed to surprise him.

The scent of her arousal floated around him, clinging to the moist early morning air in a mist of pure seduction. He inhaled, pulling her scent into his body, absorbing all he could of Jax. God, he loved her and fuckin' hell he had to have her now!

Ian dove to the leaf-covered forest floor and grabbed Jax's ankle, tumbling her to the ground. She cried out as he clasped her other ankle and flipped her over, sliding her across the ground toward him.

Before she could react, he was on top of her, pinning her arms to the ground above her head. Their gazes met as hovered over her, his breathing ragged, his body primed to mate. Ian pressed his erection against her sex and Jax spread her legs in open invitation.

In one swift plunge, Ian slammed into her body, wringing a cry from deep within her. He reveled in the lust reflected in her glazed over emerald gaze.

Do you feel the need to feed, Jaqueline? Do you want my blood as much as I want to slam into you again and again until we're both spent in exhaustion?

Ian drove deeper as he slid his hands up her arms and laced his fingers with hers. She whimpered and rocked against him, wrapping her legs around his hips. He groaned at the feel of her warm walls already contracting around him. He had to mentally shake himself to keep from losing it.

Her soft body cradled his and her tight nipples had turned a dark, dusky rose as her arousal peaked. He couldn't resist sucking on one bud and then the other. When he met her gaze once more, he whispered in her mind as he withdrew and sank back home, *I want you to know my blood as well as my mind and body, Jax.*

Jax smiled, displaying her fangs. The incredible, erotic sight caused his stomach to knot in anticipation and his lower muscles to flex while his balls tightened against his body.

Jax tugged at his hold on her and Ian released her hands. As soon as her hands were free, she reached up and pulled him down on top of her, replying in his mind while she laved at his neck, *And so do I*, a chroí.

When Jax sank her teeth into his neck, Ian closed his eyes and groaned. His hips moved of their own accord, thrusting into her body as she took his blood, greedily, lustfully, and like everything else Jax did...wholeheartedly.

His entire being shook from the deep, passionate experience. Not only did he feel his own orgasm raging to the forefront of his body, but as Jax's mouth pulled at him so did her sex, the warm, moist glove clasping him tight with orgasmic contractions. She unwittingly projected her own sensations and he absorbed every one of her electrifying responses. The sensual combination more than rocked his world. He groaned his satisfaction as he came in explosive bursts of heat and passion, hips grinding against hips, flesh rubbing against flesh.

As his heart settled and his body stilled within her, Jax's intoxicating, exotic scent coupled with the rich, earthy smell of the forest around them imbedded itself in his memory. He vowed to himself he'd find a way to make love to Jax outside as often as possible.

Ian rested his forehead on hers and said, "*Thug muid roinnt dár gcuid fuil chroí dá chéile; tugadh agus glacadh fuil go toilteanach. Tá muid inár lánúin anois.*"

Jax laved the wounds on his neck then kissed his jaw. "What did you just say?"

He pressed his lips to her temple answering in her mind, *I said, "Your life's blood for mine; given and taken willingly. Now we're mated"*

As he finished his words, he kissed the wound on her breast then swiped his tongue across the soft skin to start the healing process.

Moving to her side, he propped himself up on his elbow and gave her a rakish grin. "Care to return the favor?"

Jax looked down at his semi-erection and smiled when the flesh jumped and swelled to full attention. A devilish grin tilted the corners of her lips and she grasped his cock in her hand.

"No, I don't think so."

"What?" he looked at her, his expression confused.

She ran her thumb over the wounds she'd inflicted. "You see, this reads, 'marked and owned by Jax Mordoor'. I'd like to keep it that way for a little while."

Ian chuckled. "Possessive, aren't you?" he said and started to pull her on top of him.

They both froze at the sound of sirens in the distance.

"They sound like they're at the house." Ian stood and pulled her to her feet.

He sniffed the air, his expression grim as he brushed the leaves off her back. "I smell smoke." Grasping her hand, he turned saying, "Come on, let's go."

Ian kept a firm hold on her hand as they exited the woods and started up the hill toward the house. When they saw the plumes of dark smoke billowing up to the sky, Ian picked up his pace.

As they rounded the side of the house and the acrid smell of burning wood assailed her senses, Jax's insides quivered in hopes that everyone had made it outside unharmed.

Firefighters doused the left side of the house, near the kitchen area, while everyone stood outside watching the emergency workers do their job. Jax breathed a sigh of relief to see the guests safely outside.

When everyone turned and looked at them as they approached and Ian suddenly moved in front of her, too late, it dawned on her that she didn't have a stitch of clothes on her body. Jax's cheeks suffused with heat. She clasped Ian around the waist and pressed her warm cheek against his back.

Ian whispered in her mind, *Now that you've fed, you should have the strength to project clothes.*

I don't know how, she responded.

Yes, you do, he replied in a patient but determined tone. *Just picture yourself dressed…will it so.*

As soon as he said the words, Ian's body was immediately clothed in jeans, boots, and a navy sweater.

Jax closed her eyes and concentrated. When she opened them again and looked down, she was surprised to see herself dressed in jeans, tennis shoes and a gray sweat jacket…well the illusion of dressed anyway. *Hey, this is kinda cool. Talk about taking the whole, "imagine what this outfit will look like on you" idea to a whole new level.*

Jocelyn walked over to them, her stride brisk as her long, red silk robe flapped in the wind. When she reached them, she let out a relieved breath. "Thank God you two are all right. We were worried when we couldn't find you."

Jax smiled at the concern in Jocelyn's voice. She truly cared for this woman who had become like a mother to her in such a short time. "We're fine." She cut her gaze over to Ian and gave him a secret smile. "We were exploring your property."

"What happened here?" Ian asked as Roderick, Lucian and Rana approached.

Roderick pulled Jocelyn back against his chest and wrapped his arms around her. "We haven't a clue."

"It was arson, near as I can tell," a fireman replied as he walked up. "Once we put the fire out, we did find remnants of a crude but effective igniter near the kitchen curtains." He pulled off his hat and scrubbed his jaw, a quizzical look on his face. "Yeah, I'm surprised the fire didn't spread further, what with a houseful of guests all snug in their beds. Being the time of day it is, it's not like folks would've been up at three o'clock in the morning," he finished with a laugh.

They all shared a silent, amused moment before Roderick followed the fireman back to his truck to discuss the paperwork that still needed to be taken care of.

"This was Drace's doing," Ian said between clenched teeth. "I feel it in my bones."

Jocelyn nodded as she wrapped her arms around her body and shivered. "He wasn't too happy with me when I refused to let him stay here."

Ian gave her an apologetic smile. "I've been meaning to ask you about Drace, but I've been a bit distracted since we got here," he said as he pulled Jax into his arms and kissed her neck.

Roderick walked back over to them saying, "Well, the fire chief suggested we find other arrangements since there's still a good amount of smoke that needs to be aired from the house."

Jocelyn sighed, disappointment evident. "Guess it's a good thing most of the guests had planned to leave today anyway."

"Come stay with us," Lucian addressed Roderick. Turning to Ian he continued, "Why don't you and Jax come too, Ian. We've got plenty of room."

"Ooh, I'd love for you all to visit with us for a while," Rana echoed her husband's invitation.

"Sounds great," Ian replied.

Jax looked up at him in surprise. "We've got to track down Drace."

Ian kissed her temple. "Drace can wait for now. I need to discuss some Ruean business with Lucian."

Turning Jax toward his car, Ian called over his shoulder, "We'll meet you there."

As they walked away, she pulled him to a halt. "Hey, I'm not leaving my weapons or Pawn."

Ian gave her a quizzical look. "Pawn?"

"You know, the black cat that's been hanging around our balcony."

"You've already named her?" he said with a laugh.

"Of course. I don't blame the cat." She shrugged and grinned. "She was Drace's pawn, that's all. Hence the name."

After a long, meaningful stare where she refused back down, Ian finally said grudgingly, "I'll get the damned cat and your stuff."

Jax stood on her toes and kissed him on the cheek, an appreciative smile on her face. "Thanks and don't forget our clothes, okay?"

Ian wrapped his arms around her and nuzzled her neck as he pressed his erection against her belly. "I don't know about the clothes part. I kind of like the idea of you walking around stark naked."

With the heightened emotions surging through her body, Jax's mental capacity stuttered, causing her clothes illusion to flicker in and out. She looked around in embarrassment. Thank goodness all the other guests seemed to be too busy walking to their cars to notice them. She pushed on his chest with a laugh. "That's exactly why I need clothes."

* * * * *

Jax shrugged into her clothes as Ian drove to Lucian and Rana's house. While she moved around, struggling to get her clothes on in the confined space, Pawn tried to make a bed in Ian's lap. At Ian's hissing intake of breath, Jax remembered he didn't have any clothes on. She quickly moved to grab the cat before it lost one of its nine lives.

"The only claws I want digging into my thighs are yours," Ian said in a gruff voice as she pried the cat off his leg and set it on a towel in the backseat. When Pawn circled and curled into a ball, Jax turned and leaned back in her seat to enjoy the scenic view as they drove up the long, winding driveway to the Trevane estate.

Jax sighed as they pulled up to the circular entryway. Ian looked over at her and she gave him a half smile saying, "I just realized I haven't slept in my own bed in over a month." Her forehead puckered as she drew her brows downward. "Um, speaking of home. Where...?"

Ian read the uncertainty in her expression. He cupped the back of her neck and kissed her. When he pulled away, her emerald gaze, languid and more confident, locked with his.

"We'll live wherever you want, *a ghrá*." He drew a finger down her cheek. "I do own a modest place that overlooks the river. We'll have to use the Ruean estate from time to time for meetings and such since my other house is not as large, but it would be a wonderful place to raise a family as well as suit our need for privacy."

Ian's chest tightened as he awaited Jax's response. He'd live anywhere she wanted, but what if Jax didn't want kids? She certainly hadn't had the best childhood.

She smiled and slid her fingers through his hair, pulling him close once more to whisper in his ear, "I would love to have your children, Ian, a whole houseful."

Ian's heart soared at her words. She pushed away from him with a determined look. "But for now, let's concentrate on getting Drace, then we'll talk about our future."

Ian chuckled as she scooped up Pawn into her arms. Her nurturing nature had emerged full force with that cat. His stomach clenched and his groin tightened at the idea of conceiving a child with Jax, the thought of her holding his child, breastfeeding the baby, gently cooing...well, maybe not the cooing part. Jax wasn't a cooing type of woman.

As he rounded the car to help Jax down , Ian had no sooner dismissed the idea of his *Sonuachar* cooing over an infant only to see Jax lift the cat close and rub noses with it, saying in a soothing voice, "We'll be home soon Pawn, no worries."

He couldn't help the wide grin that spread across his face. Jax would make a wonderful mother.

Once they entered the house, Sabryn approached with the two ever-present wolves loping along beside her. At the sight of the dogs, the cat arched her back, hissed, and took off toward the back of the house.

"Pawn..." Jax started to call her.

"She'll be fine, Jax," Sabryn reassured her while she nodded to the butler to take their bags.

"Thanks but I need to put on clothes anyway," Ian said, shrugging off the help.

Sabryn stroked one of the wolves between the ears. "Rana asked me to greet you. She promised a guest of ours, Trish, a game of chess thinking she'd be just a few minutes," Sabryn paused and grinned before continuing, "But it turns out the two are so evenly matched, the game has become quite a tournament. Uncle Vlad is glued to a chair watching the drama unfold," she finished in an amused tone.

"Jocelyn and Roderick will be a bit later arriving. They had a few loose ends to tie up with the fire chief. Why don't you two get settled in?"

Ian pulled Jax's bag over his shoulder along with his and headed for the stairs. Sabryn called after him, "Lucian's in his office, Ian."

Nodding to acknowledge Sabryn's comment, Ian continued up the stairs with Jax following close behind.

Once he reached the guest bedroom, Ian set their belongings on the bed and pulled out some clothes for himself. While he put on jeans and a hunter green shirt, Jax grabbed her bag and headed for the bathroom.

At the same time Ian sat down on the bed to pull on his socks, a horrible retching sound came from the other room. His heart raced and his stomach felt like it had dropped to the floor. Ian took the distance to the bathroom in two long strides. He slammed open the door to see Jax squatting next the toilet, her long hair pulled back in one hand and an oval plastic container in the other.

She glanced up at him, a pained expression on her face. "Ugh, I suddenly felt like crap," she commented.

Ian plucked the packet of pink pills from her hand and tossed it in the trash. At her cry of outrage, he stated in a calm voice, "You're no longer human, Jax. Human birth control pills aren't effective on vampires. That's why your body rejected them."

Jax stood and then swayed, grabbing the sink for support. Ian placed his hands on her upper arms to steady her.

"Well, what am I supposed to use for birth control now that I'm a vampire? I suppose we could use condoms."

"Like hell!" Ian could see the frustration in her expression, but he wanted to be honest with her. He shrugged. "We don't use birth control. There are so few blooded- vampires as it is. Why would we try to slow the growth of our race?"

He touched her chin and lifted her head so she had to meet his gaze. "You did say you wanted to have children, *a chroí*."

"Yes, but Drace—"

"We'll get Drace, don't worry," Ian cut her off as he splayed his hand across her lower belly. "You could already be pregnant."

Jax jerked her gaze back to his, her expression incredulous. "No, Ian. I was on the pill—"

"Which ceased to become effective the minute you became a vampire," he finished for her.

Several expressions flitted across her face—confusion, outrage, frustration, awe before a stubborn one finally settled. "Fine, I could be pregnant. Don't think for one minute that's going to stop me from finding Drace."

"You'd put our child in harm's way?" Ian asked as anger rose within him.

"No," she shot back. "But I'll be damned it you'll use this as an excuse to shut me out of the hunt, Ian." She raised her hands in exasperation. "For that matter, more than likely I'm not pregnant and this whole argument is moot."

Ian pulled her to him and wrapped his arms around her. "Even if you weren't pregnant, I'd still feel protective over you, *a ghrá. Is tú mo shonuachar.* You're my soul mate. I couldn't bear it if anything happened to you." He heard the raw emotion in his own voice and realized he'd never spoken so candidly to anyone in his life, but he wanted Jax to understand how deep his emotions ran for her.

She wrapped her arms around his waist and held him tight as she buried her nose in his shirt and inhaled. Even though her body was toned, he still appreciated her curves that felt so right pressed against his body. Ian threaded his fingers through her silky hair and kissed the top of her head as she mumbled against his chest, "I love you and I feel the same. I wouldn't want anything to happen to you either."

She gave his butt a whack and stepped away with a smile. "Now go and meet with Lucian. I think I'll work out while Rana is occupied with her chess game."

Ian chuckled, raising an eyebrow. "You know you don't have to exercise anymore."

Twisting her hair up and securing the thick mass with her chopsticks, she replied, "I find working out to be very rejuvenating."

As Ian turned to leave, she called out, "Oh, and when you're done with Lucian, how about we give Sebastian a call? He started to tell me something about Drace last night. I think he knows where the vamp might be."

Ian couldn't help the gut clenching, possessive feeling that swept through him at Jax's mention of the Norriden leader. He'd seen the way Sebastian looked at Jax, remembered the way the vamp had taunted him as he held her in his arms. If he didn't owe the man his life, he'd have challenged Sebastian last night for daring to touch his mate.

He kept his expression neutral as he walked out of the room.

Chapter Eighteen

"So what Ruean business did you need to discuss, Ian?" Lucian asked as Ian entered his office.

Ian walked over to stand in front of the desk. Crossing his arms and propping his hip on the corner of the deep cherry wood, he addressed his friend, "Nothing. I just want your help keeping Jax busy while I go after Drace."

Lucian laced his fingers behind his head and leaned back in his chair, a big grin on his face. "You plan on going after him without her?"

A sense of panic gripped Ian, knotting his stomach at the idea of Jax being harmed during a hunt. Drace had it in for both of them. The vamp wouldn't be merciful if he had the slightest advantage. He'd use their love for each other as a weakness.

Ian rubbed his chin and chuckled to release the tension in his body. "I don't really relish the idea of compelling Jax to sleep while I hunt down Drace. I'm hoping Rana will be able to distract her."

"You're not afraid of Jax, are you?" Lucian teased.

Ian shot his friend a look of steel. "No, but I've compelled my mate to sleep quite a few times in the recent past. As you know, Jax can be a force to be reckoned with. Now that she's a vampire," he paused, thinking about the way Jax had "marked" him earlier. He finished with a wry smile, "Let's just say I'm well aware of the damage she could inflict."

Lucian started to answer when someone knocked at the door.

Ian stiffened at the scent that invaded his senses. He narrowed his gaze saying, "Sebastian. What's he doing here?"

Lucian shrugged. "There's only one way to find out, my friend." He called for Sebastian to enter.

Sebastian entered Lucian's office with the same grace he always entered a room. Ian had to hand it to him, as the Norriden leader, Sebastian was the epitome of elegant, yet cynical, old-world charm. With the calm, self-assured confidence he exuded, women, human and vampire alike, flocked to the bastard and he welcomed them all with open arms.

Ian set his jaw. Why did he have a feeling Sebastian's presence had something to do with Jax?

"Good morning, gentlemen." Sebastian approached them with a wide grin on his face.

"Something must be damn important to keep your from your bed and a warm, willing woman, Sebastian," Ian said.

Sebastian flashed him a rakish smile. "Actually I was lying in bed thinking about Jax…"

Ian's entire body tensed and he clenched his fists by his sides, ready to knock the vamp into next week.

Lucian spoke in his mind in a calm tone. *Calm, my friend. He's trying to rile you.*

"Your point, Gauthier," Ian bit out.

Sebastian gave him an innocent look before continuing, "I tried to tell Jax where Drace was last night, but she interrupted me, saying that you and she would find him on your own."

She'd had a chance to learn where Drace was and she didn't act on it? Pride surged through Ian, its warmth spreading throughout his body.

"So why are you here?" Ian asked, his patience running thin.

Sebastian shrugged. "As I said, I was lying in bed, thinking about how lovely Jax is and that I would hate to see something happen to that gorgeous body of hers if she tangled with Drace." He paused, his gaze twinkling as he finished, "So I thought I'd tell you where to find Drace so you can take care of the bastard yourself."

Surprised by Sebastian's generosity, Ian could only stare at the vamp.

"He's at the Ruean estate."

"That's impossible. The place is locked down," Ian countered.

Sebastian's expression hardened for a brief second as he narrowed his dark, probing gaze on him. "I know my information is correct, Mordoor. Check it out for yourself."

His face relaxed and he sat down in a winged back chair, crossing his legs in a nonchalant manner. Picking at a piece of lint on his black slacks, he glanced up and said, "I don't mind if *you* go head-to-head with Drace. After all, there is the possibility you will lose and Jax will be all alone."

Ian's anger rushed to the surface. He took a step toward the vamp, ready to inflict bodily harm at his taunts.

Let's go about this in a different way, shall we? Lucian spoke in a warning tone in Ian's mind.

Ian stopped in his tracks at his friend's subtle yet effective words.

"Since you're in such a generous mood, Sebastian, why don't you go with Ian and help him eliminate Drace."

Ian suppressed the laugh that threatened at the surprised look that crossed Sebastian's face before he masked it. The arrogant vamp hadn't seen that one coming...for that matter neither had he. He grinned inwardly. Yep, there was a reason Lucian was their leader. Ian had never regretted casting the final vote to make Lucian Vité.

Sebastian affected a bored expression as he glanced at his watch and stood up. "Much as I would love to join in the fray, as I said, I was in bed. I'd like to get back before the sun rises in an hour and a half and I'm forced to remain here until the sun sets tomorrow night."

He cut his gaze over to Ian, saying in a dry tone, "But as we know, our hybrid friend's activities aren't bound by the rising and setting of the sun."

Touché, you fuckin' bastard, Ian thought, respect dawning for the vamp's ability to think so quickly on his feet. Just a few years younger than Lucian, Sebastian was a very powerful vampire in his own right. He could easily help if he wished. Not that Ian would accept his help. He'd tell Gauthier to go to hell first.

Ian pushed off the desk and headed for the door without looking back.

"Aren't you even going to thank me, Mordoor?" Sebastian asked in an amused tone.

As he opened the door, Ian ground out, "Yeah, go to hell, Gauthier."

Sebastian's bark of laughter followed him out the door as he replied in his mind, *In due course, Mordoor.*

Ian opened his cell phone and dialed Mark's cell phone number. *I'll need a couple of hours, Lucian. Have Rana keep Jax occupied until I get back,* Ian made the mental request as he walked outside and climbed into his car.

* * * * *

Jax made her way downstairs and watched the chess tournament that now had other members of the household gathered around. The butler and a woman wearing an apron stood in the doorway of the library to cheer on Rana and Trish. Jax watched the precocious redheaded teenager as she taunted, trying her best to egg Rana into slipping up on her moves. Shrewd strategizing already—*a girl after my own heart*, Jax thought with a grin.

"Rana won't be much longer," Sabryn said from behind her.

Jax glanced over her shoulder at Lucian's sister. "Who would you place bets on?"

Sabryn's lips twitched in amusement. "Why Trish, of course."

"You sound pretty confident." Jax faced the female vampire.

Sabryn moved to lean on the door jamb. "Trish is very bright. Even though Rana is good, Trish just brings a certain calm, methodical shrewdness to the game that is unsurpassed."

Jax eyed the teenager once more, noting the look of sheer concentration on her young face. Though she admired Trish's tenacity, she also wondered at its source. "She seems awfully young to look so serious."

"She lost both her parents a couple of months ago." Sabryn's gaze clouded and she ran her fingers across the charm on the gold chain around her neck as she continued, "Sometimes life has a way of making you grow up faster than you had hoped."

Jax sensed Sabryn's thoughts had something to do with her necklace—a necklace she realized she'd always seen the beautiful vampire wearing, even when she was decked out in her finest clothes. She nodded toward the charm.

"That's a neat charm. What flower is that inside the heart?"

Sabryn looked down at the three dimensional gold heart that held a light blue flower inside. "It's a Forget Me Not."

"It's very unusual."

Sabryn glanced up and smiled, a faraway look in her eyes. "Yes, it was a gift from someone that was very special to me many years ago."

Someone that *was* special? Jax wondered what had happened to that someone special in Sabryn's life.

As if reading Jax's thoughts, Sabryn snapped out of her reverie. Straightening her shoulders, she smiled. "Come on. Trish will eventually win but it may be a little bit. Let me show you around."

Jax nodded and followed Sabryn as she took her on a tour of the Trevane estate.

When Sabryn showed her an outside courtyard at the end of her tour, Jax lingered. The brick patio was lined with benches along the edges while trees created a natural wall, surrounding all three sides. Jax grinned her appreciation at the secluded spot. "What a great place to work out."

Sabryn gave her a strange look. "As in exercise?"

"Yes."

"I know you're a vampire now, Jax. I sense the change in you. You *do* know you no longer have to exercise, right?"

Jax laughed at Sabryn's confused expression. "Yes, I know. It's just that old habits die hard and to be honest, it helps me think."

"Ah, now I see." Sabryn nodded. "You're more than welcome to use the courtyard during your stay."

Jax looked at her watch and said, her voice hopeful, "I haven't heard any victory cries yet. Think I've got more time to kill?"

Sabryn grinned. "Yep. Rana may lose but she won't go down without a fight."

"Great. I think I'll run upstairs and change into my workout clothes. Thanks so much for the tour, Sabryn."

As she dashed up the stairs, she heard Sabryn's amused voice in her head, *Um, you do know you no longer sweat at the same rate either, don't you?*

Old habits, Jax replied mentally as a grin tugged at her lips. Though the physical aspects like racing through the house at unheard of speeds seemed to come naturally, things like remembering she could use mental communication with those other than her mate and knowing that she'd have to work really heard to break a sweat...no, she didn't know. Boy, did she have a lot to learn about being a vampire.

Once she'd changed and collected her bag, Jax walked outside in the secluded courtyard Sabryn had shown her earlier. For a moment she just stood and absorbed the sounds and scents around her. Once she'd closed the door to the house, all light from inside the house was cut off. The cloudy night hid the stars, obliterating any natural source of light and making her marvel once again at her vampire night vision.

She saw everything with perfect clarity. Never again would she need a light. The birds in the trees surrounding the courtyard started to chirp as if sensing her presence. She heard their fast little heartbeats and sensed their joy with the new day just around the corner.

"Dawn isn't for a couple of hours yet, little ones," she said in a lighthearted tone as she set her bag down and pulled out a few weapons.

She went through her stretching routine while she considered the best way to convince Ian to let Sebastian help them find Drace. She chuckled at the change she had undergone since she'd met Ian. Whereas before she'd never accepted anyone's help, recently she'd accepted Ian's, Blake's and now she was willing to accept Sebastian's help as well. She'd do whatever it took to move on with her life. A life with Ian.

The idea of having a child with Ian appealed to her on a deeper level. She wanted to be able to give her child all the things she'd missed out on—a family, a heritage, a father and mother who put family first before the hunt.

She knew the hunter instinct would always run in her blood. But instead of teaching with vengeance in mind, now she could teach her children with defense and justice as the two main drivers in their education.

After she'd exercised enough to sufficiently loosen her muscles, Jax began to strap on her weapons.

She pulled the crossbow pistol from her shoulder harness and slid a bolt into place. Holding the weapon close to her chest, Jax took a deep breath and closed her eyes for a second to focus on her goal—a knot she'd seen on a tree 30 feet away. But something happened when her eyes closed. All her keen senses kicked in, causing her to take a deep breath at the barrage of sensations—crickets and animal sounds grew louder, pine and oak scents almost overwhelmed her, the very air around her seemed to cling to her skin, giving her insight into the slightest change in her environment.

Look out Dare Devil, she thought with a smirk as she felt the air shift right before a small animal rushed past her. Another bend in the air preceded a scent that announced someone's arrival behind her. Sensing a benevolent presence, Jax resisted the urge to open her eyes and look. Instead, she focused her attention on the sound of a crisp leaf floating through the air in front of her. She grinned and aimed her pistol, letting instinct tell her when to pull the trigger.

When the bolt made a sliding thud into the tree truck, someone said from beside her, her voice full of awe, "Wow, that was so freakin' cool and you didn't even look!"

Jax opened her eyes and saw her bolt embedded in the tree, the leaf impaled dead center between the bolt and the knot in the trunk. She looked at the young girl beside her saying, "Hello Trish. I'm Jax." She grinned and finished, "I take it you won."

Trish flashed a smile, causing a dimple to form in one cheek. "Yep, of course."

"And such a modest winner, too," Jax said with a laugh as she reloaded her pistol.

Trish shrugged, an unrepentant look on her face. "Yeah, well it's the only leg up I have around these bunch of frea..."

She stopped mid-sentence, her cheeks coloring red. She cleared her throat saying, "You're like Rana. Just turned vampire, right?"

"I guess it takes one to know one," Jax said with a laugh.

Trish visibly stiffened. "I'm not a vampire," she said in an offended tone.

"Hey, whoa," Jax held her hand up. "I'm sorry. Do you want me to turn on a light then?" But she felt something from this girl. Her young body emitted a low vibration of some kind.

"No, I can see just fine." Trish shrugged her lean shoulders and dug her hands deep in her jeans. "Well, maybe it comes from just being around you guys. All I know is after my parents died I was brought here and told it was for my own good 'to keep me safe from rogue freaks that might see me as a prize'." She rolled her eyes mumbling, "Whatever that means."

Pawn walked over and rubbed against Jax's legs. Trish flashed a grin, leaned over, and called out in a coaxing voice, "Here kitty, kitty."

As Trish took a step toward Pawn, the cat made a low hissing sound and took off up one of the trees in the courtyard.

"Well, nice to meet you, too," she grumbled, straightening.

"Don't mind Pawn. She's not been in her right mind lately." Jax chuckled at her own inside joke.

Trish shoved her hands deep in her pockets once more and rocked back on her heels, saying as she looked at the ground, "Yeah, me either. This whole protection crap is gettin' on my last nerve." She jerked her gaze up to Jax's with an expectant look. "Hey, would you be willing to show me how to defend myself? Then maybe they'd let me fly this cuckoo's nest that's straight out of a Munsters Family movie. She gave a sheepish grin. "Present company excluded, of course."

Jax laughed at Trish's spunky attitude, even if it was misplaced. The girl was definitely gifted. She sensed the untapped power within her but just couldn't put her finger on what that power was.

Before she could reply, the leaves in the tree above them rustled and Pawn gave a piteous meow.

Trish put her hands on her hips and said in an exasperated tone, "Will you get down here, you silly cat."

Pawn just meowed louder.

Jax peered up into the tree limbs and saw Pawn clinging for dear life to a wide branch, her white claws imbedded in the bark. She'd obviously gotten herself stuck up in the tree, fear paralyzing her.

As she started to call to Pawn, Trish spoke up, lifting her arms in the air.

"Come here, Pawn, now." Trish's tone was so matter-of-fact and calmly commanding, Jax glanced over at her in surprise as Pawn made a flying leap and landed in the teenager's arms.

Trish rubbed her fur saying, "See, that wasn't so bad, was it?"

Jax smiled. Oh, yeah, this kid had powers. She'd compelled Pawn to jump. No doubt about it. That cat wouldn't have budged otherwise.

"You're a vampire hunter, like Ian Mordoor, aren't you?" Trish asked, her confident gaze seeking confirmation.

"Yes, we hunt rogue vampires and their transers."

"Transers?" Trish tilted her head, a curious expression on her face.

Jax nodded. "Transers are humans that rogue vampires have cruelly 'almost turned' to vampires. In their needy state to cross over, they will do whatever the vampire who created them asks. In short, they're just as much a threat."

Understanding crossed Trish's young features. She sniffed the air, then gave Jax a smug look. "I smell Ian on you."

Yep, definitely keen senses. "We are partners," Jax answered with a laugh.

"So...you even hunt together, huh?" A knowing smile tilted the corners of her lips.

Jax nodded, wondering at the girl's amused expression.

"Well then, you might want to take off after your partner. I saw Ian leave not long after the Norriden leader arrived and spoke with him in Lucian's office."

Deep hurt slammed into Jax's stomach, churning until she felt almost ill. There was only one reason Ian would leave without her.

He went after Drace.

She masked her anger as she returned Trish's steady gaze. "Thanks for the info, Trish," Jax said in a nonchalant manner as she bent over and retrieved her Bowie knife, strapping it to her leg over her tight, black workout pants.

As Jax straightened, Trish said, "He's *so* busted, isn't he?"

Even in her haze of anger, Jax couldn't help but smile at Trish's appropriate words.

She nodded. "*So* busted."

As she walked away from Trish, Jax grabbed a bolt from the special pocket on her holster and quickly threw it toward the young girl.

With lightning movements, Trish caught the bolt in the air, curling her fingers around the metal as a triumphant smile spread across her face.

The kid had keen senses, temerity, gumption and most of all, she had heart.

"Take my cat and my bag to my room for me and when I get back, I'll teach you what you need to know to protect yourself."

"What about hunting?" Trish asked, her expression hopeful.

Jax thought about all the mistakes her father had made with her as a little girl.

"Let's work on protecting yourself first, then we'll move to the offensive."

"Woohoo, Buffy the Vampire Slayer, lookout!" Trish whooped as she turned and hurled the bolt across the courtyard. The metal shaft slammed into the tree, burying itself right beside the bolt Jax had shot earlier.

Despite her anger at Ian, Trish's surprising strength made Jax laugh as she walked back into the house. But once inside, Jax picked up her pace and headed for the front door.

As she opened the door, it occurred to her that she had no way to follow Ian since he'd obviously taken off in the Hummer. Disappointment and frustration warred within her until she saw Sebastian sliding his key into his driver's side door across the driveway.

"Hey," Jax called out, clearing the steps and part of the driveway in one long leap.

Sebastian turned to her as she landed next to him, an appreciative grin on his face. "Being a vampire suits you, Jax. Such grace."

Jax didn't bother with niceties. Ian could very well be killed in a fight with Drace.

"You told Ian where to find Drace, didn't you?" she said as she met his dark, probing gaze with a bold stare.

Sebastian started to open his door. "Don't worry, Jax. Ian will take care of Drace."

"Like hell he will," she ground out as she pulled her handgun from the holster strapped to the small of her back. Pointing the weapon at his chest, she said, "I'll need your car."

Sebastian raised a dark eyebrow in amusement. "I need to get home, Jax. The sun will rise within the hour."

"Then stay here," she countered, anger simmering at his delay tactics.

"I prefer my own bed."

Releasing the safety on her gun, Jax replied, "Then you'd better get in and let me catch up with Ian so you can get home before you turn into toast."

Sebastian narrowed his gaze. "I could compel you to let me leave."

Jax gritted her teeth at the unperturbed way he spoke, as if he didn't have a care in the world. She placed the barrel of the gun over his heart. "Go ahead. Compel me, but you know what they say about paybacks, don't you?"

Sebastian sighed and pulled the door to his silver BMW Z3 all the way open. Bowing slightly, he placed the keys in her hand. "How about you drive, my dear?"

Chapter Nineteen

Jax eyed Sebastian, gauging him for possible trickery, but only bored amusement flickered in his onyx gaze. She slid the holster from her back to her side and slipped the gun into the leather holder before she climbed into the car.

Turning the keys in the ignition, she put the car in gear and punched the gas before Sebastian had even shut his door.

"Where are we going?" she asked, keeping her tone calm even though she felt like throttling both Sebastian and Ian. Damn these arrogant vampire men.

"To the Ruean estate," he replied in a bland tone.

Jax glanced at Sebastian in surprise. "I thought Drace had been removed from the estate."

Sebastian gave an indifferent shrug. "Apparently he didn't take too kindly to being tossed out on his ass."

Jax returned her gaze to the road, thoughts swirling. How could Ian just leave? They were a team, partners. He'd finally convinced her to work with another only to leave her in the dust to go after Drace alone. Her heart pounded as betrayal sliced through her, causing her to grip the wheel tighter and press harder on the pedal while she quickly shifted through the gears.

A low chuckle from Sebastian didn't help matters. Jax took a sharp turn at breakneck speed and smirked when Sebastian gripped the door handle as his body pitched sideways.

"Might want to put your seatbelt on," she said in a sweet tone.

Sebastian straightened saying, "I trust your skills."

"At least somebody does," she mumbled under her breath.

"Ian is trying to protect his mate, Jax—" Sebastian started to say.

Jax cut him off. "I don't want to hear it…" She stopped speaking mid-sentence when she spotted Ian's Hummer sitting at a red light fifty feet ahead of them.

Her adrenaline pumping, she gunned the engine and warned in a calm voice, "Your seatbelt might be a good idea right about now, Sebastian."

As the light turned green, Jax zoomed passed the Hummer and quickly pulled in front of Ian's vehicle, slamming on the brakes and jerking the wheel.

Sebastian's Z3 turned 180 degrees and faced the black Hummer before it squealed to a dead stop. Ian had to slam on brakes to avoid hitting them head on. Nose to nose the cars sat, engines rumbling as Jax stared up at Ian through the windshield.

"You and Ian are definitely made for each other," Sebastian said in an amused voice.

The strong, pungent odor of burned rubber invaded her heightened senses, nearly knocking her out. Jax shook her head to clear it as Ian climbed out of his car and approached them.

The lines of his body reflected his anger. She could tell by his purposeful step, the stiff way he held his broad shoulders, and the hard expression on his face. Jax straightened her spine and squared her shoulders, ready to battle.

With casual, unhurried movements, Sebastian hit the window's button and leaned out to address Ian, "Nice early morning drive, eh Mordoor?"

"What the hell are you doing here with my wife, Gauthier?" Ian bit out.

Sebastian raised his hands in an innocent manner. "I was hijacked."

"Hijack..." Ian stopped speaking and put his hands on the door. Leaning down so he could see Jax, he said in a brisk tone, "What are you doing?"

"I'm helping my *partner* take down a rogue vampire," Jax answered. "But somehow my dear husband forgot to tell me he was leaving. Can you imagine?" She coupled a shocked expression with the sarcastic tone in her voice as she met Ian's narrowed golden gaze.

"How about we meet you there?" Sebastian said in a light tone, breaking the tension that arced through the air between Jax and Ian.

"Jax will ride with me," Ian ground out. He looked at Sebastian. "You can go home."

"Ian, if Drace is at the Ruean estate, your friend obviously is no longer guarding the house. Maybe we could use—" Jax started to say.

"No," Ian interrupted her, his tone final.

Sebastian looked at Ian in surprise. "You had a guard on the house?"

"Of course," Ian said, giving the vamp a "would you expect anything less" look.

"Maybe I *should* go along to help," Sebastian offered.

"No," Ian ground out. "Come on Jax."

Jax opened the door and turned to Sebastian. "Thanks for the ride."

Sebastian winked at her. "Any time, Jax. Any time."

She hopped out of the car and followed Ian to the Hummer. After he opened her door, she climbed in and he closed it behind her.

While he drove, Ian leaned over and opened a compartment underneath his seat. With quick, efficient movements he pulled first one and then another semiautomatic handgun out and laid them on the seat between them. Then he pulled out his leather gun holster and muscled into it while holding the steering wheel one hand at a time.

His cold silence grated on Jax's nerves.

"I don't hear you apologizing, Ian," Jax said, her tone stilted.

"And you won't hear one, either," he shot back, his jaw ticking as he gripped the steering wheel tighter and stared at the road.

She wouldn't hear one? What the fuc... "Of all the high-handed, arrogant, lame-ass, lower than dir —"

"You are my *life*, Jax," Ian simply said. He cut his amber gaze her way for all of a second before looking back at the road, but the raw emotion she saw in his expression and the tense gruffness in his voice took the wind right out of her sails.

Would she have done the same if she thought there might be a possibility of losing him? In her heart she knew. She'd been a hunter alone too long; she would have done the same.

Jax picked up his gun and released the clip, checking to make sure he had a full one. She did the same for the other gun and then set them back on the seat between them.

Ian retrieved one gun and snapped it in the holster. When Jax moved to pick up the other gun for him, he grabbed her hand and raised it to his lips. Kissing the inside of her palm, he looked at her and said, "Stay close, *á ghra*."

Jax's heart melted at the concern flickering in his gaze. She'd never felt so cherished in her life. Squeezing his hand, she replied with a nod, "Like glue."

As he released her hand, she asked, "Do you think your friend is okay?"

Pain entered his gaze for a brief second before he masked it. "I don't know. Mark is a fighter. If he did die, he went down like a mad dog."

As Ian drove past the broken down gate and up the drive to the Ruean estate, Jax turned to stare at the house, her heart sinking at the possibility Ian may have lost someone close to him—all because of Drace.

Drace. The damn vamp had hurt too many people in her life. Today, he'd finally pay with his own. Jax sensed the tension in Ian as they approached the house.

"Why aren't we parking away from the estate?"

Drace would sense us anyway, Ian answered her mentally.

Good point. Jax met his gaze with a brief smile.

As soon as Ian stopped the car, Drace stepped outside the front door, pulling a man by his blue denim shirt along in front of him. Blood smeared the man's head from his dark blond hair, across his forehead and down his cheek. One of his eyes was swollen shut and his left arm hung by his side, apparently broken. He looked as if Drace had used him as his personal punching bag.

Jax felt Ian's emotions whirling. Anger surged to the surface, emanating from him in such strong vibrations she shivered at its intensity.

Mark? she asked.

Only the tick in his jaw told her the answer.

"Get out of the car, Mordoor."

As Ian and Jax exited the Hummer, Drace continued in a lighter tone while two of his men circled either side of the vehicle, training their machine guns on them, "How very nice of you to bring Jax right to me this time."

Ian moved to stand beside Jax. He nodded to Mark. "What are you doing with this human, Drace?"

Drace eyed Mark's sad state and shook him, causing a low moan of pain to escape the man's split lip. "Don't even try to pretend this little human shit doesn't mean anything to you, Mordoor," Drace sneered. "Why do you think I was ready for you tonight, mmmm? Your call on his cell phone came in handy."

Drace gave an evil smile as he yanked Mark's head back by his hair, exposing his neck to reveal a bite mark, bruised and bloody, his skin torn.

No! Drace couldn't have turned Ian's friend, making him a transer. Mark would do whatever Drace asked him to. Jax's heart ached for her mate's friend.

"You motherfucker," Ian hissed, ready to pounce.

"Ah, ah, ah," Drace *tsked* as he pulled a semiautomatic from his leather coat pocket and placed the barrel against Mark's temple. "I took care of all of the friends he brought with him to guard the estate, but I saved your buddy Mark here just for you. He's my insurance policy if you try something stupid."

When Ian backed down, Drace smirked. "You always were a sap when it came to humans, Ian. They are definitely the weaker half of you."

Drace threw his head back and laughed at his own pun. The sheer evil sound he made grated on Jax's last nerve. She'd kept her hands carefully to her sides, but her fingers itched to choke the bastard.

"How about a little ironic justice, hmmm?" Drace nodded to his men. "Take their weapons."

The vamps did as Drace asked. Tucking his gun away, Drace waved his hand, silently asking for one of the weapons a vamp had just retrieved from Ian. Once his man had placed the gun in his hand, Drace let go of Mark, put the gun in the man's hand and said, "Shoot Ian Mordoor."

Mark weaved on his own two feet, his left arm dangling as he raised his right arm and the gun toward Ian.

Jax's gut clenched at Mark's totally entranced expression. Oh God, he planned to shoot Ian. She dug her short nails into her palms to keep from her first gut reaction: attack the vamp near her for her gun. Noting the vamp beside her had his gaze trained on Mark, she eyed her gun he'd tucked in the front waistline of his pants. No way would she let Mark shoot Ian. She'd take him out first. Jax casually rubbed her earlobe, then touched her eyebrow before making her way up to one of her chopsticks.

"No, Mark. Fight it," Ian called out to his friend, his tone commanding, strong, compelling.

Time seemed to stand still. Tension filled the air. Jax's stomach knotted at the thought she was left with no choice but to take out Ian's friend to save her mate.

Just as she touched her chopstick in her hair, Mark said in a vengeful tone, "Nobody owns me, you fuckin' vamp," as he rammed his shoulder into Drace and popped off two rounds into the vamp next to her.

While Ian took on the vamp beside him, Jax dove and retrieved her gun from the dead vamp's pants, but before she could fire off any rounds at Drace, he'd leapt over the wrought iron railing and fled around the side of the house.

Jax cleared the steps in one leap as Mark fell to the ground unconscious. Ian's gun slipped from his loosened grip and landed with a thud on the wooden porch. Punching sounds in the background drew Jax's attention. She looked up to see Ian slamming into the vamp, disarming him as they fell to the ground.

Her heart slamming in her chest drowned out the sound of the scuffle in the yard between Ian and the vamp as she squatted to feel Mark's pulse, fear gripping her. His pulse felt weak. They needed to get him to Mora ASAP! Jax stood and jumped to the ground, intending to go after Drace.

"No," Ian said, grabbing her arm. "We'll go together."

She nodded and asked as Ian retrieved his second gun from the porch, "How was Mark able to fight off becoming a transer?"

Ian shook his head. "The only thing I could think of is that he wasn't as far gone as we thought."

As they followed the path Drace took around the side of the house, Ian jerked back, pulling her to his side.

"I feel too many vamps, Jax. We need to—"

"Now, now, don't be shy," Drace called out with a triumphant smirk as he walked around the back corner of the house toward them. Jax eyed the group of men behind him. There were six men, some transers, some vampires, but either way, the odds didn't look good, especially since the men facing them held guns ranging from Uzi's to semiautomatic handguns.

Ian stepped in front of her, forcing her to walk backward or be stepped on.

Outrage flared within her. *Ian* — she started to speak mentally to him but stopped short when she felt hard metal jam into her spine.

"Looks like you've finally walked into a scenario you have no chance of winning, Mordoor." The corner of Drace's lip curled up in a derisive smile.

Jax turned around and put her back to Ian's as she inspected the group of five men she now faced. She felt a very low vibe from every single one. Damn, all the men were transers. With the impending sunrise, she thought for sure she and Ian would have an advantage. Transers could abide the sunlight.

While Drace's men slowly spread out in a circle around then, Jax's adrenaline spiked. She raised her gun, ready to fire.

Jax, on the count of three, I want you to jump as high as you can and push away from me. It's our only chance to get out of this, Ian spoke in her mind, his tone matter of fact, but assuring nonetheless.

Adrenaline surged through her at Ian's proposal. As exciting as the prospect sounded...well, not the potential Swiss-cheese part, she wondered if her vampire powers gave her the strength to jump high enough.

You can do this Jax, Ian insisted as if he'd read her thoughts.

Jax took a deep breath before she answered, *Let's do it.*

Remember, shoot as soon as you're airborne, 'cause they sure as hell will be.

"You know I'm going to kill you, don't you?" Ian said to Drace as he counted to her mentally.

One

Two

Drace chuckled, waving his gun toward him. "Your absolute arrogance never ceases to amaze me, Ian."

Three

Jax jumped upward as fast and as hard as her legs would take her, shooting at the surrounding vampires with all she had. When she reached her full height potential, everything seemed to happen in supersonic speed. Jax pushed off of Ian and rolled in the air. The buzz of a bullet whizzing past her head reminded her to focus not only on her shooting but to listen for the bullets zinging toward her. A bullet snagged her sleeve, making her heart jerk.

As gravity took over and she began to fall to the ground, Jax looked around in surprise to see all of the transers and vamps lying flat on their backs, their weapons strewn on the ground around them.

Ian landed at the same time she did and immediately dove into Drace before he could recover from being knocked down. The two men grabbed each other's necks and rolled away from the group, grunting and hissing at one another. Jax gave a brief smile when Ian landed a hard blow to Drace's chest.

The roar of an engine drew her attention, causing her to look up from her squatted position. A man, dressed in all black leather, came barreling over the rise of the hill on a motorcycle, firing his automatic weapon toward the transers and vamps who scrambled for their dropped guns.

Duncan!

One of the downed vamps had reached his weapon and had turned it on Duncan. Jax raised her gun to take the vamp out when the vamp doubled over as if in pain, dropping his gun.

Duncan had driven his bike in the middle of all the vampires and transers and hopped off. After he took out two more bad guys with his gun, he threw it to the ground and faced the others saying, "Come on you bunch of shits. Let's see what ya got."

Jax grinned at Duncan's ballsy statement considering he now faced five men.

When the men he spoke to tried to retrieve their weapons, the guns moved of their own accord, flying a good hundred feet off into the woods.

"That should make it a fair fight, Mordoor," she heard a man's amused voice off to her right.

She turned to see Sebastian walking toward her and that's when she realized he, as a pureblooded vampire, was the only one powerful enough to have knocked back all those men at once. Of course, he did have the element of surprise on his side.

She started to mentally thank Sebastian for his help when she was suddenly knocked to the ground. Jax grabbed her head as pain shot through her skull. Someone had attacked her from behind. Anger bubbled to the surface and she rolled over to face her attacker. But when she looked up, she saw the vamp lying on the ground, his jugular torn in his neck, blood gushing onto the ground.

Sebastian grabbed her hand and pulled her to her feet, saying with a concerned expression, "Are you okay?"

Jax nodded and eyed Sebastian's silk shirt and jacket, now covered with blood. She looked again at the dead vamp, surprised to see the results of such violence from Sebastian. "Thank you," she said as she met his dark gaze.

The sound of fists, connecting with tissue and bone, drew Jax's attention. Duncan had discarded his weapon and he, the transers, and the vamps all rolled on the ground, lashing out at each other, shredding clothes, blood gushing as they fought. Every so often she heard Duncan baiting his adversaries with verbal jibes. He seemed to be thoroughly enjoying kicking vamp and transer ass alike.

A single gunshot went off near her, the sound ringing in her ears and jarring her body. *Damn my sensitive hearing.* Jax jerked her gaze toward the source of the gunshot. She met Blake's furious scowl as he pointed his gun at Sebastian.

"Get away from her," he bit out.

Jax turned to Sebastian. He'd been shot in the shoulder.

"Blake!"

As she faced Blake once more she saw her friend thrown back a good fifteen feet, landing hard on his ass. The sudden sound of weapons being cocked made Jax look up. An entire contingent of Trackers leaned over the rooftop, their sniper guns trained on Sebastian, ready to take him out.

"Blake!" she called out once more.

"Stand down," Blake called up to his men as he stood and walked toward her once more.

She knew Sebastian had to have noticed the presence of the men above him, but that didn't stop him from rolling his eyes. He pointed to himself when Blake reached them, saying with a low growl, "Good guy."

He then pointed to Duncan a few feet away, fighting off vamps. "That vamp, holding his own? Good guy."

Thumbing to Ian and Drace rolling around on the ground twenty feet away. "Dark hair, *bad guy*. Other one..." Sebastian winced as he rolled his hurt shoulder, then gave a sarcastic smile. "You guessed it...good guy." Sebastian spoke to Blake as if he were talking to a very small child.

Blake met Jax's gaze and jerked his head toward Sebastian, a pissed expression on his face. "Who's the smartass?"

"You mean the one you just *shot*?" Sebastian ground out, his expression far from pleased.

Exasperated at the testosterone-driven male machismo surrounding her while lives hung in the balance, Jax gave them both with a stern look. "Okay humans and fiends, why don't we all play nice for a bit while we kick the 'real' bad vamps' asses, hmmm?"

"But you're not human any more, are you, Jax?" Blake accused, his eyes narrowing. "I saw the stunt you and Ian pulled. That's not something a human could have accomplished."

Jax didn't feel a single twinge of guilt at his comment. "No, Blake, I'm not human anymore."

"Why Jax?" The look of disappointment on Blake's face made the guilty factor rear its ugly head.

"Because I lov—" She started to answer when a hoarse cry of pain filtered though her consciousness, drawing her attention away from Blake.

Ian! Before she turned her gaze their way, instinct told Jax that Drace was the one who had been hurt, not Ian. She looked up in time to see Drace's feet slam into Ian's chest, sending him flying. Her mate landed hard on the ground fifteen feet away from Drace.

Drace scrambled to his feet and ran toward the house, then took a flying leap and landed upon the balcony on the second floor of the house. With a roar of rage, he rammed his shoulder against the French doors, splintering them open. Ian jumped up and leapt to the balcony, pursuing Drace. Jax's heart jerked in her chest as Ian entered the house. She didn't see him carrying a weapon.

Before she could follow Ian and Drace, she was distracted by the sight of two remaining vamps fleeing toward the entrance to the back of the house as if the very devil himself were nipping at their heels. None of the transers had survived their battle with Duncan. Only when Jax saw Sebastian wince did she notice the first tendrils of yellow and orange daylight had begun to streak the morning sky. Sunrise!

Fear for her new friend gripped her, making her chest tighten. "Get inside, Sebastian," Jax ordered.

"I'm going after Ian," he stated, turning in the direction Ian had taken.

Jax shook her head as she retrieved her dropped gun from the ground. "I need you to go with Blake and keep the vamps inside the house under surveillance until they can be dealt with by Ian as the Ruean leader."

"Jax," Blake said in a warning tone as if he planned to refuse.

She faced him, her expression serious. "Do this for me, Blake. I've never asked for your help until now."

Blake touched her jaw, a tender expression on his face. "You really love him, don't you?"

She nodded.

Blake straightened, his expression turning serious as he looked at Sebastian. "Let's go, vamp."

"That's Gauthier, to you," Sebastian answered in a stiff tone.

Jax waited until Sebastian, Blake, and his men entered the house. She breathed a sigh of relief when she didn't hear any resistance from the vamps inside.

Duncan drove up on his motorcycle, the look on his face deadly and intense.

"I'm going after Drace and Ian. Where did they go?"

"No, Duncan. We need you to get Ian's friend Mark to Mora as soon as possible. He's unconscious on the front porch. Since you look like Ian, he'll trust Mora to help him."

Duncan's jaw hardened.

She put her hand on his arm. "Please, Duncan. Ian sent Mark here to protect the estate and now Mark might die. He needs attention as soon as possible. Trust that I'll do everything in my power to protect Ian."

Duncan pressed his lips together, then he gave her a slow, sexy grin. "Damn, my brother's a lucky bastard."

As she smiled back, he revved his engine and took off toward the front of the house.

Chapter Twenty

Jumping up on the balcony, Jax stepped over the broken glass and crossed the threshold into the bedroom, her heart pounding. The silence in the room made her stomach clench while the stale, stuffy air almost overwhelmed her heightened sense of smell. Looking around the room, Jax noted the sheets covering the furniture. Nothing stirred. Where were Ian and Drace?

As she walked toward the doorway to the bedroom, a gasp of pain followed by a gurgling sound pierced the dead silence. Overwhelming fear for Ian's safety stopped her dead in her tracks. She closed her eyes and tried to feel Ian's emotions.

Nothing. Not one single emotion filtered through to her. Jax followed the pained sound down the darkened hall and into a bedroom three doors away.

The bedroom was in shambles with a dresser turned over, its mirror smashed on the floor. Wooden bits of a broken chair and dresser drawers scattered every area of the room. The bed had collapsed on one end and the wrought iron headboard was bent askew. Jax noted a missing spindle from the headboard a moment before another gasp for breath drew her attention.

Drace lay on the floor a few feet from the window, his grasp weak on the metal spike imbedded in his chest while his face contorted in a mask of excruciating pain.

She looked up and saw Ian standing a few feet away from Drace. His shirt hung in tatters around his waist and blood oozed from various claw wounds and deep gashes on his chest and arms. He stared at Drace while he reflexively clenched and unclenched his fists. Relief flooded through her to know Ian's wounds weren't irreparable.

Shards of broken mirror pieces crunched under her boots as Jax walked across the room and stood beside her mate. Without a word, she handed Ian the gun so he could put an end the hunt. Taking Drace out was more important for establishing his role as the Ruean leader. She knew in her heart, Ian's destiny outweighed her need to avenge her father's death. Either way, the end result was the same. She closed her eyes, thankful it was finally over. Now she could move on with her life.

Jax glanced up in surprise at the sound that followed the gunshots. The distinctive crash of shattered glass hitting the wood floor behind the heavy, red velvet curtain drew her out of her jumbled thoughts.

She looked at her mate and her heart constricted. He refused to meet her gaze as he stared at Drace. She'd never seen such a cold, detached expression on Ian's face before and the sight scared the hell out of her. He didn't speak as he glanced at the bullet holes in the curtain…almost as if he were waiting.

When the first streams of sunlight began to shine through the curtain and slide across the floor toward Drace like a poisonous snake about to strike, Ian's intent became clear. The knowledge made Jax's heart sink and her stomach feel as if it had dropped to the floor. *No!*

Jax mentally blocked out Drace's cries of pain and the stench of burning flesh as she focused on her mate's needs.

She took the gun from Ian and stood in front of him, hoping to draw his attention from the torture he'd set in motion. Jax looked up at the man she'd come to love and met his glazed gaze, hoping her very presence would shake him out of his spiraling path of vengeance.

He looked so angry and tortured. Her heart ached for him. She licked her finger and ran her saliva across a gash on his jaw, her ministrations caring and loving. The physical contact, along with her healing touch, seemed to pull Ian out of his fury-induced trance enough for him to address his actions.

"He almost raped you, Jax. You saw what he did to Mark…your father…" He drew a deep breath, then stiffened his stance, his expression turning resolute. "The bastard deserves what he gets."

Jax gasped at the all-consuming rage that flooded to her consciousness as Ian let down the guard he'd held on his emotions. Taking a deep breath, she shook off the shared fury. "Don't let Drace turn you into the very man you've hunted your whole life."

"It's not the same," he countered with a look of righteous anger.

Jax never thought she'd see the day she'd defend the rogue vampire who destroyed her father, but if it would save her mate from turning into a heartless man like Drace, she'd let go of her revenge.

"This man I've come to admire, once said to me, 'The hunt should never be about revenge, Jax. It should *always* be about justice.'"

Her gaze never left Ian's as she lifted the gun and fired toward Drace, ending the vamp's agony.

"Justice is served, *a ghrá*. Now let's go home."

Ian looked at Drace, then met her gaze once more. Reaching out, he cupped his hand around the back of her neck and pulled her close.

Jax clasped him around the waist and laid her head on his chest, careful to avoid his wounds.

Ian's grip tightened, then slowly relaxed. Rubbing his thumb along the curve of her neck, he whispered against her hair, his tone gruff and regretful, "Thank you for reminding me who and what I am, *a thaisce.*"

* * * * *

Blake handed a box of Jax's belongings to Ian saying, "It's kinda heavy. Think you can handle it?"

Ian narrowed his gaze on Blake before he turned and walked into the house.

Jax faced Blake as he pulled another item out of the back of his utility vehicle.

"What's going to happen with the Trackers now, Blake?"

He set a suitcase on the ground. "What do you mean?"

"Now that you know most vampires are good."

Blake raised an eyebrow. "Who said that?"

Frustration mounted at her stubborn friend. "Blake!"

He set another suitcase on the ground, then faced her. "Listen, Jax. The Trackers will operate the way they have been."

At her look of outrage, he continued, "My men know who your friends are, but I make no guarantees on the others."

He held up his hand when she started to argue. "Maybe one day we can work together, Jax, but right now I'm not totally convinced. I mean, you have fuckin' fangs."

Unprecedented hurt sliced through her at his words.

Blake chucked her on the jaw and winked. "Gotcha!"

"Blake!"

He stopped laughing and his expression sobered. "All I can promise you right now is that I'll take a deeper look at the vampire I'm hunting."

She felt better but she still had to add, "Well, the least you can do is let up on Ian."

Blake turned and picked up more items. Facing her, he held a floor lamp in one hand and an empty aquarium under his arm. "I'll always look out for you, Jax."

Jax took the lamp from him. "Now that you've taken over the Trackers, don't you think you have enough to worry about?"

He shrugged. "I'll always feel a certain responsibility to know where you are and that you're all right."

Jax set the lamp on the ground, curiosity getting the best of her. "Speaking of which...how did you seem to know exactly where to find me the last few days of my hunt for Drace."

Blake gave her a smug look and touched the tip of one of the chopsticks in her hair. "They have a homing device in them."

Jax bristled. "Do you mean to tell me that I've been walking around with the ability to pick up cell phone signals in my head?"

He shrugged and gave her an unrepentant grin. "You're the one who refused to keep in touch with me on a regular basis."

Ian reached from behind her and picked up the lamp saying, "Now that Jax is with me, there's no reason for you to know her every move, Blake."

Blake straightened his shoulders and met Ian's gaze. "I promised her father and uncle I would look out for her—"

"Which is no longer necessary now that I'm her mate," Ian replied in a final tone.

Blake started to respond when a silver truck driving down the long gravel driveway drew their attention.

Mark drove up next to them and got out of his truck. "Where's Duncan?"

"My brother had a gig tonight," Ian answered.

Mark rolled his eyes. "Figures. I had no idea he was into music. He's been dodging me this past week. Don't worry, Ian, I'm going to make Duncan 'join in the fun' if it's the last thing I do." Mark grinned, then winked, continuing, "And if nothing else works, I'll just use a guilt complex on him."

Ian laughed out loud and clapped his friend on the shoulder. "That's an angle I never considered with Duncan. Good luck, Mark. Not much phases my brother's conscience."

"Well, I've only been a vamp for a week. Give me some time. I'll draw him out," he said with confidence. Mark rubbed his hands together saying, "Okay, what big stuff do you want this super-strong vampire to help you with today?"

Jax smiled at Mark's levity.

"Watch it, Devlin," Blake ground out as he handed Mark her suitcase, then turned and retrieved two more suitcases. "Talk like that will get you shot among the Trackers. It's best they don't discover you're a vampire," he finished as he handed Mark two other suitcases.

Jax smiled. No matter what Blake said, he was already starting to accept vampires at some level.

The two suitcases he'd handed Mark were full of heavy books. Jax knew Blake had handed him those on purpose. She started to take one from Mark, when Ian spoke in her mind, *No, Jax, don't help Mark.*

She gave her mate a quizzical look as Blake put the aquarium on two boxes and picked them up, saying to Mark, "Follow me. I'll show you where to put the suitcases."

Ian's gaze followed Mark and Blake inside. "Much as I hate to give the man credit, the way Blake is handling Mark is perfect."

"Perfect?"

Ian nodded. "Yeah. Mark's not showing it, but losing several cop friends in a fight with Drace and then becoming a vampire himself rocked his world."

"It's not like he was given a choice," she answered with a snort.

Ian nodded, "True, but at least Duncan gave him a fighting chance by converting him to a vampire himself."

Jax shook her head, chucking "I still can't believe Duncan fought off five Trackers to get to Mark."

Ian shrugged. "I would've done the same. You asked him to personally take care of Mark on my behalf. He had no way of knowing that Mark had made some contacts within Blake's group."

Mark and Blake came back outside and Jax switched to speaking mentally as she handed them more boxes.

Duncan sacrificed a lot to personally convert Mark, didn't he? Jax asked.

Yes, my brother has chosen a solitary, loner's life because he resents not quite fitting in either the human world or the vampire world. So, why would he want to create vampri that would face the same 'fish out of water' issues he's had to face all his life?

Jax nodded her understanding. *I'm glad he made an exception. If Mark can no longer be human, this is the perfect solution for your friend. He can still keep his police job since he's not affected by the sun.*

Why do you think Duncan converted him? My brother knew Drace had made sure Mark was too far gone, but at least with Duncan's final bite, Mark could choose what life he wanted to live — a day life or a night life.

Jax looked at Ian in shock. *Your never-say-more-than-he-needs-to brother told you all this?*

Ian gave her a 'yeah right' look. *No. He's my twin, Jax. I know he couldn't resist jumping inside Mark's head and when he did he realized Mark's job as a police officer was very important to him. He did the only thing he could for Mark.*

"Hey you slackers," Blake called over his shoulder as he and Mark walked back toward the porch, their arms full of boxes. "The operative word is we're here to help Jax move in."

"Keep your shirt on. We're coming," Jax called out and picked up a laundry basket full of odds and ends from her bedroom. As she walked toward the house, she left Ian with a mental thought. *Have I told you how glad I am you don't have Duncan's power to read minds?* Ian's laughter followed her all the way inside.

* * * * *

Jax watched the red taillights of Blake and Mark's vehicles until they turned off their driveway onto the main road.

Ian's arms encircled her from behind and he said in a husky voice as he nuzzled her neck, "Mmmm, alone at last."

Their home was near the river, deep in the woods and being so far away from the hustle and bustle of the town allowed her sense of hearing to pick up every frog's croak and every cricket's song. She'd learned to tune out the almost deafening night sounds, but tonight Jax welcomed them as dusk slipped into evening.

The hoot of an owl made her smile and Ian whispered in her ear as his arms tightened around her, "He prepares to hunt."

His seductive tone made goose bumps form on her arms.

Clasping her hand, he said, "Come, I want to show you something."

Jax followed Ian up the stairs to their bedroom and out onto the deck that backed up to the woods.

He pulled her into his arms and turned her around, facing the dense forest below.

As he unbuttoned her pants and pushed them down her hips, Ian said, "I know we have the ability to walk in the daylight, *a ghrá*, but there is something about the night that seduces me. Do you feel it calling to you?"

Jax stepped out of her shoes, pants and underwear, then drew her sweater over her head and tossed it on the deck. She shivered as Ian quickly shed his clothes. Even though her body felt cold, excitement made her pulse quicken.

Ian pulled the chopsticks out of her hair and threw them deep into the forest.

"Ian—"

"There's only one person who should know where you are at all times. You're *my* mate," he said, his tone possessive, yet so full of tender emotion.

Jax welcomed Ian's heat as his naked chest pressed against her back and his arms encircled her waist. She cried out when he suddenly jumped, taking her with him as he landed on the railing facing the woods.

She gasped at the unsettling feeling of being perched high above the ground, yet somehow Ian had them perfectly balanced on the two-by-four board. Her survival instinct peaked and she dug her fingers into his forearms.

Sudden warmth radiated throughout her body and Ian spoke to her, his voice soothing, calming, seductive, "I've given you my heat to keep you warm, my blood to sustain your life, and my heart to show you the depth of my love..." *Trust me*, he whispered in her mind, his encouraging words a persuasive echo to his spoken ones.

Jax loosened her grip on his arms and thrilled at the sensation of his fingers skimming up her ribcage and brushing the sides of her breasts.

When he ran his hands down the outside of her arms and threaded his fingers with hers, she sighed in contentment.

Ever so slowly, Ian raised her arms outward while he leaned their bodies forward. Fear rammed into her stomach, making it churn at the precarious position.

Trust me, his words echoed in her mind once more.

Ian kissed her neck and said in a husky voice, "I will always provide the blood you need, Jax, but there's one thing I want you to share with me every night of our lives."

Her vampire heart, at first slow to respond to her mental arousal, thudded in her chest. "What's that?"

Close your eyes, he commanded.

Jax did as he asked and by eliminating her night vision, the sounds of the forest seemed to intensify. Her heart beat faster.

"I want you to hunt with me," Ian rasped as he leapt them high in the air.

Panic gripped her and she tried to pull down her arms, to prepare to break her fall.

Ian's voice entered her mind, swift, commanding, encouraging as he lifted her arms up and down, "Concentrate, Jax. Tonight, we fly."

Jax focused on Ian's emotions. He seemed so confident, so assured, so...

Wind whipping around them interrupted her thoughts, causing her to open her eyes. They soared high over the trees and then crossed over the river.

Though he no longer held her hands, Jax felt Ian's presence above her, mimicking her arm movements, giving her a gentle nudge to show her when to turn. The sound of flapping wings made her chest tighten in excitement.

She looked up and gave a mental gasp to see the magnificent black raven above her. He glanced down at her and blinked a golden eye.

You're my partner in all things. Tá grá agam dhuit, he spoke in her mind, his voice filled with emotion.

Her confidence growing, Jax flapped her wings and moved to fly beside him. *I love you, too. There's no one I'd rather hunt with than you.*

Irish[1] Phrases used in *A Taste for Revenge*

Endearments

Sonuachar (son-oo-uh-k*ur) = Soul mate (or a close Irish equivalent)

A Chroí (ah khree) = My Heart

A Ghrá (ah graw) = My Love

A Thaisce (ah hash-keh) = My Treasure

A Ghrá mo Chroí (ah graw muh khree) = Love of my Heart/My Heart's Beloved

Other

Is tú mo shonuachar [2] (iss too muh hon-oo-uh-k*ur) = You're my soul mate

Tá tú go h-áileann (thaw too goh haw-ling) = You are beautiful

Tá grá agam dhuit (taw graw ah-gum g*itch) = I love you

Damnú air! (dahm-noo air!) = Damn it!

Go raibh maith agat (guh rev moh a-guth) = Thank You

Oíche mhaith (e-hah whah) = Good Night

Is liomsa í (iss lyum-suh ee) = She's mine

Bheinn sásta an bhean bhreá seo a roinnt leat, a dheartháir (veh-inn saws-tuh un van vraw shuh a roonch lyat, uh y'rawr) = I'd be willing to share this lovely woman, brother.

Thug muid roinnt dár gcuid fuil chroí dá chéile; tugadh agus glacadh fuil go toilteanach. Tá muid inár lánúin anois.

= (exact translation) We each gave each other (some of) our heart's blood; blood was given and accepted willingly. We're mated now.

= (as stated in the book). Your life's blood for mine; given and taken willingly. Now we're mated.

Notes:

1. **Irish** is the proper name of the language. Irish, Scottish, and Manx belong to the language subgroup called **Gaelic**.

2 *Is tú mo shonuachar* literally means: You are my good spouse. This is the closest the Irish language can get to the meaning of the English term 'soul mate'.

Kendrian Vampire Terms

Pureblood - Pure vampire

Hybrid - Part pureblood vampire

Vampri - Humans made into vampire. Their powers, though vampire-like, are less than the vampire who created them. They must drink blood to survive. Only Hybrids and Purebloods can make vampris. Vampris made by a pureblood vampire will not be able to walk in the sun. Vampris made by a hybrid vampire will have the same tolerance or aversion to the sun the hybrid does.

Transer - Human on the brink of becoming a vampri. He's so close to being a vampri, he will do anything for the vampire to take that third bite and make him a vampri.

Anima - The mate of a vampire. If the person is a human turned vampri by his or her vampire mate, then by the nature of being mated to a vampire, he/she will have equal powers/limitations to his/her vampire mate.

An Excerpt From
BAD IN BOOTS: HARM'S HUNGER

Chapter One

"What do you mean, you don't know where she is?" Ty Hudson raised his voice and switched his cell phone to his other ear. His dark brows drew together as he rubbed the back of his neck, clearly agitated. "Her flight was due in at three. Did you call her cell phone?" Ty cast Harm an apologetic glance.

Harm placed his booted foot across his knee and leaned back in the seat sighing. Looked like he might be here a while.

"She probably forgot to turn it back on once her plane landed. Check that she did actually get on the plane and call me back. I appreciate it, Colt." He snapped the phone closed. "Sorry about the delay, Mr. Steele. I know you're anxious to get the papers signed and get back to your ranch, but my sister owns half the property, so I need her signature as well." He ran a hand through his close-cropped hair. "I don't know why our great-aunt Sally stipulated we handle the transaction in person if we decided to sell the property."

Harm rose and placed his black Stetson back on his head. "Sally Tanner was a fine woman. I'm sure she had her reasons. I can hang out for a couple more hours. He patted the cell phone clipped to his belt. You've got my number. . Call me when you locate your sister."

As he walked toward the elevators, Harm wondered for the fiftieth time why Sally deeded the land to the Hudsons. They were from the east coast, used to city living, not ranching. Sally had been a great neighbor, letting him use a large portion of her property to rotate his cattle. She'd always claimed, "It's the Texan way, Harmon. You take care of my horses and I let you use the land." And it was as simple as that for Sally. He'd miss the old girl.

As he pushed the button for the lobby, just his luck, the elevator skipped right past the lobby and descended to the basement level. When the elevator doors slid open, two long, shapely legs attached to a very curvy body stepped into the elevator.

Maybe his luck was about to turn.

"Hi." The blonde woman with crystal blue eyes smiled at him as she leaned over to push the button for the eighth floor. She was wearing a barely there two piece candy apple red bikini, her hair and skin still wet from the hotel pool she'd obviously taken advantage of. He smiled back and out of habit, ran his fingers across the brim of his hat. "Ma'am."

She looked him up and down and quipped with a grin. "Ooh, a real live cowboy."

"Born and bred." He grinned back.

When the elevator stopped on the lobby floor, Harm was thankful no one was there waiting to get on. He hit the Close Door button, fully intending to bask in this woman's beauty as long as he could. A lift of her eyebrow was the only indication she noticed he didn't punch a button for a different floor, only the eighth floor button was lit.

As the elevator started to ascend, Harm asked, "Not from around here I take it?" He couldn't place her accent. Virginia maybe? But she had the huskiest voice, like Lauren Hutton's. It was so damn sexy he wanted to keep talking just to listen to her speak.

She gave a throaty laugh. "No. Just visiting."

As she stared up at the elevator lights, he took a moment to enjoy her luscious curves. Not one ounce of fat graced her nicely built body. She looked to be about five-eight or nine. A nice fit for his six foot three frame. The first stirrings of arousal made itself known in his tightening crotch when he noticed her hard nipples pressed against her wet top. He let his gaze drop to her flat stomach and firm thighs. Nice. He'd bet his last dollar she had an ass that begged to be squeezed. But unfortunately she had her hands crossed behind her back, holding a small hand towel against her damp suit.

The elevator stopped on the six floor but the doors didn't open. They both looked at each other and then he punched the button for the eighth floor to get it going again. Nothing happened. He hit the Open Door button but the doors didn't budge.

Harm lifted the emergency handset and dialed the front desk. Once he'd set the receiver back on its cradle, he turned to her and grinned. He couldn't help it. Now he had a few more minutes with her. It would take the front desk at least fifteen minutes to find maintenance. "Well, looks like you're stuck with me for a few."

He put his hands on the guardrail and leaned his back against the sidewall. She adopted the same position on the opposite wall, laughing. "So sit a spell and all that, huh?"

He chuckled. "Yeah, something like that. Where are you from?"

"Maryland."

"Here for long?"

She shook her head, her eyes twinkling. "Not officially."

A long moment of silence ensued as they both assessed each other. She had a beautiful oval face with almond shaped eyes and eyebrows slightly darker than her hair. But it was her lips that drew his attention. Free of lipstick, her full, naturally rosy lips made him throb. Those lips were made for kissing.

Her unabashed gaze roamed his face and his body while he did the same, this time appreciating the full frontal view. If only he could see her breasts. Were her nipples large quarters or small dimes? He was dying to peel away her bathing su—. Just then, he couldn't believe his eyes, the front snap on her bikini top gave way and her luscious breasts spilled out as the lycra material snapped backward.

Her sharp, embarrassed intake of breath had him averting his gaze and turning his head while trying not to grin. Dimes. Perfect rose tipped dimes. She faced the wall and made frustrated sounds as she tried to get her suit back together.

"Um, excuse me. Would you mind doing me a favor?" She called over her shoulder?

She's kidding, right? He cleared his throat. "Sure, can I turn around?"

She laughed. "Yes, you'll have to in order to help me."

Harm turned and immediately saw her problem. One of the hooks had caught on the back of her bikini top and she wasn't able to reach it. He had to touch her back in order to release the hook. The brief brush of his fingers against her soft skin only made his cock throb harder.

"Thanks." She let the towel drop so she could fix her top.

Holy shit! What a beautiful ass. He couldn't tear his gaze away from the firm round flesh that the red straps of the g-string bikini framed quite nicely.

She faced him, her eyebrow arched. "Enjoy the view?"

"Hell, yes," he admitted before he thought better of it.

She didn't look angry, just amused. Shrugging, she picked up her towel. "I was trying to avoid that."

His lips quirked upward. "I figured as much." He hadn't moved away and now only a foot separated them. Her scent reminded him of warm sunshine right after a spring rain.

She leaned back against the wall, putting her hands on the handrail for support. "You know, I—" Her bathing suit popped open again, exposing her breasts once more. "...am apparently going to keep flashing you," she gritted out, her cheeks turning red as she dropped the towel once more to grab the errant fabric.

"You won't hear any complaints from me. Flash away." He gave his best roguish grin.

"Har-har." She looked up while trying to snap the scraps of material closed.

The elevator started moving and her sarcastic expression turned to panic as they neared her floor. He reached out and pulled the red emergency button to stop the elevator. When he turned back to her she looked about ready to spit nails.

"Can I help?" he offered.

She threw her hands up in frustration, obviously beyond embarrassment at this point. "Have at it."

As he moved closer, she added, "The bikini top, I mean..."

About the author:

Born and raised in the southeast, Patrice Michelle has been a fan of romance novels since she was thirteen years old. While she reads many types of books, romance novels will always be her mainstay, saying, "I guess it's the idea of a happy ever after that draws me in."

The tone of Patrice's paranormal and contemporary novels may range from intense to light hearted, but she says one thing will always hold true with her writing—"I will always write a deep, emotional connection between the heroes and the heroines in my books."

Patrice welcomes mail from readers. You can write to her c/o Ellora's Cave Publishing at 1337 Commerce Drive, Suite 13, Stow, Ohio 44224.

Also by Patrice Michelle:

A Taste for Passion
Bad in Boots 1: *Harm's Hunger*
Cajun Nights
Dragon's Heart
Ellora's Cavemen: *Tales from the Temple II*

Why an electronic book?

We live in the Information Age—an exciting time in the history of human civilization in which technology rules supreme and continues to progress in leaps and bounds every minute of every hour of every day. For a multitude of reasons, more and more avid literary fans are opting to purchase e-books instead of paperbacks. The question to those not yet initiated to the world of electronic reading is simply: *why?*

1. *Price.* An electronic title at Ellora's Cave Publishing runs anywhere from 40-75% less than the cover price of the <u>exact same title</u> in paperback format. Why? Cold mathematics. It is less expensive to publish an e-book than it is to publish a paperback, so the savings are passed along to the consumer.

2. *Space.* Running out of room to house your paperback books? That is one worry you will never have with electronic novels. For a low one-time cost, you can purchase a handheld computer designed specifically for e-reading purposes. Many e-readers are larger than the average handheld, giving you plenty of screen room. Better yet, hundreds of titles can be stored within your new library—a single microchip. (Please note that Ellora's Cave does not endorse any specific brands. You can check our website at www.ellorascave.com for customer recommendations we make available to new consumers.)

3. *Mobility.* Because your new library now consists of only a microchip, your entire cache of books can be taken with you wherever you go.

4. *Personal preferences are accounted for.* Are the words you are currently reading too small? Too large? Too...**ANNOYING**? Paperback books cannot be modified according to personal preferences, but e-books can.

5. *Innovation.* The way you read a book is not the only advancement the Information Age has gifted the literary community with. There is also the factor of what you can read. Ellora's Cave Publishing will be introducing a new line of interactive titles that are available in e-book format only.

6. *Instant gratification.* Is it the middle of the night and all the bookstores are closed? Are you tired of waiting days—sometimes weeks—for online and offline bookstores to ship the novels you bought? Ellora's Cave Publishing sells instantaneous downloads 24 hours a day, 7 days a week, 365 days a year. Our e-book delivery system is 100% automated, meaning your order is filled as soon as you pay for it.

Those are a few of the top reasons why electronic novels are displacing paperbacks for many an avid reader. As always, Ellora's Cave Publishing welcomes your questions and comments. We invite you to email us at service@ellorascave.com or write to us directly at: 1337 Commerce Drive, Suite 13, Stow OH 44224.

Printed in the United States
22631LVS00007B/79